DYING
TO KILL

DYING TO KILL

PATRICIA H. RUSHFORD

Revell
Grand Rapids, Michigan

Published by Fleming H. Revell
a division of Baker Publishing Group
P.O. Box 6287, Grand Rapids, MI 49516-6287
www.revellbooks.com

Printed in the United States of America

Library of Congress Cataloging-in-Publication Data
Rushford, Patricia H.
    Dying to kill / Patricia H. Rushford.
        p.   cm. — (An Angel Delaney mystery ; bk. 2)
    ISBN 0-8007-5848-X (pbk.)
    1. Policewomen—Fiction. 2. Family violence—Fiction. I. Title.
II. Series: Rushford, Patricia H. Angel Delaney mystery ; v bk. 2.
PS3568.U7274D95 2004
813'.54—dc22   2004015534

ONE

Sunday, May 4

Dear Dr. Campbell,

For obvious reasons, I can't tell you who I am. For now, consider me a guardian, an avenger, an angel of death—your alter ego. I think that if you were not constrained by your position, you would do the same. You talk against violence, but deep down, you know it's the only way.

The police are calling what I did to Jim Kelsey a murder. That's far too strong a word. I didn't murder the man, I simply disposed of a piece of garbage. Men like Jim Kelsey deserve to die. Don't you agree?

This isn't a confession letter, if that's what you are thinking. I have no real guilt about it other than being incensed that the police would stoop so low as to think his sweet wife would kill him. She didn't.

Perhaps that's why I write—to somehow free her from police tyranny once and for all. And that brings me to the second part of my letter.

Something needs to be done about Phillip Jenkins. After his last episode . . . That's what his wife calls them—episodes. I call them blowouts. Like the tires on a car when the pressure builds up and makes them explode, spewing rubber all over the highway. Phillip explodes, spewing his rage all over the people who should mean the most to him.

Seeing Candace all beat up and crying, after his last "episode," I swore it was the last time he would ever hurt anyone again. He should go to prison for his crimes. And that's what they are—crimes. But Candace won't take a stand, so someone has to.

Rage seeps into my bones just thinking about the injustice. I laid awake all night staring at the ceiling, praying for an answer. Then it came, bright and clear as crystal. Having made the decision, I feel stronger and more powerful.

I know something Phillip Jenkins doesn't know. I know the very day and hour he will die.

Dragonslayer

TWO

___

By 7:00 on Tuesday morning, Angel had run two-and-a-half of her five miles; then she detoured inland from the hard-packed sand left by high tide and aimed for what had become her favorite house in Sunset Cove.

The newly remodeled two-story home held her admiration for three reasons. First, the place had become a work of art. The owner had turned the rundown shack into a showplace. Second, a cute little dog waited for her at the door every morning. Third, and most important, the house belonged to the new love in her life, Callen Riley, Detective Callen Riley with the Oregon State Police.

She imagined the handsome detective pulling her into his arms and telling her how much he'd missed her. She sighed and reined in her fantasy. There would be no hugs and kisses this morning. Callen had been gone for nearly a week, working a case involving a missing high school girl from Florence, a town about one hundred miles south of Sunset Cove on the Oregon coast.

God, please keep her safe. Let her be found alive. Angel prayed for the Grant girl every day. And every day, Angel hoped that she'd turn on the news and learn that the teenager hadn't been abducted—that she had simply gone off on an adventure.

Callen was helping with the search and following up on leads. When she'd talked to him the night before, he told her he'd be coming home today. So, until tonight, she'd have to settle for doggy kisses.

Angel's jog slowed to a plodding walk as her feet sank into the soft sand. She loved the Oregon coast despite the rainy season, which sometimes seemed to last all year. Behind her and to the west lay the Pacific Ocean. The Coastal Mountains rose to the east, creating peaks and valleys covered with vast green forests through which creeks and rivers tumbled from deep snowbanks into lakes and coves, finally making their way into the ocean. Clouds hovered over the water today, creeping closer to shore and threatening rain.

The sun had risen in a glorious array of colors, reminding Angel of the old fisherman's ditty, "Red sky at night, sailors delight; red sky in morning, sailors take warning."

Sunset Cove lay at the base of the Coastal range. The sloping hills were perfect for building elegant ocean-view homes. The cove itself lay between two hills, forming a bowl at their base. A channel ran from the cove to the ocean. While Angel appreciated the luxurious developments on the hillsides, she preferred the diverse oceanfront properties with homes of various shapes and sizes and values. Maybe because she'd grown up about a mile north of Callen's home, with the beach in her backyard and the ocean only a hundred or so yards away at high tide.

Angel had recently moved out of her parents' home to a place not far from the beach. She now had the view and the rent payments to go with it. The rent, unfortunately, had become somewhat of a problem of late. But that was another story.

Mutt, Callen's dog, barked when she came up over the dunes where he could see her. Every morning he waited for her at the sliding patio door. And every morning he yelped a greeting that had all the earmarks of a scolding mixed in with obvious glee.

"Morning, Mutt!" She pulled out the key Callen had given her, unlocked the door, and carefully slid it open, holding back the exuberant white ball of fluff with her foot. Once she'd squeezed inside, she scooped the dog into her arms and buried her face in his silky fur. She still couldn't get used to calling the bichon frise "Mutt."

Mutt hadn't been Callen's first choice for a dog. His wife, Karen, had loved the breed, and Callen couldn't have refused her anything in those last months of her life. Karen had lost her battle with cancer two years ago, but Mutt stayed on, having secured a place in Callen's heart. Even though the breed didn't seem to go with a macho detective, Angel couldn't imagine a better fit.

"Did you miss me? Oh, poor puppy. You're lonesome for Callen, aren't you?"

Mutt barked in agreement.

"Me too. Okay, let's take you potty, then we'll get you some fresh water and food." Angel winced at the tone of her voice. Never did she think she'd be talking baby talk to a dog.

Mutt whimpered when she put him down, lifting his paws and prancing around on his hind legs. Angel reached for his leash and fastened it on his collar. "Ready to go outside?"

He cocked his head from side to side, sticking his nose against the glass.

"What am I saying? Of course you are. Okay, let's go." Angel opened the door and followed as he strained at the leash, acting as though he hadn't been outside in days. She closed the door behind them and allowed him to pull her across the stained wooden deck and down the two steps to the beach.

Mutt was definitely in his element, sniffing at the sea leavings and barking at seagulls that ventured too close. Down on the beach, he scampered into the water and out, shaking vigorously after each dip and gifting Angel with saltwater sprays. He pushed through a clump of seaweed with his nose and sneezed.

After ten minutes of romping and exploring, Mutt headed back to the house, pausing to do his duty on the way. Inside, the dog settled into the business of eating breakfast, and when he finished, he curled up on his pillow for a nap.

Ordinarily, Angel might have hurried the process along, but not today—and not this week. She wasn't in a hurry to go anywhere or do anything. Without a job, life had become unbearably boring. While she didn't especially enjoy a life of leisure, the prospect of going back to work at the Sunset Cove Police Department seemed overwhelming.

When Mutt fell asleep, she quietly let herself out and resumed her run, heading back to her apartment, a much-needed shower, and her own breakfast.

Guilt niggled at her as she ran. *You should be working. The department is way behind because of you.*

But I need this time away. Nearly everyone agreed—Callen, her mother, her brothers, her counselor, her lawyer. Even Joe, Sunset Cove's chief of police. With budget cuts and a less than adequate staff, Joe needed her at the department. Even though it irked him to lose an officer, he had signed the papers giving her additional time off without pay.

Her father was another story. Disappointment glinted in Frank Delaney's eyes every time he looked at her these days, making her feel like a traitor. Her mother tried to assure her that the look wasn't meant to be critical—at least not toward her. "He's angry, Angel," her mother had said. "Angry with the doctors, angry with himself and me and the whole world."

Angel didn't buy it. Yes, he'd had a heart attack that had led to surgery, then a stroke. He was angry, but that was not the emotion she saw reflected in his eyes. He was disappointed that she had buckled under pressure. Her father had never tolerated weakness in any of his children—why would he start now? In his eyes, she was a quitter—at least that's how she saw it.

Her chest constricted, more from heartache than from exertion. Angel stopped running and closed her eyes, then, tipping her head back, said, "I wish you could understand, Dad. I'm not doing this to hurt you." She had become a police officer to please her father, and now she needed to take a step back. She needed time to recuperate and determine what she wanted to do with the rest of her life. At least that's what she kept telling herself.

Though she didn't want to admit it to anyone, and hadn't, except to Janet Campbell, her counselor, and Callen, she wasn't certain she could work as a police officer again. Two events, both tragic, had left her reeling.

The first tragedy had happened in Florida, where she'd gone to work as a rookie after college and the police training program. She'd been partnered with an officer named Daniella Ortega. Dur-

10

ing the two years they'd worked together, Angel and Dani became closer than friends—more like sisters.

A tear slid down Angel's cheek. She brushed it away, wondering if she'd ever be able to think about Dani without crying and being angry at God for letting her die. But slowly the anger had begun to lessen as she kept reminding herself that God had not killed Dani, the gunman had.

Angel still wondered why Dani had been the one to die; she'd had a husband and two children. Dani and Angel had been the first officers to arrive on the scene of a hostage situation in a day care. The last words Angel had heard her partner say were in the form of a prayer. *"Heavenly Father, don't let any of those children be harmed."*

Thinking about it now, Angel could still hear the sirens and feel the tightness in her chest as they entered through the back door, hoping to negotiate with the man who'd taken a day-care worker and six children hostage. Two other police officers were supposed to come in from the front. The man must have heard them as he stepped into the hallway at the same moment as Dani and Angel. He fired twice and ducked back into the room with the children and their caregiver, shouting at the police to stay away or he'd kill them all.

His first bullet slammed into Dani's forehead. The second hit her neck. She staggered back and fell into Angel's arms, dead before she hit the floor.

God had answered Dani's prayer that day. The children were spared and the gunman stopped. But Dani was dead, and Angel still bore the emotional scars.

The department had given Angel two weeks off. When she insisted on going back to work, they put her on a desk job. She'd hated it and fought going to counseling, making only the mandatory visit. She realized now that she'd been operating in the same mode as her father, dealing with emotions by stuffing them inside. For far too long, Angel had been in denial, refusing to admit how much Dani's death had affected her. Delaney pride and stubbornness died hard if it died at all.

She'd eventually quit her job in Bay City and come back home

11

to Sunset Cove to heal, lick her wounds, and start over. At first, she'd lived with her parents and eventually moved into her own apartment. Police Chief Joe Brady hired her mostly as a favor to his old friend, Frank Delaney, who had served on the Sunset Cove police force for forty-some years.

Angel had worked for the Sunset Cove PD for less than a year when tragedy struck again. This time it came in the death of a twelve-year-old boy who'd been at the scene of a gang-related burglary at a pharmacy. She learned later that he wasn't one of the gang members after all, and that his gun had been a toy, but by then it was too late.

Images flooded her mind as they often did these days. Janet called them flashbacks, the result of post-traumatic stress. Images of her pulling the trigger, of Billy falling to the floor, of her covered in his blood. She shoved the thoughts aside.

You can't keep blaming yourself. It's over. You have to move on. And she would someday. But Dani's and Billy's deaths were carved into her life. Two deep and still bleeding wounds.

Her mother often reminded her that God worked all things for good for those who love the Lord. There had been some good things in her life. She'd made her peace with God and she'd met Callen. And she was growing closer to her mother. Healing came softly in often imperceptible ways. Angel marveled at how differently she felt now as compared to just a few weeks earlier.

Angel continued her run, stopping when she reached her apartment complex. She let herself in, locked the door behind her, and headed for the shower. She wished she could turn off her brain with as little effort as it took to turn off the water faucet. Unfortunately, the worrisome thoughts continued to swirl in her head. As she dried off, she decided she needed something constructive to do with her day so she could quit ruminating about the past and her tenuous future.

"You could look for a different job," she muttered aloud to the steamed-up image in the mirror.

She'd been off work for nearly six weeks and missed it. Part of her wanted to go back to being a police officer. But part of her wanted nothing more to do with law enforcement.

Problem was, she couldn't think of anything she would like better than being a cop. Secretarial work got two thumbs-down. She needed to be active and involved with people. Her counselor had suggested that with her degree in criminal justice she could get a job teaching at the local college. Not a bad idea, but would the college hire someone with only four years of experience in the field?

"You'd better make up your mind soon." Angel brushed through her dark, dripping curls. With her paid leave at an end, the stack of bills lying on the kitchen counter would only get higher.

Angel had enough money for another month, then she'd either have to go back to her old job, quit and go on unemployment, or find another job. At the moment she didn't feel like doing any of the above. Maybe she could find a cheaper apartment. Or move back in with her parents again.

Angel cringed at the thought. Her mother would love that. Anna Delaney lived to take care of others.

Determined not to dwell on her problems, Angel focused on Callen's homecoming. She wanted to do something special to welcome him back and knew just the thing. Once she'd dressed in her daily uniform, jeans and a lightweight knit top, she picked up her phone and dialed the Delaney residence.

"Hey, Ma," Angel said when her mother answered. "What's your schedule like today?"

"Tell me what you want, and I'll see if I can work it in."

"I'd like you to teach me how to make soup. Callen's coming home tonight, and I want to surprise him."

"That's a wonderful idea. The way to a man's heart is through his stomach."

Angel laughed. "Not Callen's. He's a better cook than . . . than I am." Which wasn't saying much. Everyone cooked better than she did.

"Speaking of Callen, have you talked to him today?"

"No, why?"

"I was watching the news this morning. The police think they've found the car they've been looking for. You know the one they think that high school girl got into with that man. It doesn't look good."

"Have they found her?"

"Not yet."

Angel ran a hand through her damp curls. "There's still hope."

"I know. My heart aches for those poor parents. I don't suppose you'd want to call Callen. Maybe you could find out more."

"I don't think that's a good idea right now. He most likely has his hands full. We'll see him tonight, and he can fill us in then."

After agreeing to come over for lunch, Angel hung up and finished getting dressed. She couldn't help thinking about the fate of the high school cheerleader who should have known better than to get into a stranger's car. If he was a stranger. He could well have been a classmate or relative or friend. Though she'd told her mother there was still hope, Angel couldn't quite convince herself.

If she were still working as a police officer, she'd have all the facts by now. She might even be part of the team trying to piece clues together. *But you are not working, Angel Delaney*, she reminded herself. *You are not part of the team. You are a civilian and you are about to learn how to make soup.*

Whoopee.

THREE

Callen pushed a tree limb aside and ducked under it. He wished he were home with Angel and Mutt, watching the waves roll in and sitting by the fire, instead of tromping through the soggy woods. He was bone tired and cold.

They'd been searching for Christine Grant for five days and were about ready to give up when they found the abandoned vehicle, a burgundy '87 Buick LeSabre with Oregon plates and a fish symbol on the bumper. The vehicle, registered to a Mitchell Bailey from Sunset Cove, had been reported stolen the day after Christy disappeared; Bailey had said he'd noticed it missing the day before. Callen had asked the Sunset Cove Police Department to check the guy out. Later, he would interview the car's owner himself, but for now at least, the guys at the PD could do a preliminary interview. Bailey might be telling the truth—or he may have been setting himself up with an alibi.

Though Callen hated to admit it, he didn't hold out much hope for the girl's survival, not with the large amount of blood evidence they'd found in the trunk. Nonetheless, he offered up another prayer for her safe return.

While the CSI technicians processed the vehicle, he and other members of the search-and-rescue team scoured the wooded area near where the car had been found. Callen continued to operate under the premise that Christy had been in the trunk and that her abductor had either taken off with her or dumped her body.

A shout from one of the search-and-rescue members brought him up short. His pulse shot up as he crashed through brush and skirted around trees.

"Over here." One of the Lane County sheriff's deputies waved at him as he came to a clearing.

Callen's heart dropped to his feet when he saw the cadaver dog sniffing at a large mound of leaves and branches. The sheriff's deputy, a young guy named Dan Riggs, had already begun to remove the brush. Riggs stopped suddenly, his face pale as he backed away. He tossed Callen a guilty look. "Sorry, I . . ." The young man ducked behind a bush and heaved.

The smell of carrion emanating from the mound stopped Callen too, turning his stomach inside out. He took a stick of Mentholatum from his pocket and spread the stuff on his nostrils to hide some of the smell. Breathing through his mouth, he carefully moved forward to get a closer look. Though the body had begun to decompose, he knew all too well who she was.

Callen closed his eyes for a moment. He'd seen a lot of death in his years as a detective, but no amount of experience could lessen the impact. He stepped back physically and emotionally. When he found his voice, he spoke into his radio. "We've found her."

He gave his coordinates, then called the medical examiner and the CSI team. Callen reassured Deputy Riggs that his reaction was to be expected, then sent him back to the main road to kennel the dog and get the camera. Once the others arrived he began delegating the tasks that went along with securing and processing the body dump. Considering the large amount of blood in the car, he surmised that Christy had been alive when the killer put her into the trunk and was probably dead when he took her out. Dead bodies didn't bleed much, and they found little blood evidence around the body dump site. She could have been killed in the trunk, or he might need to look for a primary crime scene.

One certainty remained. The search for Christy Grant was over.

His mind whirred with possibilities. They were at least fifty miles north of Christy's home and only about fifty feet from where they'd found the deserted vehicle. Who and where was the driver? They'd have to continue to comb the woods. Would they find him dead? Alive? Or would they find him at all?

Too many unanswered questions at this point and too soon to speculate. They'd have to sift through the evidence one painstaking step at a time.

Callen shivered as water from an overhanging fir branch dripped down the back of his neck. Looked like he wouldn't be going home anytime soon.

FOUR

Tuesday, May 6

Dear Dr. Campbell,

I'm back, but then you wouldn't know that since I decided not to send my letters—at least not yet. I don't want you to get them and feel obligated to call the police or try to stop me. For now it is enough to write them and store them in my own files.

It took an entire day of planning, and I almost backed out, but everything went off perfectly. When I picked up Phillip's gun and it fit my hand like it belonged there, I knew I was doing the right thing.

The handle felt smooth and cool against my damp palms. I was frightened at first. Sweat beaded up on my forehead. My mouth went bone dry. What if he realized why I was really there? I didn't think he would. He was so caught up in his ball game.

Just before I pulled the trigger, I remembered something I'd memorized in Sunday school, Thou shalt not kill. Okay, maybe God thinks killing someone is wrong, but when nothing else works, you have to do something. You have to stop the madness.

Dragonslayer

FIVE

_____

A ngel set the wide-bladed knife down and lifted her hand to
her eyes to wipe away her tears.

"You're almost done." Anna handed her a tissue.

Angel sniffed and blew her nose. "Remind me again why I'm
doing this?"

Anna chuckled. "Because it won't be _minestra di cavolfiore_
without the onions. And because you're in love."

"Humph." A half smile tugged at the corners of Angel's
mouth.

"Well, you are, and there's no use denying it."

"Don't start, Ma. It's too soon to be in love. And we're not getting
married, at least not anytime soon." She slid the onions into a dish
and moved six stalks of celery onto the cutting board. "Neither
one of us is ready for that kind of commitment."

Her mother didn't comment. If she had, Angel knew exactly
what she'd say. "I know love when I see it." Maybe she did. Anna
had been the one to bluntly tell her she hadn't been in love with
her longtime boyfriend, Brandon. Of course, Angel had known
that all along. She just hadn't wanted to admit it. What she hadn't
considered and what Anna had called her on was that she'd been
using her relationship with Brandon. His proposal forced her to
take a good look at their relationship, which in the end proved to
be a friendship, a safe haven for both of them. Brandon had since

fallen in love with Michelle Kelsey, widow and suspect in her husband's murder. Poor Brandon.

Angel caught the contented look on her mother's face. Anna was thrilled about her daughter's new love, and not a day went by that she didn't say so. Even so, Angel suspected the delight in her eyes went deeper than that.

Anna slipped an arm around Angel's waist. "It's a miracle, that's what it is."

"What's a miracle?" Angel sliced the celery, two stalks at a time.

"You are. Imagine, my baby girl standing right here beside me, learning how to cook."

Angel cleared her throat. The tears were no longer coming from the onions. She used her wrist to brush them away. Growing up, Angel had avoided anything feminine or domestic, preferring blue jeans and trucks to dresses and dolls. She and her mother had nothing in common, or so she'd thought. For years, Angel had worked hard to fit in with her four brothers, vying with them for her father's attention and approval.

She doubted her father ever realized how important his acceptance was to her. Angel adored him and constantly tried to please him, even to the point of becoming a police officer herself. Her efforts were finally rewarded. When he'd seen her in uniform, no one could miss the pride and delight in his eyes.

Angel saw no pleasure in those eyes now—only sorrow and disappointment. Disappointment in her and, of course, in himself.

The stroke had affected his right side, leaving him without the use of his right leg and arm. When he tried to talk, only odd, garbled sounds came out. Now he had stopped talking completely. After his release from the hospital, his doctor suggested placement in a combination rehabilitation unit and nursing home. Anna wouldn't hear of it. "He's my husband. I can't leave him in a place like that. I want him home where he belongs."

Angel had tried to talk her mother out of bringing him home, but Anna insisted that she could care for him. "At least hire someone to help you part time," Angel had suggested. "We can get an aide to come to the house."

Relief had flooded Anna's face. "How did you get so smart? Of course. Why didn't I think of that?"

So Tom Carpenter came in every day, bathing and dressing Frank and putting him through his paces in a rehabilitation program that would hopefully allow him to regain at least partial use of his limbs. If Tom did his job half as well as his daily journal indicated, he was an angel sent directly from God—at least that was Anna's opinion. Frank had seemed belligerent and uncooperative at first. Now he seemed to look forward to Tom's daily visits.

Frank Delaney had lost far too much—Angel felt the loss as well and wished there was something she could do to help him. She hated seeing her father struggle with every daily task. He'd been so strong and capable. Even though her hero worship had diminished as she grew older, a part of her clung to the man her father had been and refused to acknowledge what he had become.

Angel didn't like to think about her father or even spend time with him these days. In fact, she often went out of her way to avoid him. In time, maybe she'd get used to seeing him this way. *You're a coward*, she told herself. Maybe she was, but it hurt too much to be around him.

She brushed thoughts of her father aside and focused on her mother, who seemed willing to accept Angel regardless of what she did or didn't do. Anna had always wanted her daughter to learn to cook; now, thanks to Callen, she was getting her wish.

Anna flashed her daughter a wide grin as she took a large pot out of the cupboard and set it on the stove.

Angel smiled back. "You think Callen will like this?" After placing the cut celery on a plate, she picked up the knife and resumed chopping.

"Of course he will. Everyone likes my soup." Anna rinsed off more celery stalks and set them in front of Angel on the cutting board. "He'll be surprised and pleased. Not just because it's delicious, but because you made it."

"I hope so. I hate to admit it, but I'm feeling intimidated. He's like a real chef."

"Yes, but still not as good as your mama." Anna wasn't boasting, just stating a fact. She'd learned to cook as a young girl from her Italian mother and grandmother.

They were making up one of the family's favorite recipes, with, of course, some minor changes. Angel doubted her mother had ever followed a recipe to the letter. "What makes this soup so good," Anna said, "is that you can use it as a base, then add meatballs, sausage, chicken, or whatever you have handy. I even use it as a base for my bouillabaisse."

"Yum. That's my favorite. Could we do that?"

"Of course. While this is simmering we'll make a list and you can go to the market."

"What now?" Angel placed the rest of the celery into the dish with chopped onion and cauliflower, then dumped the leavings into a bucket that would eventually become compost for the garden.

"Pour some olive oil into the pot, let it heat up a little, then put your vegetables into it. Then you're going to sauté them for a few minutes."

"How much oil?"

"Just a smidgeon."

Angel rolled her eyes and dumped oil in until it barely covered the bottom of the pan. "It's easier to do this if you give me exact amounts."

"Nonsense. Cooking isn't a science. It's an art. A dab of this, a dollop of that. You'll get the hang of it."

"I hope so." Angel slid the cut-up veggies into the hot olive oil, then leaned back as the steam rose into their faces. She stirred the mixture around, coating all the pieces evenly with oil, drawing in a deep breath of the mouth-watering scent as it filled her nostrils with gastronomical promise.

After a few minutes, Anna peered into the mixture. "Perfect. Now turn down the heat, season with salt and pepper and your spices, and keep stirring." She had told Angel earlier to have all of the ingredients ready to go before starting the cooking process. Angel had dutifully measured out minced garlic, cilantro, basil, and some red pepper flakes along with two bay leaves. She sprinkled those spices in and stirred.

"Now, mix that up a little more, then you can put in the tomatoes."

Angel grinned. "Hey, I'm actually making soup." Who would have thought that such a simple task could make her feel so giddy?

Anna peered over Angel's shoulder.

"Tomatoes now?" Angel picked up a jar of homemade canned tomatoes.

Anna nodded. Another smile spread across her face. Angel hadn't seen her mother so happy since her grandchildren's births. The idea that she was making her mother happy pleased her. Angel dumped in the two jars of diced tomatoes and stirred the mixture with a wooden spoon.

"Now add the chicken stock. Then all you have to do is cover the soup and let it simmer until the vegetables are tender."

"What about the pasta?"

Anna smiled. "That comes just before we serve it or the noodles would turn to mush."

"Oh." Angel added the last of the ingredients, stirred, then took a sip of the broth and raised her eyebrows. "Hmm. It's missing something."

Anna laughed. "Well, of course it is. The ingredients need time to marry. Now, what have I been telling you all these years? Cooking isn't so hard."

"I don't know about that." Angel's lips parted in a teasing smile. "It had me in tears."

"Me too." Anna's eyes filled, but her gaze stayed on Angel.

A psychiatrist might have called what passed between them a bonding moment. Angel saw it as so much more. A bridge was beginning to span their separate lives, bringing them together on a level neither had experienced before.

The phone rang. "I'll get it. Might be Callen." Angel wiped her hands on her apron as she hurried into the living room. "Hello?"

"Anna?" The voice sounded breathless, fearful. Angel couldn't place it.

"Um, no, this is Angel. Did you want to talk to my mother?"

"No," the voice said quickly. "Actually, I wanted to reach you. I . . . I need your help." The woman's breathing seemed labored.

"Who is this? Is something wrong?"

"Candace . . . Candace Jenkins. It's my husband. I can't explain it on the phone. I need . . ."

"Do you want me to call the police?" Angel remembered meeting Candace on a domestic violence call after Phillip Jenkins had used her as a punching bag. She'd taken Candace and her three children to the women's shelter.

"N-no. Please don't. I was hoping you could come out to the house."

"I'm not working for the police department right now."

"I know. Please. I need your help."

Suspicious now, Angel asked, "How did you get this number?"

"Your mother volunteers at the shelter. She told me to call if I ever needed help. Please, come."

Angel struggled with the odd request. "All right," she finally agreed.

"Thank you." The call ended with a breathless sob.

Angel hung up and headed back to the kitchen.

Anna looked up and frowned. "What's wrong?"

"I'm not sure. That was Candace Jenkins. She sounded upset. I think she was crying."

"Oh, that poor woman. Don't tell me that wretched husband of hers has beat her up again."

"I don't know." Angel removed the apron her mother had insisted she wear and draped it over a chair. "I didn't realize you knew her."

"From the women's shelter."

Angel nodded. "That's what she said. She asked me not to call the police. She wanted me to come out."

"You? What for?"

Angel bit her lip. "Maybe she feels comfortable with me. I went out to the Jenkins's farm on a domestic violence call several months ago."

"That's when you brought her to the shelter." Anna gripped the back of a chair and shook her head in disgust. "That poor woman.

She had a swollen eye and a huge bruise on her face. She tried to cover it up, but . . ." Anna pinched her lips together, anger sparking in her eyes. "It infuriates me no end, Angel. The abuse cycle goes on and on. We tell them they don't have to stay in an abusive relationship. We offer a way out, and they go back. I tried to talk her out of going back to her husband, but she was so sure things would improve." Anna sighed. "Sometimes they listen. Most of the time they don't. I haven't seen Candace in a while. I was hoping things had actually worked out between them."

"I hope she's okay. I guess I can understand why she'd want me since I'm familiar with the situation."

"I'm not sure it's a good idea for you to go out there alone. Why don't you call Nick?"

Angel considered it. Nick Caldwell was a longtime friend and a police officer. "Not yet," Angel decided. "She specifically asked for me. I'd like to see what's going on. I have my cell phone so I can call in if there's any trouble."

Anna went back to the stove and picked up the wooden spatula. "Go then. I'll take care of the soup." She stirred the mixture and settled a lid on the pot. "But just for the record, I don't have a good feeling about this."

"Neither do I," Angel muttered as she headed for the door.

SIX

———

Angel ran for her car, dodging bullet-sized raindrops. May on the Oregon coast could be cold—especially when the wind blew in from the north, which was what it had been doing for much of the morning. She was glad she'd taken the opportunity to run during the brief sun break. The persistent wind and rain almost made her miss Florida, but not quite.

She ducked into the car and snapped on the seat belt. Turning the key brought the engine to life and a rush of emotion. Angel's 1972 cherry red Corvette had belonged to her older brother, Luke. The Corvette had been his pride and joy. He was the oldest of the five Delaney kids. Dad's favorite. At least he had been until he disappeared. Luke was a lawyer and had been involved in some sort of criminal case when he went missing. On occasion, Angel thought about trying to find him. She certainly had the time now and determined to think more about that possibility later. At the moment, however, she needed to pay a visit to a very distraught woman.

While she maneuvered the Corvette out of the driveway, Angel forced her thoughts to more pleasant matters. Like the warm and wonderful-smelling kitchen she'd just left and how Callen would react when she served him her homemade soup. The silly grin she'd been wearing earlier came back.

Her stomach did a little flip as she thought about Callen again. The intensity of her feelings both surprised and frightened her. She didn't like someone having so much power over her. On the other hand, Angel hadn't felt so alive in years. Part of her wanted to cut her losses and run. The other part wanted to stick around and see where the relationship would lead. She'd promised herself and Callen that much, but with the hours he had to work, developing a relationship could take a while.

Callen had come to a dead end on the Kelsey murder investigation. Jim Kelsey had been killed nearly three months ago. Since drugs had been found in his garage, they originally thought he'd been one of several people murdered by a drug dealer, but the evidence didn't support their theory. His wife, Michelle, had been a suspect as well, but again they had no substantial evidence linking her to the crime other than the fact that Jim Kelsey had abused her. Michelle was first on their list, however, and falling in love with her lawyer hadn't helped her situation any.

The Kelsey case had become a sore spot for the Sunset Cove Police Department as well as the Oregon State Police. The police chief, Joe Brady, didn't like loose ends, but he didn't have enough officers to spare. Her leave had left them short staffed, and with budget cuts they really couldn't afford to hire replacement officers. So they coped, dealing with the priority cases first.

As an Oregon State Police detective, Callen had been assigned to lead up the investigation, but he'd come to a standstill as well. Whoever had killed Kelsey had done a great job of eliminating any evidence linking him or her to the murder. Before leaving, Callen had confided in Angel, saying they'd had to put the investigation on the back burner while he worked on finding the missing girl in Florence.

Angel wished there was something she could do to help him—to help the department.

Maybe there would be if you went back to work. Soon after starting with the Sunset Cove PD, Angel had considered taking the tests to qualify as a detective, but that was before the shooting incident.

Taking additional leave is the right thing to do, Angel reminded herself. *You have to take some time to heal and to figure out who you*

27

are and what you want to do. At the moment her excuses seemed lame. She'd been a police officer for four years, but did she really want to be one? Sometimes she thought she did. Like now, on her way out to the Jenkins's place.

She again reinforced her decision to extend her leave. She was backing up and taking a new direction, determined to achieve some balance in her life. Learning to cook was one of her new goals. Not just for Callen or her mother but for herself. She'd never be the domestic diva her mother was, but she wanted to be able to hold her own if and when Callen asked her to marry him.

Marriage. She and Callen had talked about it once or twice, but Callen needed as much time to adjust to their relationship as she did. Both had been surprised by the depth of their feelings for each other. *No*, Angel thought, *marriage is a long way off. A very long way off.*

At Highway 101 Angel headed south, then turned east along the road that bordered Sunset Cove. Phillip and Candace lived with their three children in a renovated two-story farmhouse on twenty acres. They weren't into big-time farming but did have a few head of cattle, horses, and other animals along with a super-sized garden. Phillip Jenkins had a construction business while Candace kept up the farm.

Seeing the farm just ahead turned Angel's thoughts back to the woman who'd called. Like so many women, Candace had gone back to the abuse. Angel couldn't help but speculate on what had happened. Had Phillip beaten her again and left her incapacitated? Why hadn't she just called 911?

Her thoughts drifted again to Jim Kelsey and the unsolved murder. Kelsey could have been Phillip Jenkins's twin. Both men were big, burly, and abusive.

Angel's anxiety level rose as she drove into the Jenkins's long driveway. After several minutes, she pulled up between a big black truck with the logo Coast Contracting and the family's white van. The truck meant Jenkins was there, and that probably meant a confrontation. Not something Angel looked forward to. *You could call Nick*, she reminded herself.

28

Not yet. The PD had other things to do. If she could handle the situation herself as a civilian, she would. If not, she'd call.

The sliding door on the driver's side of the van stood open. Groceries in plastic bags from Andy's Market littered the floor and backseat.

Her gaze moved to the front porch, where Candace sat on one of the two white wicker chairs. She had on jeans and a pink knit top, mostly covered by a denim jacket. Her shoes were a popular style of hiking boot—a good choice for someone living on a farm or just living in Oregon.

Candace stood when Angel approached, and walked across the porch, then gripped the railing as if she needed the support. Angel looked around but saw no sign of Phillip Jenkins. She maneuvered around the mud holes and made her way to the sidewalk that led through a grape arbor. The rain had eased up, but wet branches dripped water on her head and down her neck as she walked under them. The air smelled fresh and clean. Rays of sun poked through the multiple layers of clouds. She bypassed the walk that led to the front of the house and headed toward the side porch and Candace.

"Thank you for coming." Candace's gaze flickered over Angel and darted to the open door of the house and back.

"Are you okay?" Angel looked the woman over for signs of injury. There were none—at least not on her face. "Did he hurt you?"

She shook her head. "No. He's been good for the last few weeks. He . . ."

Candace crumpled, and Angel hurried to her side, intent on catching her before she fell. She helped the woman back into the chair. "What's wrong? Has he hurt the children?" Angel looked around, her mind conjuring up images of a murder-suicide.

Candace shook her head and lifted her haunted gaze to Angel's. "He's in there." She pointed to the door. "In the living room."

Something about her expression and the way she moved set Angel's stomach on edge. "What happened?"

"I don't know. I went shopping and picked the kids up from school. When I got here, I found him right where I'd left him, in front of the television set. He'd stayed home today to watch a game. The Mariners were playing Oakland. That's where he's from, Oakland. Only when I came back, he . . ." She gasped and covered her mouth with a closed fist.

"He's inside?"

She hauled in a deep breath and nodded. "There was a gun in his hand, one from his collection. He . . . he . . ." She stared at her hands. "He shot himself."

Angel stopped breathing. She leaned against the porch railing to put her thoughts in order. The porch was one of those wide, wraparound types with plenty of room for sitting. The floors and walls were painted white, now muddied by her own footprints leading from the rain-soaked driveway.

A porch swing creaked back and/forth as the wind swirled around them. Crisp, clean cushions in a tropical print adorned the pristine white wicker furniture. Pages of a *Woman's Day* magazine flipped up and fluttered on the glass-covered coffee table. An assortment of plants finished off the scene. The place could have been featured in *Better Homes and Gardens*—certainly not the scene of a suicide.

Angel pocketed her hands and hauled in a deep breath, wishing she hadn't agreed to come. The last thing she wanted to do was walk into that house, but she had to, and when she'd seen Jenkins for herself, she'd call dispatch. This was the part she'd hated most about being a police officer—looking at death. It reminded her how fleeting life could be. How a bullet to the head had stopped her partner in her tracks. How a twelve-year-old boy had died in her arms.

Stop thinking about it. Angel ordered the images away and stepped closer to the door.

"I have to take a look," Angel heard herself saying. Blood pounded in her ears. Her stomach knotted as she steeled herself and headed for the open doorway.

"Wait," Candace ordered. "Take your shoes off. Please." Her tone softened. "It's a house rule. He hates it when the floor is dirty."

The man is dead. I doubt he cares. Angel kept her thoughts to herself. The woman was obviously in shock. A dirty floor was the least of her worries, but Angel obliged, leaving the dazed woman on the porch alone. She slipped out of her loafers and set them just inside the door on a rug apparently placed there for that purpose. The rug held a pair of man-sized work boots, which she surmised belonged to Phillip, along with several pairs of children's shoes.

Not certain as to why, she tiptoed across the highly polished white linoleum floor, noticing the immaculate kitchen and the gleaming counters. When she reached the center of the room, Phillip Jenkins came into view. She stopped, frozen in place.

Phillip Jenkins sat in his brown leather recliner with his stocking feet up and head back, looking as though he'd fallen asleep. A bowl half filled with popcorn and a can of beer sat on the end table to his right. A gun hung from his left hand. The bullet had entered his skull just above his left ear. Not much blood, Angel noted. Candace had said he'd killed himself, but in Angel's mind, suicide didn't jive with what she was seeing. Jenkins had settled in to watch a baseball game on television. The set was still blaring. The game over.

She felt more than heard Candace come up behind her. "I cleaned him up the best I could."

"What did you say?"

But Angel had heard every word. She just couldn't believe them.

SEVEN

———

"There was mud on the floor and blood on the chair and the carpet," Candace explained. "Phillip hates things to be messy and . . ."

Angel groaned and rubbed her forehead. It wouldn't be the first time a person had cleaned up a crime scene. And this was obviously a crime scene. The man had been murdered. "You may have destroyed vital evidence."

"Evidence? I don't understand. He killed himself. Why do you need evidence?"

"Come on." Angel led Candace out of the kitchen and back to the porch. "I need to call the authorities."

"I know. I suppose I should have called them instead of waiting for you, but I couldn't. You understand, don't you?"

"Yeah. I understand." But she didn't, not really. Why had Candace called her mother's place asking for her? To give her more time to clean things up? For moral support? Angel put her shoes back on and joined Candace on the porch. Pulling the cell phone out of her pocket, she dialed 911 and reported the death.

"I'm sorry," she said to Candace when she'd finished making the call. While she wanted to believe the woman's story, she couldn't quite dismiss Candace as the killer. Destroying evidence

32

and failing to call the police provided more than enough reason for suspicion.

Angel glanced at the still-open van door. "Where are the children?" Her mind jumped in with more scenarios. Had Phillip injured or killed the children? Had Candace come to the end of her rope? Had she gone psychotic and killed them all?

"They're in the barn. I told them to feed the animals."

Thank God. Angel released the breath she'd been holding.

"Mommy?" One of the children stood in the barn's yawning dark doorway. "Can we come in the house now? We're cold."

Candace turned toward the child. "Not yet."

"Do they know about Phillip?" Angel asked quietly.

"No. I came in with some of the groceries and asked them to bring some in too. When I saw him, I sent them to the barn. I don't know how I can tell them. They loved their dad. He was good to them when . . ."

When he wasn't drinking. She'd heard the line a hundred times before.

Candace frowned. "I should put the rest of the groceries away."

"No, just leave them where they are. It's fine." Candace had done too much already.

The woman didn't argue. She assumed the same position she'd been in when Angel had first pulled into the driveway, straight backed and staring at some spot on the cloud-scattered horizon.

Angel watched the sky as well. Another storm system was approaching. Her morning patch of sunshine had already become a distant memory.

Angel looked over to the barn. The children stood just inside the doorway, apparently reluctant to disobey their mother's orders. "Mom!" one called out. "We're hungry."

Candace lifted her gaze to Angel. "Can I get them a snack? I have some cheese and crackers and fruit in the van."

"Sure. I'll come with you."

They were heading down the porch steps when Nick Caldwell pulled up in an unmarked car and whipped into a parking spot beside her Corvette. Being a friend of her brothers, Nick had practically lived at the Delaney house while they were growing

33

up. Angel loved him like a brother and had a lot of respect for him as a fellow officer.

"Hey, Angel, what are you doing out here?" Nick was six years her senior, tall and slim but muscular. He'd been her oldest brother, Luke's, best friend.

Angel left Candace at the van and hurried over to talk to Nick, relieved to be handing the problem over to the authorities. After a quick hug she filled him in. "Mrs. Jenkins asked me to come out. I thought maybe he'd beaten her up, but . . ." She nodded toward the house. "He's dead."

Nick groaned, his feelings apparently echoing her own. The last thing they needed in the small coastal town was another murder.

"It gets worse." Angel ran a hand through her thick curls still damp from the earlier downpour. "She cleaned the place up."

"That's just great." He rubbed his neck. "Did she shoot him?"

Angel shrugged. "I don't know. Says she didn't. She claims she went shopping and picked her kids up from school, then came home and found him. She seems to think he killed himself—at least that's the story she told me."

"You don't agree?"

Angel shook her head. "He was stretched out in a recliner, watching a baseball game."

Another vehicle pulled in, Bo Williams, a sheriff's deputy. Behind him came an ambulance, Dr. Bennett, the medical examiner, and two people in a white SUV. The place was beginning to look like a used car lot. Bo and Nick began setting up the crime scene, roping off the house with yellow tape. A man and a woman stepped out of the SUV. The OSP insignia blazoned on their navy blue caps and coveralls indicated they were from the Oregon State Police crime lab. They were wearing black boots and carried their evidence-gathering equipment in aluminum cases.

"You must be Angel Delaney." The woman stretched out her right hand as they fell into step beside Angel. "I'm Jill Stafford, and this is Terry Bartlett."

"Hi." Angel shook the extended hands in the order they were offered.

34

"Detective Riley has been telling us about you." Terry winked. "Nice to finally meet you."

"Thanks. It's nice to meet you too. What has Riley been telling you?" She grinned. "On second thought, I don't think I want to know."

Jill chuckled. "It wasn't what he said so much as the way he looked when he said it. You've made quite an impression on him."

Callen had made quite an impression on Angel as well, but she didn't say so. She walked as far as the door and debated whether or not to stay with Candace to lend moral support.

Nick took over as lead and asked Bo to keep an eye on Candace until he could question her. "Angel," he said, putting an arm across her shoulder, "I'd like you to come in with us. I need you to go over things with me again. Tell me exactly what happened."

"Sure." Relieved not to have to stay with the widow, she put on the shoe coverings he handed her then followed him inside. The lab techs had already begun processing the crime scene, with Terry taking photos and Jill making preliminary assessments.

While watching the medical examiner check out the body, she told Nick again what had happened, then added, "I just don't think Phillip Jenkins would kill himself. Not just because he was watching a game. He was too . . . arrogant and self-assured. That night I came out on the domestic violence call, he didn't seem the least bit repentant. He was more upset about our being there and interfering than he was about hurting his wife." She glanced at the television screen that was still turned to a sports channel. "Look at the food and beer and the recliner. He was all set up to enjoy the game, not to kill himself."

"Was he here alone?" Nick asked.

"Candace didn't mention anyone else being here. You'll have to ask her."

"What do you know about the family?" Nick hunkered down beside the medical examiner to get a closer look at the head wound.

Angel told him about the domestic violence call, when she'd first met Phillip and Candace and their three children. "One of the kids called us. The oldest one, I think. By the time I got here, things were under control. Candace refused to press charges. She did go to the shelter for a while though, then went back to him." Angel chewed on her lower lip.

"Maybe if she had followed through and left him, he'd still be alive." Nick straightened and met her gaze.

Angel didn't answer. It was far too soon to be making allegations against Candace, but she couldn't fault Nick for doing the same thing she'd done herself.

"Where are the kids now?" Nick glanced over at her, hands resting on his hips.

"The two younger ones are in the barn. I don't know about the oldest."

Angel watched Jill Stafford pick up something off the floor with tweezers and tuck it into an evidence bag.

"You're right about one thing, Angel," Dr. Bennett said. "The guy didn't commit suicide."

"How can you tell—other than the fact that it doesn't make sense?"

"His wound indicates that he was shot from about four to five feet away."

"So someone did kill him." Though Angel had no authority here, she couldn't help thinking about motive. Candace certainly had that, but somehow Angel couldn't see the woman as a killer. Candace had other options and knew it. She could have gotten a restraining order or gone back to the shelter. And hadn't Candace told her that Phillip had been doing better, that he hadn't hurt her lately? Of course, she could have been lying.

Angel hung around until Nick and the ME placed Jenkins in a body bag and onto a stretcher. Once they removed the body, she breathed a little easier. Terry photographed the empty and stained recliner. A remote control unit lay on its side against the right arm of the chair. That and the fact Jenkins had placed his snacks and drink to his right indicated that he might be right-handed. If that was true, why had the gun been placed in his left hand? If Candace had killed him, wouldn't she have known to place it in his right hand? Maybe she was too frightened or distracted. Of course, it could mean nothing at all, since a lot of left-handed people are ambidextrous, and his food may have been on his right because that's where the end table was located. Still, she made a mental note to ask Candace and to mention it to Nick later.

Angel took another look around the tidy living room. Photos on the mantle depicted a happy family. One showed them posing together on a beach. They were all tan, with sun-bleached hair. There were other photos leaning against the wall, some professional, some from school, some not.

No dust. The meticulous environment niggled at her. Had Candace and the children been forced to keep the house perfect for Jenkins? Had Candace snapped, unable or unwilling to accommodate him anymore? Had he pushed her too far?

"You might as well go home, Angel." Nick settled a hand on her shoulder. "We can take it from here."

Angel almost wished she was still working so she'd have a reason to be there other than curiosity and concern for the family. She didn't want to go—didn't want to be left out of the loop. Nick was right, she should leave, but his suggestion annoyed her.

There's nothing more you can do, she told herself. Nick and the others would gather and sort through the evidence. The medical examiner would perform an autopsy. They'd put all the pieces together and hopefully come up with a suspect.

Angel made her way outside. Bo stood near his car, talking into his cell phone and looking toward the barn.

"They're going to need a place to stay while we're processing the scene." Jill came up behind Angel. "We won't be able to let them in here for a day or two."

"I can take care of that," Angel said, relieved she'd be able to hang around a bit longer.

Jill nodded. "I'll tell Nick. We'll need to go over her car as well. If she shot him, it would have been before she left to pick up the kids—there may be evidence. So maybe you can drive them into town."

"Sure. I'll get them into a hotel—or maybe the shelter." Angel glanced at the wicker sofa where Candace had been sitting. It was empty.

"She's in the barn, with her kids," Jill offered. "Said she needed to get them a snack and tell them about their dad."

"Thanks." Angel removed the shoe coverings and placed them in a box by the door.

Candace was sitting on a bale of hay just inside the double doors, her gaze directed toward the house. Her youngest child, a girl about five, huddled beside her. The second child, a boy, glanced over at Angel. He stood on a gate looking into a stall and jumped down when Angel entered the barn and joined his mother. Standing behind Candace, he placed what looked like a protective hand on her shoulder. Did they know yet? With his father gone, had he already slipped into the protector mode? Protector? Maybe the poor kid had been in that mode for a long time.

Angel hunkered down in front of Candace. "How are you holding up?"

Candace turned to look at her then, her eyes unfocused and confused. "Is he . . . is his body still in the house? The kids are getting hungry. I need to start dinner."

"He's gone, but you can't go in there for a while. The police are still gathering evidence. You'll need a place to stay tonight. Do you have any family or friends you could stay with?"

She stared off toward the house again. "No. No one. Our families are in California. We haven't really made any friends—not people I could ask. We haven't lived here very long, and we live so far out."

Isolation. Another pattern of abuse. Angel thought about the soup in her mother's inviting kitchen. "We'll figure out something. In the meantime, you can come to my parents' place for dinner."

"Oh, we couldn't."

"Yes, you can. We have a huge pot of soup on the stove. My mom would be very unhappy if I didn't bring you over." Angel took out her cell phone and dialed her parents' number. When Anna answered, Angel explained the situation.

"Of course. Bring them, and tell Candace she and the children are welcome to spend the night."

"Uh, Ma, I'm not sure that's a good idea."

"Nonsense. They need a place to stay, and we have plenty of room."

"All right. We'll see how things go."

After hanging up Angel relayed the message.

"Your mother is so sweet. But we couldn't stay. I wouldn't want to put her out."

"Like she says, they have plenty of room. Besides, she'll be upset with me if I don't bring you."

"I don't know. We have sleeping bags and camping equipment. We could sleep in the barn."

"That's not a good idea." Angel glanced at Bo, who had moved from his car to the porch and was having a conversation with Nick. Both officers looked their way.

"The police are going to need to question all of you. You'll need someone to watch the children when they do." *They may even arrest you.*

Candace stared at the hay-scattered floor and soothed her little girl's golden curls. "Are you sure she won't mind?"

"Positive."

Pressing her hands to her knees, Angel straightened. She glanced from one child to the other. "Do they know?"

Candace nodded.

"I'm so sorry about your dad," Angel said to them.

"Don't be sad." The little girl slipped her hand into Angel's. "Daddy's in heaven with Jesus. Want to see our baby goat?"

"It's a kid," the boy corrected.

"Sure." Angel allowed the little girl to pull her into the depths of the old barn. They led her back to the stable where the boy had been when she'd first come in. He climbed on the wooden door and pointed into the corner of the stall.

"He's adorable." Angel watched the kid take several wobbly steps. "When was he born?"

"It's a she," the boy said. "Night before last."

"We named her Midnight," the girl said, "'cause she's so black and that's the time she was borned."

"That's a nice name. What are your names?"

"Dorfy," the little girl answered. "My brother's name is Brian."

"She means Dorothy, after the girl in *The Wizard of Oz*. That's our mom's favorite movie. She's got a tooth missing, so she can't talk very good."

"Hmm." Angel felt a wave of sadness wash over her. *Kids shouldn't have to suffer like this. Please, God, let their mother be innocent. They shouldn't have to lose both parents.*

Dorothy clasped Angel's hand even tighter than before. "Are you taking us to your house?"

"To my parents, yes."

She frowned. "We can't go until Sissy comes home. She won't know where we are."

Brian jumped backward off the gate. "You don't need to worry. Mom will pick her up."

Candace glanced at her watch. "Brian's right. We need to go. Gracie will be waiting." She nodded toward the officers. "They told me to stay here, but . . ."

"Let me check with Officer Caldwell. Maybe they'll let you go with me now and question you later." She'd also need to borrow a vehicle, as hers was a two-seater. Maybe Nick would let her use his.

Candace sighed. "I don't know how I'm going to manage without Phillip."

"You will." Angel told her the crime lab would be going over the van and that she'd have to drive them. "Wait here while I make arrangements."

"How will I get my van back?" Candace glanced worriedly at the groceries still sitting in the back. "Who will take care of the groceries? I put away the perishables, but . . ."

"I'll bring you out here tomorrow, or whenever the police are finished." *If you're not in jail.*

"But our clothes. I don't have anything for the children to wear tomorrow for school."

School? Your husband has just died and you're worried about what the kids are going to wear to school? Angel kept her thoughts to herself. Candace apparently was still in shock. "They won't let us in the house right now, but I'll come back out later and pick up a few things."

40

Candace hesitated, a deep frown etched into her face. She clearly didn't want to give her home over to strangers. Finally she nodded and stood in the driveway, an arm around each of the children, while Angel went back to the house. She found Nick still inside talking to the lab techs.

"Hey, Nick, Mrs. Jenkins needs to pick up her daughter from school. How would you feel about my taking her and the kids into town? They're going to need to eat, and I think it might be best if we get them out of here."

"I need to question them." Nick walked over to her. "Besides, you can't take them in the Vette."

"I know, I'll need to borrow yours."

"No way. I can't let you do that. In case you've forgotten, you're technically a civilian. If something happened to the car, it would be my neck."

"Come on, Nick. We can't let them stay out here. You're not going to be done for hours yet. I'll take them into town and bring the car back."

"I don't know."

"They'll be at my parents' place," she assured him. "Don't worry. I'll keep an eye on them."

He rubbed at the lines of indecision on his forehead and pulled a set of keys from his pocket. "Okay, but make sure she doesn't go anywhere else. And give me your keys in case I have to leave . . . and put the out-of-service sign on the car door."

From the look on his face when she handed him her car keys, she suspected he didn't mind exchanging vehicles as much as he wanted her to believe.

Angel led them to Nick's car and opened the doors. The children scrambled into the back, with Brian going on about how neat it was to ride in a police car. "Wow. This is so cool. Can you put the siren on?"

"Maybe later," Angel told him. She opened the trunk and retrieved the magnetic sign, placing it squarely on the driver's side door.

To Brian and Dorothy's delight, she turned on the siren once they reached the main road, letting it run for a full minute before suppressing it again. Ten minutes later, they pulled up in front of Sunset Cove High School.

Gracie was waiting on a bench in front of the school, arms folded and mouth set in a grim line. She eyed Angel suspiciously and frowned when her mother stepped out of the car. Something told Angel that Gracie didn't share her brother's enthusiasm for riding in an official vehicle. Candace took three steps toward Gracie and stopped.

"You're half an hour late." Gracie stood and picked up her book bag.

"I'm sorry." Candace just stood there, arms stiff at her sides.

"What's wrong?" Gracie demanded. "Where's the van? Who is she? Why are you riding in a . . . a police car?" Gracie was a tall, slender girl with her mother's silky blonde hair and blue eyes. She glanced around, a panicky look in her eyes. Angel half expected her to bolt.

"I . . . honey, it's your father. He's . . ."

"What? What's wrong?"

"He's dead."

Gracie's eyes narrowed as she assessed her mother. The girl said nothing, but Angel noticed the strange, almost conspiratorial, look that passed between them.

Candace wrapped an arm around Gracie's shoulder. "Come on." She introduced Angel before opening the back door to let Gracie climb into the backseat with her siblings.

Minutes later they pulled into the driveway of the Delaney home. The single-story rambler had a warm brick exterior and was surrounded by lush plants, with rhododendrons four to six feet in height, all in bloom.

"Oh, the rhodies are gorgeous," Candace commented as they exited the car.

"My mother's pride and joy." Angel ushered Candace and the children inside and stood aside while her mother hugged them all, murmuring words of comfort and assuring Candace that she and the children were more than welcome to stay as long as they needed to.

Before showing them to their rooms, Anna took Angel aside.

"Don't look so worried. You've done the right thing bringing them here. Now run to the market and get some romaine and tomatoes so we can have salad with your soup."

"Should I get the seafood too?"

Anna pursed her lips. "Better not. The children may not like it. I'll just toss in some sautéed chicken."

On the way to the market, Angel thought again about Candace cleaning up the crime scene. She thought too about the look that had passed between Gracie and her mother at the school. Did Gracie know something? Did she suspect her mother?

Concern shivered through her. *What have you done, Angel?* At the time, bringing Candace and her children home to her parents had seemed the logical solution. Now she wasn't so sure.

43

EIGHT

Angel picked up the groceries, adding strawberries, angel food cake, and whipping cream to her list, along with some snacks for the kids, then went back to the house. She still hadn't heard from Callen and decided that if he didn't call by 9:00, she'd call him.

Anna met her at the door, taking one of the bags and heading into the kitchen. Angel hurried behind her, noting that the children were lounging on the sofa, Gracie writing in a notebook, Brian and Dorothy reading. "You guys look studious."

"We are." Dorothy gave her a toothless grin. "We're doing our homework. We hafta, or we can't watch TV after dinner."

Gracie glanced up and rolled her eyes. "Right, like you really have to study."

"I do. Mom says."

Gracie moved her head from side to side and continued writing. They seemed oddly unaffected by their father's death. Candace apparently believed in maintaining normalcy at all cost.

Angel ducked into the kitchen and set the groceries on the counter. Candace stood at the sink, folding a dishcloth. The table had already been set.

"Looks like you've been busy," Angel said.

44

"Everything's ready except the salad," Anna told her. "I'll let you put that together while I check on your father."

"Is he eating with us?"

"I'm working on it."

Minutes later, Candace, the children, and Anna gathered around the table. Anna asked that they hold hands for grace. Her brief prayer offered thanks for the food and blessings for family and friends. She omitted any mention of Phillip Jenkins's death, most likely for the children's sake. She concluded with an amen, and they all raised their heads. All, that is, except Dorothy.

With her eyes tightly shut, she added a petition of her own. "And bless my daddy and Jesus in heaven. Amen."

"Thank you, Dorothy." Candace, eyes filled with tears, ran a hand over her small daughter's hair and kissed her cheek.

"Who sits there?" Brian pointed to Angel's father's place at the head of the table.

"My husband, Frank," Anna answered. "He's not feeling well."

The place had been set as it usually was but remained conspicuously empty. Eating was a chore for Frank. He had to wear a bib to catch the drool that flowed out of his drooping mouth and down his chin.

"When are the police going to talk to me?" Candace asked, bringing Angel out of her reverie.

"I'm not sure. Tonight, maybe tomorrow."

"You said you would go back out to the farm and get what we'll need to stay overnight. I probably should go with you, but I hate to leave the kids." Candace still wore a confused expression. Tears gathered in her eyes, and she dabbed them away with a tissue. She stirred her soup and took a tentative sip.

"You don't need to come with me. Just tell me what you need, and I'll go as soon as we've finished eating."

Candace nodded and turned toward Anna. "It's so good of you to have us."

"I'm happy for the company."

Shifting her gaze to Angel, Candace said, "I don't know what I would have done without you today. Thanks again for coming."

Angel wasn't sure how to respond, so she didn't. She examined the spoon as she dipped it into the soup, filling it with vegetables and a piece of chicken, and lifted it to her mouth. The soup was as good as it looked. Too bad Callen wasn't there to enjoy it with them.

Candace sighed. "I suppose I have to make arrangements for the funeral. I still can't believe he's gone."

"We can call Tim after dinner if you like," Anna offered. "He's the pastor of St. Matthews. Unless you have a church."

"Tim? Oh, you mean Pastor Delaney. He's related to you?"

"My son."

"I hadn't made the connection. We only went once. Phillip said we should start going to church again." She glanced around the table. "I liked him. I think Phillip did too. Yes, if he wouldn't mind."

"He'll be more than happy to help with the arrangements." Anna picked up the basket of homemade rolls she'd made and passed them around.

Gracie, who'd been brooding since they sat down, took a roll and buttered it. She gave Candace a hard, cold stare. "Why are you acting so sad? I'm glad he's dead, and so are you."

Candace stiffened and sucked in a sharp breath. "Gracie, you mustn't talk like that. Your father loved us."

Gracie sneered. "Yeah, right. He hurt you. He deserved to die."

Turning her apologetic gaze to Anna then to Angel, Candace said, "I'm sorry. She isn't usually like this."

"Like what?" Gracie threw down her napkin. "Honest? You're right about that. It's hard to be honest around a person who slaps you when you try to express an opinion that happens to be different from his."

"It was the alcohol. We've talked about that." Candace clenched her fist around the cloth napkin in her lap. Tears gathered in her eyes again. "He promised he'd quit. He was trying. He was a good man, but the alcohol made him lose control sometimes."

Gracie threw her roll on the plate and pushed her chair away from the table. "If he loved us, he would have stopped, Mama.

46

He would have." Turning to Anna she said, "May I be excused, please?"

"Of course," Anna told her.

Gracie headed for the door.

"Where are you going?" Candace called after her.

"Out." Gracie grabbed her coat from the entry closet and yanked open the door.

"I'd better go after her." Candace apologized again and followed Gracie outside.

"Whew." Angel set her napkin beside her plate. "That was interesting."

"Gracie is a brat." Brian pierced several romaine leaves with his fork and stuffed them into his mouth.

"Mama says it's because she's a teenager and her 'mones get mixed up," Dorothy said.

"Not 'mones. Hormones." Brian picked up his milk and chugged the rest of it down. "And that's just a dumb excuse. Dad said."

"She's upset and rightly so." Anna stood and began picking up the dishes.

Angel got up to help. Gracie had an attitude. But she also had a point. Apparently Gracie prided herself on being honest. How much of Candace's grief was genuine? How much an act?

Angel had almost finished clearing the table when Candace and Gracie came back in. They seemed to have worked things out between them. Gracie was more subdued, though she didn't apologize for her outburst.

After taking off their coats, Candace sent Gracie into Angel's old room to do her homework, then turned on the television set for Brian and Dorothy. Once the kids were settled, she came into the kitchen, offering to help Anna clean up so Angel could make a run out to the farm. "I don't mean to rush you, but I like to have the little ones in bed by 8:00. That gives them some time to read before lights-out."

Angel gladly handed over the dishtowel. "Is Gracie okay?"

"She's upset and angry. I understand that." Candace frowned. "She didn't mean what she said. You know how kids her age can be. Their emotions are all over the board."

47

Angel didn't remember being that volatile, but then she hadn't had an abusive father. And her father hadn't been murdered. But Gracie's reaction did concern Angel. Not all that long ago, she'd read about a case in which a fourteen-year-old girl had murdered her mother in a fit of rage. And another in which a thirteen-year-old boy had killed his parents in cold blood because they wouldn't let him go to a party.

"He deserved to die," Gracie had said. Thinking about the comment now and the hard look that went with it sent a chill through Angel. Had Gracie's anger reached the boiling point? Had she killed her father?

NINE

Wednesday, May 7

Dear Dr. Campbell,

*My joy at ridding the world of one more abuser was short-lived
as I watched the news tonight and saw the horrific details of
the murdered girl from Florence. My heart aches when I think
of the cruelty that poor child endured at the hands of her killer.
Oh, dear God, why couldn't I have known? Why couldn't I have
been there to stop him?*

*I know I shouldn't beat myself up over it. Like you've often said,
you can't fix everything or everyone. You have to choose your
battles. Perhaps that's the hardest part, choosing one's battles.
It's too late for poor Christy, so I must focus on those women
I can help, the women right here in Sunset Cove. There are so
many to choose from—so hard to determine which abuser will
be the next to die.*

Dragonslayer

TEN

Angel called Nick to let him know she was on her way out to the farm to return the squad car and to pick up clothing for Candace and the kids for their overnight stay. He told her it was about time.

Nick stood on the porch, eyeing her when she drove up, then coming down the steps to meet her.

"How's it going?" She stepped out of the car and shut the door.

"Slow. Have to hand it to these people, they're thorough. We should be wrapping things up soon. At least for the night." He gave his watch an impatient glance. "I hope." He stretched and rubbed the back of his neck, stretching the blue uniform tight across his muscular chest.

"Poor baby," she teased.

He frowned and raised an eyebrow. "Hey, smart mouth. You try pulling two shifts every day for two weeks. This is all your fault, you know. If you'd come back to work, the rest of us wouldn't have to put in such long hours."

The comment surprised her. Nick had encouraged her to take the time off. "No way am I taking the blame. Our fine citizens voted down the tax increases, and the powers that be started cutting where it hurts."

50

He sighed. "I'm sorry. And you're right, I shouldn't be blaming you. The Oregon State Police got it worse than we did. Speaking of which, where's Detective Riley? I thought he was due back today. I was hoping to run some things by him."

She shrugged, trying not to let her concern show. "He hasn't called. I heard they'd had a break in the investigation involving that high school girl."

"Yeah, glad I'm not working on that one. They found her in a shallow grave late this afternoon."

"Oh no." Angel leaned back against the car. "I was hoping . . ."

"Me too, but I had a hunch it would turn out this way—especially when I heard about the blood evidence in the trunk of the car they found."

"I imagine Callen will have to stay there a while longer with everything breaking loose." Angel didn't bother to hide her disappointment.

"For sure. You could always go down there to see him."

Angel shook her head. "I could, but I won't. I'd just be in the way."

"Well, fortunately, we aren't going to need the state detectives or a lot of manpower on this one."

"What do you mean?" Angel peered at him, then let her gaze drift toward the house.

"It's an open-and-shut case. Obviously, his wife killed him."

"Nick, don't you think it's too soon to make that kind of assumption?"

"What's that supposed to mean? You don't think she did it?"

"No, I don't." Angel couldn't have told him when she'd come to that conclusion—or if she really had. "At least not yet."

Nick shook his head. "Because she's a woman?"

"No. Of course not. But there are other possibilities." She didn't mention Gracie, and wouldn't—not until she checked some things out.

"You got some intuition thing going? Or maybe you know something I don't."

"It's just something she said. Candace thought Phillip was doing better. She said he hadn't hurt her lately. They were working things out, and he was seeing a counselor."

"What she says doesn't mean a heck of a lot. She's probably wanting us to think that. You know how it goes."

"Maybe I just don't think you should rush to judgment on this."

"Look, Angel. We've been friends for a long time. You were a pretty good cop. But you're not in uniform. You're a civilian, and that means your opinion is just that—an opinion."

"My brain didn't fall out when I gave up the uniform," Angel snapped back.

"No, but you're not a detective. And dating one doesn't give you the right to act like one."

"That is totally unfair." Angel threw up her hands. "Fine. You don't want my opinion, then figure it out on your own."

"I plan to."

Angel brushed by him. "I'm going inside to get some stuff for Candace and the kids."

She paused at the entry and took off her shoes, noticing the huge amount of mud that had been tracked in onto the porch and entry. No wonder Candace insisted everyone leave their shoes at the door. Candace had said something about cleaning up muddy tracks. Had they belonged to Jenkins's killer?

Oh, Candace, why did you have to clean things up? We might have been able to prove you didn't do it.

Unless . . . Maybe she had cleaned up the prints because she recognized them. A woman comes home and sees her husband has been shot. Any normal woman would have called the police right away. She hadn't. Candace had washed the floor, eliminating the muddy prints. Was it because she thought the prints belonged to Gracie? Maybe that's what the look that had passed between them at the school had been about—a mother protecting her daughter.

On the other hand, the woman did seem obsessed with keeping a clean house. As she walked through the house and up the stairs, Angel was again taken aback by Candace's housekeeping skills. Her own mother was a terrific homemaker, but even she couldn't keep things this neat all the time. Angel went from room to room, and each one, even those belonging to the children, was surprisingly tidy.

As a kid, Angel's own room had been a disaster most of the time. She smiled, thinking about her mother's insistence that at least once a week she should be able to see the floor. Sometimes Angel would push stuff under the bed in an attempt to tidy up. That worked for all of two Saturdays until Anna got suspicious about the lack of dirty laundry. Angel had been grounded for two weeks.

She knelt on the floor and lifted the dust ruffle on Gracie's bed. The hardwood floor was spotless, gleaming from the scant light that managed to sneak in from the ceiling light. "Not even a dust bunny," she said aloud. "Now that's scary."

"Hey, Angel. I thought I heard someone in here." Jill, the CSI tech, came in just as Angel was getting up.

"Oh, hi." Angel flushed, feeling like a kid caught in the act. "I was just noticing how neat everything is. Not normal."

"I noticed that too." Jill smiled. "Some women are like that. Me? I'm lucky if my house sees a dust rag once a month. Guess it's a matter of priorities."

"I guess." *Or necessity.*

"Did you get everything you needed?" Jill asked. "We're about to lock up."

"Yeah. I think so." She took another look at the two suitcases Candace had told her she'd find in the master bedroom. Along with the clothes, she'd tucked in a couple of stuffed animals from each child's room. In Gracie's, she looked around and picked up a handheld CD player and headset along with a couple CDs. Just as she was leaving, she grabbed a teddy bear off the bed. "Just in case," she told Jill.

"Nice gesture."

"Jill . . ." Angel hesitated, not sure how her request would be taken. "You probably heard that I'm on leave from the Sunset Cove PD."

She smiled. "Nick told us. Said you'd taken leave—of your senses."

Angel laughed. "Nick's just jealous. Anyway, I was wondering if you could keep me in the loop on this. Since I was the first one to talk to Candace and call it in, I'd like to know what you find."

"I'm sorry, but I don't think that would be a good idea." She bit into her lower lip. "It's not that I don't trust you. I could lose my job . . ."

"Sure. I understand. Um, don't say anything to Nick about my asking. He's a bit testy about my being interested in the investigation."

Jill nodded. "I wouldn't take it personally. He's probably overworked like the rest of us."

"Do you think Candace killed her husband?"

"Tough call. If she hadn't cleaned everything up, we'd be able to come closer to answering that."

"I'm not sure why, but I don't think she did it."

"You may be right. At this point I couldn't even venture a guess. We'll know more when we process the evidence—which may be a while. We're backed up six weeks at the lab."

"That's a long wait."

"Don't I know it. But we'll do some of the preliminary work-ups. That will help."

After saying good-bye, Angel hurried downstairs, where she traded keys with Nick and placed the bags in her trunk. She climbed into her own car and waved at Nick and Terry as she started the engine.

After dropping the suitcases off at her parents' house, Angel headed to Callen's house to feed Mutt. Halfway there, her cell phone rang.

"Callen." If hearts could dance, Angel would swear hers was doing a jig. "Where are you?"

"Still in Florence. We had a breakthrough today." He sounded tired, and Angel wished she could feed him soup and massage his shoulders.

"I heard. Nick said you found her body."

He cleared his throat. "Unfortunately."

"I'm sorry. I kept hoping it would turn out differently."

"Looks like she's been dead for about two days."

"Any idea who did it?"

54

"We have a car and are tracking down the owner." He cleared his throat again. "Angel, if you don't mind, I'd just as soon not talk about the case. Tell me about your day. How are you liking the life of leisure?"

"What leisure?" Angel filled him in on the Jenkins murder. "I wish you were here. Nothing against Nick, but the Sunset Cove PD could use your expertise."

"Ah, so it finally comes out. You only want me for my brains."

"Shoot," she teased, "I didn't mean for you to find out so soon."

"Sounds like they're doing fine without me."

"I don't think so. Nick has his mind made up that Candace is guilty, and he hasn't even questioned her yet."

"Nick's a good man. I doubt he'd come to that conclusion without good cause."

"Humph. He's tired and overworked and I'm afraid he's taking the easy way out. By the way, I made soup for you today."

"You made me soup?"

"Uh-huh. My mother's specialty. Is that so hard to believe?"

"Yes. Now I'm even more disappointed about not being able to come home."

"Well, it's all gone. Ma and I ended up feeding it to Candace Jenkins and her kids."

"That would be the murder victim's family?" He sounded none too happy at the news.

"Right. They're staying at my parents' house."

"Is that a good idea? If Nick thinks the wife killed him, your parents may be in danger."

"I don't think she did it. Besides, if she did kill her husband, it was because of his abusive behavior. It's not like she's a serial killer or anything." Once again Angel's thoughts shifted to Gracie, and once again she kept silent about the girl's possible involvement.

"Let's hope not. Anna is the kindest woman I know, but this wasn't a wise move on either of your parts."

"Callen, I don't need a lecture." She sighed, wishing she hadn't brought it up.

"Sorry. I'm worried about you is all. Did this Jenkins guy leave a suicide note?"

"I don't think so—at least not in plain view. Nick would have said something."

"Do you know if they checked his computer?"

"I imagine they will." Angel doubted Nick had. "Besides, he didn't kill himself. The ME said he was murdered."

"That may be, but they need to look at every possible angle. Someone may have written a note for him."

"I agree. Maybe you should talk to Nick. Seems like he could use a mentor."

"Maybe I will."

"Could we talk about something else?" Angel asked. "We keep gravitating to murder."

"Sure." He chuckled. "I miss you."

"I miss you too. When are you coming home?"

"I'm hoping I can get away this weekend. I really want to get up there and talk to the guy who owns the abandoned car. There's no doubt the victim was in that trunk." Callen sighed.

"The owner lives here, in Sunset Cove?"

"Yeah, we're checking him out."

"Who is it? Maybe I can help."

"Mitch Bailey."

Angel raised her eyebrows in surprise. "No kidding. He's been our family mechanic for years. Nice guy."

"He's not a suspect—at least not at this point. He reported his car stolen last week."

"If he said it was stolen, then I'm sure it was. Mitch is a solid guy." On the other hand, how well did she know him?

"Hmm. Like I said, I'll be questioning him."

"Is there anything I can do for you up here?" Angel said, then wondered if she should have.

After a moment's silence Callen asked, "You applying for a job? Maybe as crime lab tech?"

"Not exactly."

"Let me guess. You're wishing you hadn't extended your leave and had gone back to work at the PD."

"No. I need more time away, but . . ." Angel hesitated. "I was thinking today about finding a different type of job. As strange as it may seem, law enforcement is the only thing that sounds appealing."

"I'm not surprised. You're a good cop. I know you have some decisions to make, but going into police work to please your father isn't such a bad thing. Besides, knowing you, I really doubt that's the case. You don't strike me as the submissive type."

"What's that supposed to mean?"

"Just that your father may have influenced you, but I doubt you'd have gone into law enforcement unless you really wanted to."

"Maybe." Angel chewed on her lower lip. "But what about my aversion to guns?"

"Normal reaction considering what you've been through."

"Are you saying I should go back to work for the PD?"

"Not yet. It's too soon."

"Yeah," Angel agreed. "It is."

Out on the main road, Angel turned south toward Callen's beach house. "Hey, I'm on my way to your place right now to take care of Mutt."

"I feel terrible having to leave him alone so long. Should have brought him with me." He sighed. "But then he'd have been cooped up in the hotel room."

"You could always come back and get him tonight." Angel was surprised at the longing she heard in her tone. "And you could see me at the same time. I could try making that soup again."

"You have no idea how good that sounds. But I can't."

"It was just a thought. Anyway, don't worry about Mutt. I'm taking good care of him. It's you I'm worried about." She thought again about driving down to Florence to see him, but she couldn't leave now—not with Candace and the kids staying at her parents' house.

"Angel, are you still there?"

"Yeah. Just thinking. I'm pulling into your driveway. If you want to hang on a minute, you can say hello to your dog."

Mutt looked longingly at her through the picture window, wiggling and bouncing from the window to the door. When Angel finally got the door open, the white fluff ball pounced on her, licking and barking in delight. Angel laughed and leaned down to pick up the wriggling pup. "Hey, Mutt. Are you glad to see me? I have a surprise for you. Callen is on the phone. Want to say hi to him?"

She could have sworn Mutt nodded.

Chuckling, she put the phone to the dog's ear. Mutt squirmed and whimpered at the sound of Callen's voice, then barked his own greeting as if to chew his master out for not being there.

Angel put the phone back to her own ear. "I think he's telling you to come home."

Callen groaned. "I have a call coming in. I have to go. I love you."

"I love you too."

"I'll call you tomorrow."

Angel pressed the button to end the reception and slipped the phone into her pocket.

I love you too. Had she really said *I love you*? The words had slipped out so naturally, as if they'd been saying them for a long time. Maybe in her heart she had. Sudden tears dripped onto Mutt's silky white fur. The dog whined in sympathy and licked the tears away. Angel shook her head. "I know. I'm being ridiculous." She pulled a slightly used tissue out of her pocket and blew her nose.

"Come on, dog. Let's get you something to eat." She set the wiggle worm on the floor and headed for the kitchen.

Minutes later, Angel sat on the couch watching Mutt devour his special blend. The dog eyed her warily as if he were afraid she'd leave him. When he'd gobbled up the food, he ran toward her and leaped into her lap. After thoroughly kissing her hands and face, he settled into a ball beside her and heaved an enormous sigh.

"You silly little thing. You're lonesome, aren't you? If I could have pets at my apartment, I'd take you home with me." She stroked his head and back, feeling like an ogre at the thought of leaving him again. "Tell you what. How would you like it if I stayed here tonight?"

Mutt peered up at her, his tail whipping back and forth.

"I'll take that as a yes."

Mutt jumped off her lap and went to stand at the patio door. Good thing he was trained. She'd forgotten about taking him outside. She took his leash off a peg by the door and slipped it onto his collar. Mutt charged ahead, leading the way over the dunes.

While Mutt did his job, Angel stood with her head tipped back, watching the stars overhead. The half-moon shone like a beacon, lighting up the waves with silver highlights.

The night was crisp and cool. She watched the whitecaps roll in, thinking of the times she and Callen had walked along this stretch of beach, and how much she wanted him beside her right now.

Once inside, Angel removed her jacket and hung it in the closet, then scoured the refrigerator for something to feed her own growling stomach. Callen, being the efficient chef that he was, had cleaned out everything perishable. The cupboards yielded a wide array of snacks, from roasted soybeans to rock-hard peas with a hot wasabi coating. Angel settled on a bag of microwave popcorn.

While it popped she borrowed a T-shirt from Callen's dresser that would double as pajamas. Tomorrow she'd pack a bag. Maybe she'd stay until Callen came back. Mutt would love that.

The microwave beeped, and Angel padded barefoot to the kitchen to retrieve her snack. Once she'd poured herself a ginger ale, she settled into Callen's recliner and used the remote to turn on the television set. The action brought back the image of Phillip Jenkins settling in with his popcorn and beer.

Had he known his killer? She suspected he must have, since there had been no sign of a struggle. Still, how could they know that for sure, since Candace had cleaned up the place? Had Jenkins invited someone over? Had he known what was coming? She thought again about the footprints that might have been tracked into the house. The prints Candace had mopped up.

Angel surmised that from where Phillip Jenkins had been sitting, he would have seen anyone coming into the room either from the kitchen or from the front door. Of course, all that was speculation. She'd have to take a closer look at the house to know for certain.

Still, she couldn't help but wonder. Had Candace removed a gun from his collection at an earlier time, hidden it upstairs, and waited for the right moment? Had she crept into the room while Phillip was absorbed in the game, shot him, placed the gun in his left hand, cleaned up the mess, then gone to pick up the kids?

Angel still had a hard time seeing the small, soft-spoken woman as a killer, but she'd been wrong before.

She thought again about the remote control and the snacks being on the right side of the chair and the gun being in his left hand. If Candace had killed him and if he was right-handed, wouldn't she have placed the gun in his right hand? Not necessarily, but it was worth noting. She'd forgotten to mention her observation to Nick and promised herself she'd do so the next day. Not that he'd appreciate her opinion.

And what about Gracie? Where did she fit into all of this?

Why are you even thinking about it? Nick was right; dating a detective doesn't make you one.

Detective or not, Angel felt a part of it. She had to know one way or another and planned to talk to both Candace and Gracie in the morning. Allegedly, neither had been home when Jenkins was shot. Candace had been shopping, Gracie at school. She'd have to check out their alibis.

Angel finally drifted off sometime around midnight, with Mutt curled up beside her. His occasional shifting and moaning along with thoughts of Jenkins and his killer kept Angel on the verge of sleep most of the night.

Morning came far too soon with Mutt barking and insisting she let him out and feed him. Angel dressed hurriedly in the clothes she'd worn the day before. At the patio door, she attached the leash to Mutt's collar and slipped outside.

She was not in the mood to run or play, and told the dog so. Mutt seemed to understand, doing his business then heading back to the house. Of course, his lack of ambition may have been due to the relentless mist. After feeding him, Angel collected her jacket and left Mutt to fend for himself. "I'll be back later. Try to stay out of trouble."

Mutt barked and ran to the window to watch her go. Nose against the pane, he whined, his big liquid eyes pleading with her not to leave him. "I'm sorry, Mutt, but I can't hang around here all morning." She felt guilty leaving him, but what could she do?

Back in her apartment, Angel took a long, hot shower. As she stepped out of the bathroom her phone rang. She ignored it until the answering machine beeped and she heard her mother's frantic voice. "Angel, are you there? You are not going to believe what happened. Nick came by this morning and took Candace into custody. He read her her rights and cuffed her right in front of the children."

"I want my mommy!" Dorothy wailed in the background.

"Angel." The distress rose in Anna's voice. "You have to do something."

Angel picked up the phone. "I'm here, Ma. Calm down." Angel figured Candace would be taken in, but not this soon or quite so dramatically. "He probably just wants to question her."

"Angel Delaney. Your father was a police officer for thirty years. Don't you think I know the difference? She's been arrested like a common criminal."

ELEVEN

"The children are upset," Anna said, "and I don't blame them. Gracie insists she has to go to school. Brian and Dorothy are . . . well, Brian is just sitting there trying to take it all in. And poor little Dorothy. That's her you hear crying."

While her mother lamented, Angel padded to the walk-in closet. She grabbed clean jeans, a white turtleneck, and a burgundy sweater from the shelf.

"Calm down, Ma. It's going to be okay." Angel felt odd comforting her mother. Anna was usually calm and collected. Angel wished she'd taken Candace and the children to the shelter instead of her parents' home. "Take a deep breath. We'll handle this together, okay? I'll come over and take the kids to school. We'll have to find a place for them to stay."

"They can stay here. I told Candace I'd take care of them until she got out."

"Ma, you can't. You sound totally frazzled. And what about Dad?"

"I can manage. I don't want them in foster care. They'd probably be split up. They're darling children and . . . I want to do this, Angel. I need to."

"A day or two, maybe, but Candace could be in jail for a while."

"That woman is innocent. I can feel it in my bones. You've got to get her out of there."

"I'll do what I can. Which isn't much, I'm afraid."

"We can at least get her a lawyer."

"Good thinking," Angel agreed. "Maybe Rachael will represent her."

"That's exactly who I had in mind."

Angel struggled into her jeans, not an easy task with one shoulder supporting the phone against her ear. "Okay, I'll take Gracie to school, then go down to the station to see what I can find out."

Anna released a heavy sigh. "Thank you."

"I'll be there in fifteen minutes."

Angel finished getting ready while she mulled over the conversation. Taking the children on wasn't a very good idea, but she wouldn't argue the point. At least not today. When Anna Delaney made up her mind, nothing could change it. But maybe after a day or two, Anna would reconsider. Even the best-behaved children could be a handful. She was sixty-two and already had more than she could handle with her invalid husband.

Angel pulled on socks and shoved her feet into her loafers, then ran a brush through her hair, trying to rearrange the curls into some sort of order. Her hair would have to air-dry this morning.

The minute Angel stepped inside her parents' house, Dorothy squealed. Holding her teddy bear in a death grip, she scrambled off the sofa and threw her arms around Angel's legs. "I knew you'd come. I knew it."

Angel picked her up and hugged girl and bear. When she let go, Dorothy looked up at her. "Mrs. Delaney said you were a real Angel."

Angel laughed. "That's my name, but I'm not—"

"That means you can help my mommy, right? Mrs. Delaney said you would take care of everything."

Angel blinked back tears. "I'll try." What was her mother thinking, telling the kids she'd take care of everything?

"Breakfast is ready," Anna called from the kitchen.

Angel set Dorothy down. "Better go eat."

"Are you coming too?"

"In a minute." She turned her attention to the other side of the room, where Tom was bringing Frank out to his chair.

"Hey, Angel. Haven't seen you for a while." Tom nodded at her.

"That's because I'm usually sleeping at this hour."

Tom's comment pushed a guilt button. The half-teasing, half-accusing look in his eyes told her he thought she should come around more often. Angel shed her coat at the hall closet and waited until her father was seated before leaning over to drop a quick kiss on his cheek. "Morning, Dad. You're looking good."

He teared up as he so often did since his stroke. Once again expressing his disappointment. He glanced away as if he wanted nothing to do with her. Angel straightened and headed for the kitchen, determined not to feel the sharp barbs of his dismissal.

"Did you make enough for me?" She headed straight for the cupboard and extracted her favorite coffee mug, one from a local artist, with clusters of grapes painted on a pale yellow background speckled with purple.

"Don't I always?"

Angel kissed her mother's cheek and helped herself to a cup, then dished up a portion of the eggs that had been scrambled with mushrooms, onions, broccoli, and yellow pepper then topped with cheese. "The kids have settled down."

"Yes," Anna whispered. "I told them their mother would be home soon."

"Right," Angel said, "and that I'd take care of everything. Ma . . ."

"Shush. We'll talk about that later."

Once they were seated around the table, Anna offered the blessing.

Dorothy peered at her eggs and wrinkled her nose. "Mommy never puts green stuff and shrooms in our eggs."

"Pick them out, then," Gracie told her.

"You're lucky Dad isn't here," Brian said, "or he'd make you eat it for a week." He paused, giving Anna a stricken look. "I guess he can't do that anymore, huh?"

64

Anna smiled. "Would you like me to make some plain eggs for you, Dorothy?"

"Yes, please." She handed her plate up.

Brian lifted a bite of the eggs to his mouth and grimaced. He swallowed without chewing and washed it down with milk.

"Broccoli isn't your favorite, either?" Angel grinned.

He glowered. "I eat whatever's on my plate."

"Better make some plain eggs for Brian too." Angel reached over and patted his arm. "It's okay," she assured him. "My mom used to have to leave stuff out of my omelettes when I was your age."

"I'm sorry, kids. I wasn't thinking—it's been a busy morning," Anna said. "How about you, Gracie?"

"It's good." She was halfway through. "I like my eggs this way."

Anna good-naturedly scrambled more eggs and put the untouched portions of the original omelettes into a container for the refrigerator. Serving the untarnished eggs, she asked, "Is this more to your liking, *Signor* Brian? *Signorina* Dorothy?"

They giggled at her Italian accent and thanked her with a unique version of their own accents.

While they ate, Angel made a point of watching each of the children. They were already dressed and ready for school, eating greedily, now that they had eggs with no gross stuff, and acting as if yesterday had never happened and that their mother hadn't been arrested. What were they thinking? Their actions gave little indication of the trauma they had to be going through.

"Are you sure you want to go to school today?" Anna asked, apparently picking up the thread of a previous conversation.

"I have to," Gracie said. "I have a test in language arts and after school I have cheerleading practice." She bit her bottom lip. "I mean . . . it's not like we could do anything except sit around if we stayed here."

"It's better if we go." Brian propped his elbows on the table and rested his head on his hands.

"Yeah, better." Dorothy mimicked his pose.

"All right," Anna relented. "But if you change your mind, you can come back. One of us will come get you. Now, elbows off the table," she admonished. "Use your manners."

The children quickly complied.

"We'll be fine," Gracie said. Her anger from the night before seemed to have dissipated, though she seemed thoughtful and subdued. "As long as we don't have to talk to the cops anymore."

"Officer Caldwell questioned all of you?"

"Yeah, before he took our mom away." Brian frowned. "We told him she didn't do it, but he wouldn't listen."

Angel was determined to talk to Nick about his actions, but she had some questions of her own. "Gracie, were you in school all day yesterday?"

Gracie's head snapped up. "Yeah. Where else would I be? I don't have a car."

Angel shrugged her shoulders. "I just wondered. A lot of kids go home for lunch, and I wondered if you had and if you might have seen or heard anything unusual if you'd been there."

"No. I didn't." She picked up her orange juice and started drinking.

Something about her demeanor told Angel she was lying. She wanted to pursue the conversation but decided now wasn't a good time. Not with her mother giving her the not-at-the-table glare. Anna liked to reserve mealtimes for pleasant conversations, not controversy.

When they finished eating, Anna sent the children to the bathroom to brush their teeth and finish getting ready. "Angel, could you see to the children while I feed your father?" She set their lunch bags on the counter and walked into the living room without waiting for Angel's response.

"Can I get you a cup of coffee or anything, Tom?" Angel heard her mother ask. Always the hostess.

Angel paused in the doorway. "I can get it, Ma."

"I'm fine." Tom smiled at Angel then picked up his jacket from the sofa and shrugged into it. "Thanks anyway."

"Are you finished for the day?" Anna asked. "He hasn't exercised."

"I have another client to look in on this morning. Thought I'd

66

come back around 10:00 and work with him on his exercise routine, if that's okay."

"Sure." She glanced at Frank. "Is that okay with you, sweetheart?"

Frank grunted and dipped his head in the affirmative. She squeezed his hand. "Good. That will give us some time to have a cup of coffee together. We need to talk."

Talk? Angel didn't know how they'd manage that. For days after having the stroke, Frank had tried to communicate with them. When nothing came out right, he'd tear up and stop trying. Though everyone would reassure him, he eventually stopped trying to talk altogether. Her mother had learned to interpret Frank's signals, and much of the time she could tell what he wanted.

"Well, I'll leave you then." Tom lifted Frank's limp right hand and shook it. "I have a surprise for you today. If the weather holds up, I thought maybe we'd go to the pier this afternoon and take in a little fishing."

Frank lifted his head and gave him a lopsided grin. At least it looked like a grin to Angel. Her heart did a little flip. He so rarely displayed any emotions but sadness and anger.

"That's a wonderful idea." Anna hesitated. "Tom, are you sure?"

"Trust me, Anna. A guy needs to get out every now and then. Frank was telling me the other day how much he missed fishing."

He'd talked to Tom? Well, apparently Tom had found a way to communicate with Frank. Better than Angel had done. She envied the rapport Tom had with her father. *You might have the same rapport if you'd stick around a little more.*

Anna smiled. "What would we do without you, Tom?"

When Tom left, Anna brought a cup of coffee and a plate of food and set it on Frank's tray. As if it were the most ordinary task in the world, she tied the ends of his terry cloth napkin around his neck. She refused to call it a bib and told Angel and her brothers that babies wore bibs, not sixty-five-year-old men. "There you are."

With a shaky left hand, Frank raised the cup to his lips. Anna always cooled his coffee slightly so he wouldn't be burned if he

67

happened to spill it. He looked almost like his old self this morning, except for the drooping facial features on his right side.

Anna settled herself on the ottoman to Frank's left. She gave him a warm smile and tipped her head to the side. "This is nice."

Angel had to admire her mother for taking everything in stride, and wished she could have a little of that patience.

Frank picked up his coffee and took another sip. He had always been such a handsome man, rugged and strong. He looked thinner now, pale, but his hair was still ample with that wonderful salt-and-pepper look. Anna's hair was still black and thick, thanks to Nice 'n Easy. Had he ever noticed that while he was graying, his wife never had? Probably not.

"I suppose you're wondering what these children are doing here," Anna said to him. "I didn't have a chance to talk much about it yesterday, and when I finally got to bed, you were already asleep." She told him what had happened to Phillip Jenkins and that Candace had been arrested.

He grumbled and wagged his head from side to side.

"I know what you're thinking." Anna squeezed his good hand. "We shouldn't get involved. And you're worried that Candace may have killed her husband. And that we were taking a risk having her here." Anna took a sip of her coffee and set the cup back in the saucer then scooped up a spoonful of eggs and eased it into his open mouth. "Not that we need to worry now. While you were in the shower this morning, Nick Caldwell came by. He questioned the kids and arrested Candace." Anna shook her head, not bothering to hide her disgust. "I thought that boy had better sense than that."

A frown creased Frank's forehead, leaving Angel to wonder what he thought about the situation or if he even knew what his wife was talking about.

Angel turned away and began making her way down the hall to check on the kids. The hall bathroom door was closed, and she knocked. "Hurry up in there. You're going to be late."

"Coming," Gracie said. "I'm helping Dorothy."

Brian stepped out of the room once occupied by her twin brothers, Peter and Paul. "I'm ready."

68

"Grab your lunch and get into the car," Angel said. "Hopefully the girls will be out soon."

He rolled his eyes. "Don't count on it. We taking your car?"

"No." She chuckled. "We won't all fit in mine, and I'm not driving you separately."

Brian sighed and headed outside, letting the door slam behind him.

Turning to her mother, Angel said, "I'll have to use your car."

"The keys are in the usual place." Anna glanced at Angel, then turned back to Frank and continued the one-sided conversation. "Nick seems to think Candace killed her husband. She didn't. I'm quite certain of that. You should have seen the way Nick came in here and Mirandized her. I wish you had been out here. Maybe he'd have treated her with more respect. Not that he was mean, just brisk. Barely said a word to me. In fact, when I told him he had no right to take her, he told me it wasn't my concern. Can you believe that? We practically raised that boy."

Anna sighed and went on. "Of course, they'll give her a polygraph—he offered her that much, and that will show she's telling the truth."

"Hopefully," Angel murmured.

Brian raced back inside, grabbed his lunch from the kitchen counter, and hurried to the door. "Can I start the car for you?" he asked Angel.

"No."

He shrugged and headed outside again at the same time the girls emerged from the bathroom. "Dorothy wanted me to braid her hair," Gracie said. "That's what took so long."

"Looks nice." Angel eyed the two evenly spaced French braids.

Before going to the car, Dorothy, still clutching her teddy bear, gave Anna a hug then placed the bear on Frank's lap. Frank patted her small hand, and Angel saw the makings of a smile.

Tears clouded her own vision as she waved at her parents and followed the children outside. *Oh Dad, why can't you look at me like that?*

TWELVE

———

Angel dropped Brian and Dorothy off at Beachwood Elementary School, then proceeded to Sunset Cove High School, which was on the other side of town. Tension emanated from both occupants, with Angel wanting to ask Gracie more questions and Gracie staring out the passenger side window, apparently not wanting to talk at all. Gracie wore little if any makeup, Angel noticed. Not that she needed it. She had pink cheeks and full lashes. She wore her blonde hair swept up in a ponytail, which she'd curled around and pinned in a haphazard bun.

"Do you enjoy cheerleading?"

"Yeah." She turned to Angel and offered a genuine smile. "I want to go to nationals and maybe to cheerleading camp this summer."

"Sounds like fun."

"It will be now that he's gone," Gracie said.

"Meaning that he wouldn't have let you go?" Angel finished the thought and apparently guessed correctly.

"He didn't like us to be away from home." Gracie pinched her lips together.

"Did he tell you that you couldn't go?" Angel asked.

"Yes, but Mom was going to talk to him about it."

Angel couldn't help but wonder just how much of a rift there

70

was between father and daughter. "Bet that made you mad—that he said you couldn't go."

Gracie leveled a critical gaze on Angel. "He always said no. No matter what I wanted to do. The answer was always no."

"Must have been hard." Gracie certainly had motive to kill Phillip, but was the anger she obviously felt for him intense enough for her to act on it?

"I'm going to see your mother after I drop you off," Angel said after several minutes of silence.

Gracie nodded. "I know. Mrs. Delaney told us you would."

"I didn't mean to embarrass you back at the house. Or accuse you."

"You mean when you asked if I'd gone home yesterday afternoon?"

"Right. I'd like to help your mom, but I need a better picture of what went on during the hours or days before your dad was killed."

"Phillip was not my dad." Gracie's tone was bitter and terse.

Angel tightened her grip on the steering wheel. "Oh . . . um, I didn't know. The way your mother talked, I just assumed . . ."

"She divorced my real father when I was five. He didn't want her to. My dad is a great guy. He lives in California, and I'm thinking about moving there. I stayed with him last summer. He's a set designer for a movie studio. He's married and has a couple little kids." Gracie turned away; the sadness in her eyes didn't match the praise in her words, leaving Angel to wonder just how great a guy her real father was.

"Should I contact him?"

"What? . . . Um, no. I'll call him later."

Angel had barely come to a stop when Gracie unbuckled her seat belt and pushed open the door. She scooted out, but before closing the door, she leaned back in. "My mother didn't kill Phillip. She wouldn't do that. She loved him, and besides, she wouldn't have the guts."

But you do? Angel leaned toward Gracie. "I hope you're right. But for what it's worth, I don't think she did it either."

Gracie stood there a second, then said, "You should talk to

71

Darryl. He's Phillip's nephew. Darryl was mad at Phillip for not loaning him money. Maybe he did it. He stole one of Phillip's guns." She slammed the door shut, adjusted her backpack, and practically ran up the walk.

Angel waited until Gracie entered the building before she parked in the closest space she could find, about a block away, and walked back. Climbing the same concrete steps that she'd climbed every school day for four years gave her a sense of déjà vu. High school had been a blur of activities, mostly sports. She had studied hard and played hard and come out with a four-point average. Frank Delaney had been proud of his Angel then.

The school was an old brick building that had seemed ancient when Angel had gone there. She climbed the patched concrete steps and made an immediate left into the office.

Considering the confidentiality laws, Angel doubted she'd get the information she needed, but after explaining the family's situation to the principal, Mary Johansson was more than happy to comply.

"Something Gracie said this morning concerned me and, well, I'm afraid she may be skipping classes. If she's having problems, I'd really like to know. Was Gracie in school all day yesterday?" Angel asked.

Mrs. Johansson turned to her computer and after a few clicks said, "Gracie didn't check out, but according to the study hall roster, she wasn't there."

"When is her study hall?"

"Right after lunch, from 1:00 to 2:00." Mary set her glasses on a stack of papers next to the computer. "It's not something I'd be too concerned about. She may have gone out for lunch or to the public library to study."

"And you're okay with that?" Her teachers would have given out detention notices.

"In her case, yes. Our library is rather small and outdated. The important thing is that she was back for her 2:10 class. Gracie is a good student—one of our best. I was shocked and sorry to hear about her father. And then to have her mother arrested . . . unthinkable. Do you think Mrs. Jenkins did it?"

72

"I don't know."

"Well, I hope for the children's sake she didn't."

"Me too." Angel uncrossed her legs and started to stand.

"Are you working on the case?" Mary asked.

"Me?" Angel rubbed the back of her neck. "No. I'm actually on leave from the police department."

"Oh." She acted like she wanted to say more.

"Why do you ask?"

"I doubt you could do anything about it, but if you get a chance, maybe you could find out who'll be handling the business affairs now that Phillip is dead and Candace is in jail."

Angel frowned. "I don't understand."

"He . . . uh, Phillip owed my husband a lot of money. Around five-thousand dollars for updating their house. Greg, my husband, is an electrician. He finished the work three months ago and hasn't been paid. I suppose it seems a little crass of me to bring up money—I mean, the man has just died—but we have obligations too." .

"I suppose I could look into it for you, but . . ."

"Never mind." She stood and escorted Angel to the door. "I'm sorry I mentioned it."

"That's okay. I guess if I were in your shoes, I'd be concerned too."

"I'm glad you stopped by. It's good to know someone responsible is caring for the children." Mary stopped in the doorway, waved, and went back into her office.

Once in the car, Angel digested the information she'd obtained. Gracie could have left the school and gone home, killed her father—correction, her stepfather—then gone back to school. *You're reaching, Angel. Gracie is a cheerleader and a good student. Mary seemed to think well of her—and she's just a kid.*

Still, it's something to consider.

There were other things to consider too. Phillip owed money to Greg Johansson. How many others was he indebted to? Phillip may well have accumulated a few enemies outside the family circle. She'd have to ask Candace about that.

In the meantime, Angel decided to follow up on Gracie's absence yesterday afternoon. The librarian knew Gracie well and confirmed that she often came in to study.

"Was Gracie here yesterday from say noon to 2:00?" Angel asked her.

"No," she answered without hesitation.

"How can you be sure?"

"I have several books on hold for her. If she'd been here, I'd have given them to her."

"Do you have any idea where she might have gone?" Angel asked.

"Goodness, no. I don't have time to keep track of these kids." The librarian tapped her pen against her hand. "Gracie often studied with Justin Bailey. She'd been tutoring him lately. Come to think of it, he wasn't here yesterday either."

"Okay, thanks for the information."

After speaking with the librarian, Angel took her parents' car back and picked up her Corvette. She headed toward city hall but made a detour on the way to talk to her favorite attorney. Minutes later, Angel pulled into the parking lot at St. Matthew's Church. Rachael Rastovski was the only attorney Angel had ever met whose office was housed in a church. The situation was as unique as Rachael herself.

The stone church had been built in 1896, the structure as sturdy today as it had been back then. The steeple, with its belltower and ornate cross, reached toward the heavens, ringing every day at noon and on Sunday mornings and for special occasions. Angel bypassed the massive church doors and headed for the addition that had been built ten years ago to accommodate the offices, classrooms, and fellowship hall. Passing her brother's office, she stopped and poked her head in.

"Oh, hi, Angel." Paula, the church secretary, looked up from her computer. "Pastor Tim is in a meeting. Can I help you?"

"No, I just thought I'd say hello. I'm actually on my way to see Rachael. Do you know if she's in?"

"As far as I know. I'll tell Tim you came by."

Angel thanked her and made her way down the hall to Rachael's office. The office, if you could call it that, was a tiny cubicle that had once been a storage room. There was barely enough room for the desk, file cabinet, bookshelves, and a chair.

Rachael sat at her desk, head bent over a thick book. Sherlock, her cat, had draped himself atop the monitor of her computer. When he saw Angel he stretched and jumped down, then leaped to the top of the bookcase.

Angel knocked on the open door. "Hi. Hope I'm not interrupting something important."

"Angel." Rachael grinned, revealing a deep set of dimples. "What a surprise." She stood and made her way around several piles of paper. Giving Angel a hug she asked, "Is this a social call or are you in trouble again?"

Rachael had represented Angel when she had to go before a grand jury for the shooting incident. She was also dating Angel's brother Paul.

"Neither, actually. Do you have a few minutes?"

"Sure. Want to go into the conference room?" Her grin broadened.

Angel laughed. "Why not?" Since Rachael's office barely had enough room for her and her cat, the attorney often used the church sanctuary to conduct her meetings.

Once they'd settled into a pew, Angel asked, "Have you been keeping up with the news?"

"Sort of. Why?" Rachael cocked her head. "Something going on I should know about?"

"Have you heard about Phillip Jenkins?"

"Who hasn't?" Rachael wrote the date and time on the yellow legal pad she'd brought with her.

"I'd like you to consider representing his wife, Candace Jenkins. Nick arrested her this morning."

"What's he got on her?" Rachael jotted Phillip's and Candace's names on the pad and drew a line connecting them.

"I'm not sure." Angel told Rachael about her involvement in the case and how Candace had cleaned up the murder scene. "I'm struggling with this. Part of me refuses to believe she's guilty, but I can't see Nick making the arrest unless he has some hard evidence."

"Whether she's guilty or not, she needs an attorney."

"Which is why I'm here." Angel let her gaze wander to the large stained-glass window at the front of the church—the one that had fascinated and warmed her since childhood.

"Are you sure she doesn't already have one?"

"I doubt it." She looked back at Rachael.

"All right. Tell you what. Let's go talk to her, and afterward you can buy me a latte."

"Deal. Do you want to meet me there or go in my car?"

"Are you kidding? I'll go with you. My bucket of bolts needs a tune-up—it barely managed to get me to work this morning. Tim offered to take it to his mechanic this afternoon."

"That would be Mitch Bailey?"

"Right." She frowned. "Is there a problem?"

"No," Angel said quickly. "He's good." She thought it best not to say anything about Mitch being the owner of the abandoned car Callen had mentioned. She doubted Callen would want the information made public at this point. "Let's go." Angel grabbed the pew in front of her and pulled herself up.

"I have to pick up my briefcase. I'll meet you at the car."

It took about four minutes to drive from the church to city hall and find a place to park. City hall was situated at one end of the courthouse, along with judicial offices, the police department, and a small jail. They went into the door at the north entrance that led to the police department and the jail. Angel stopped at the front desk to greet the receptionist, Rosie Gonzalez.

Rosie buzzed them in and pulled Angel into a bear hug. "It is so good to see you, girl. Where have you been? Just because you got some time off doesn't mean you can't come around here now and then. Are you doing okay? Tell me you're here because you want to come back to work early."

Angel laughed. "It's good to see you too, and I'm doing okay." Rosie had a velvety smooth Southern drawl. She and Nick had been dating for several weeks, and Rosie, who'd been drooling over Angel's brothers for years, now seemed content.

"And the job?" Rosie looked hopeful.

76

"Sorry." She introduced Rachael. "We're here to see Candace Jenkins. I understand Nick arrested her this morning."

"Uh-huh." Rosie shook her head. "That is one sad story."

"What happened?" Angel asked, hoping her friend might share some pertinent information.

"She claims she came home and found her husband dead. Her prints were on the gun, and they found gun residue on her hands. She apparently put the gun in his hand to make it look like a suicide. Can you believe that? Then she cleans up the place."

Angel wasn't really surprised at the prints or the gun residue. Candace had probably touched the gun while she was cleaning up the scene. "Is there any other evidence to implicate her?"

"You'd have to ask Nick. He questioned her and scheduled her for a lie detector test tomorrow."

"Where is Nick now?" Angel asked.

"Out at the Jenkins's farm. He went to see how the lab techs were doing."

"They're still not finished?" Angel leaned an elbow on the counter.

"Not quite." Rosie shrugged. "Guess they're still going over the vehicles."

"We'd like to see Mrs. Jenkins," Rachael said. "I assume she can have visitors?"

"Sure." Rosie turned back to Angel. "What's your interest in this?"

"Candace called me to come out there after she found him dead. I called it in."

Rosie raised her eyebrows. "Strange. Why didn't she call herself?"

"I don't know. Fear, maybe. She told me she thought he'd killed himself. Maybe she just didn't know what to do. I brought Candace and her kids to my mother's place last night. Ma is pretty upset about the arrest. Figured the least we could do was get her a lawyer."

Rosie nodded. "Go on through. I'll call the jail and let them know you're coming."

77

"So Nick made a formal arrest." Rachael hesitated. "He didn't just bring her in for questioning?"

"Nick says this is an open-and-shut case." Rosie went back to her desk. "I think he's right. I mean, who else would have done it? She had motive, means, and opportunity."

"Rosie . . ." Angel leaned forward, placing her hands on the desk. "Do we have an estimated time of death?"

"Yes. Between 1:00 and 3:00 p.m."

"Then Candace couldn't have done it. She told me she'd gone shopping and then picked up the kids from school."

"Well, she did that." Rosie shuffled through some papers and picked one out of the pile. "Nick had me check out her alibi. She had a receipt for the grocery store that put her in the store at 1:30, then she went to Joanie's for coffee. Joanie verified that, but she left right away—about 1:40. She didn't pick up the kids from school until 2:45. That's over an hour unaccounted for. Candace claims she went to the beach to read, but she can't prove it."

"Have you talked to Candace?" Angel asked.

Rosie nodded. "Just briefly when Nick brought her in. She looked pretty shaken up. Worried about her kids."

Rachael frowned. "She hasn't confessed, has she?"

"Not that I know of, but I have a feeling she will when Nick talks to her about the evidence they've uncovered."

"He's not planning to talk to her without her lawyer present, I hope?" Rachael seemed annoyed that the woman had been questioned at all.

"She hasn't asked for a lawyer," Rosie said. "Candace seemed like such a nice gal. Hard to picture her killing anyone, but it sure doesn't look good for her."

THIRTEEN

Angel and Rachael passed through the doorway leading to the jail. Once they'd gone through the security checkpoint, they were ushered into a small interview room.

A guard led Candace in several minutes later. She wore an orange uniform that washed out her already pale skin. The guard seated her at the table across from Rachael and Angel, then stationed herself just outside the door.

Tears gathered in Candace's eyes as she looked from Angel to Rachael. "I didn't kill him. Why won't anyone believe me?"

Angel didn't know how to answer. She wanted to believe Candace, but according to Rosie, Nick thought they had sufficient evidence against her. "Have you called a lawyer?"

"No. They told me I could, but I don't know anyone."

"I do." Angel nodded toward Rachael. "Candace, meet my friend Rachael Rastovski."

"You're a lawyer?" Candace met Rachael's eyes, then looked away.

"I am. And if you want me to represent you, I will." She glanced at Angel. "To answer your question, Candace, I want to believe you. Give me a reason why I should."

"I can't give you a reason other than I'm innocent. I would like to hire you. I have money—I can pay whatever it costs. Phillip had a good life insurance policy and his business was doing well."

She won't get a dime of that insurance money if she's a murder suspect. Angel hoped that wasn't the case.

"All right. From now on, I don't want you to say anything to the police," Rachael told her. "If they want to question you, have them call me. As soon as we're finished, I'm going over to the DA's office and see exactly what they have. First, though, I have a few questions." Rachael glanced at Angel. "Just one thing before we get started. Angel can be compelled to testify about what you say. She doesn't hold the confidentiality status of a priest or lawyer. If you say something that implicates you, Angel could be made to testify."

"Are you saying I should leave?" Angel asked.

"It might be best," Rachael answered.

"No. I want her to stay. Please." Candace raised her head and straightened her shoulders.

"All right. I just wanted you to be aware."

Candace nodded. "Did Angel tell you what happened? That I cleaned things up after I found Phillip? I know now I shouldn't have touched anything, but at the time . . . I don't know what possessed me." She glanced down at her clenched hands. "I just couldn't let people see the house all messy like that."

"Angel told me, but even without cleaning things up, you would have been a suspect. This only gives the DA more ammunition. And you may have destroyed evidence that could have cleared you and perhaps even told the police who actually killed him."

"Why did you clean up?" Angel asked.

"I—I had to. The floor was dirty. Someone had tracked in mud. And there was blood. I couldn't let them think I was a bad house-keeper. Phillip was so particular, you know. I didn't think about the evidence. I thought he'd killed himself and I just wanted to fix up everything."

"Did you recognize the footprints?" Angel persisted.

Candace's eyes widened as she sucked in a sharp breath. "No! What are you talking about?"

"Were they Gracie's?"

80

Candace leaped to her feet, mad as a mother bear with a cub in trouble. "How dare you? How dare you come in here and accuse my Gracie? I thought you were my friend."

"Take it easy." Angel stood up and held out a hand. "I'm not accusing Gracie of anything. I'm just trying to get a better picture of what happened."

The guard opened the door and took a step inside. "You need some help?"

"It's okay." Rachael waved her away and gave Angel a "stifle yourself" look. Turning to Candace, she said, "Sit down."

Candace complied. "Gracie was at school."

"Where are you going with this, Angel?" Rachael tapped her pen on the pad.

Angel looked at Candace. "I'm trying to understand your motivation and piece together what happened. If the police do any investigating at all, they're going to find out what I have. And they'll see that you aren't the only one with motive, means, and opportunity." Angel lowered herself into the chair again. "I think Gracie went home yesterday between noon and 2:00."

"No! That's impossible." Candace pressed her fist to her mouth.

"I know she skipped study hall and she wasn't at the library. I also know that Phillip wasn't her birth father."

Candace leaned back and closed her eyes. "Gracie didn't like Phillip, that's true, but she wouldn't kill him. Last night she told me she had to go home to get a paper she'd forgotten. Phillip was fine when she left." Straightening again, she asked, "Have you told the police about Gracie?"

"Not yet," Angel said.

"Well, don't. If you do, I'll tell them I did it."

"All right, then," Rachael said. "Give us some idea of who else might have been at the house."

"I can't. I have no idea. Phillip wasn't expecting anyone that I know of." Candace folded her long, thin arms on the table and lowered her head to them. "If I have to stay here, what's going to happen to my children?"

"The kids will be fine," Angel assured her. "My mother will

see to that. They wanted to go to school this morning, so I took them."

Candace hauled in a deep breath, working to regain her composure.

"Did your husband have any enemies?" Rachael asked. "Anyone who might want to see him dead?"

"Officer Caldwell asked me that. I can't think of anyone. He's had some people mad at him from time to time. He was a contractor and owed his subcontractors money, but they always got paid. You know how it is . . . you have to wait until someone pays you in order to pay someone else. It would be stupid to kill someone who owed you money. If they were dead, you might never get it."

Angel nodded. "This morning Gracie mentioned that Phillip had a nephew who wanted to borrow money. She indicated that this nephew might have taken one of Phillip's guns."

With a short, unpolished fingernail, Candace traced a name someone had carved into the table. "That would be Darryl. He didn't take the gun. We thought he had, but Phillip found it the next day. He'd been cleaning it and hadn't put it back in the gun case. That was the last time Phillip . . ."

"Beat you up?" Angel finished the sentence when it didn't look like Candace would. "Was that the time Gracie called the police and I responded?"

"Yes. She was afraid Phillip would hurt me."

"Which he did."

"Yes, but he apologized."

"I'm sure he did." Angel folded her arms. "So tell us more about Darryl."

"He comes around every week or so. Sometimes he comes to visit, other times to borrow money."

"Did Phillip lend it to him?"

"Usually, though he didn't call it a loan. Phillip preferred to call it a gift—that way if Darryl paid him back, great, if not, that was okay too." She hesitated. "The last time he wanted money, Phillip told him no. Phillip was afraid Darryl was gambling too much. Darryl was pretty upset when he left, but . . . I don't think he killed his uncle."

Rachael jotted the information on her notepad. "Where does Darryl live?"

"Here in Sunset Cove. Um, I don't have the exact address. He has an old travel trailer, so he's probably in one of the parks. He hasn't been here long—six months, maybe. He came from California like we did." She rubbed at the goose bumps on her arm.

The room was too cool for short sleeves. Maybe the guard could see that she got a sweater. "Anything else we should know about him? Had he and Phillip argued recently?" Angel asked. "Did they get along?"

"They usually got along well. Darryl's dad deserted the family. Phillip never forgave his brother for that. He felt obligated to be a father figure. Phillip gave him a job and loaned him enough for rent. He also let him use his motorcycle so he'd be able to get around. Darryl isn't a bad kid, just a little mixed up."

"Mixed up?" Angel repeated. "In what way?"

"Choices. Like a lot of kids, he does some drinking and maybe drugs, gambles a little. Phillip got on him for all that."

"And how did he react to Phillip's parental role?"

"Good, actually. I think Darryl likes the fact that someone cares that much about him. He wanted to get straight. It was hard for him, and Phillip understood that all too well."

"When was the last time you saw him?"

"Last week."

"Any chance he might have been there yesterday?"

She shrugged. "I suppose he could have come while I was gone. You don't think he killed Phillip, do you?"

Rachael looked at Angel and nodded. "We have our work cut out for us, but we'll find out." Rachael pulled a card out of her pocket and handed it to Candace. "If you think of anything, give me a call."

"Like what?" Candace stared at the card. "I've already told you all I know."

"Maybe, but there are little things you might remember. Did you pass a car going home yesterday afternoon? Has Phillip had any confrontations with anyone lately? Any unusual comments he may have said to anyone—that sort of thing."

Candace nodded. "All right. I'll think about it. Thanks for your help."

Angel stood. "One more thing. Was Phillip right- or left-handed?"

"Right."

"The gun was in his left hand."

"I—I didn't notice. I put it back the way it was." She covered her eyes. "It was so awful. I just wanted to get it done. Whether he was right- or left-handed didn't even occur to me. Why? Is that important?"

"I don't know. It might be useful information later on."

Angel and Rachael stood up to leave, and Angel alerted the guard that they were leaving. The guard came and led Candace out first.

"Wait!" Anxious and tearful, Candace turned back to them. "The animals. Someone needs to feed and water them. They're probably starving by now. We feed them at around 6:00 in the morning and in the evening."

"I'll take care of it," Angel volunteered.

"Thank you." Candace tipped her head down and plodded ahead of the guard.

"She's the real victim in all of this," Rachael said as the door shut and locked behind them. "She and the children."

"Let's hope you can get her out of jail and keep her out."

FOURTEEN

W hat was that work thing all about?" Angel buckled her
seat belt and turned the key in the ignition.

"What?"

"You told Candace that we had a lot of work to do. What did
you mean by that?"

Rachael tossed her a dimpled smile. "So you caught that,
huh?"

"Hard to miss it."

"I want to hire you." Rachael twisted in her seat and fumbled
with the seat belt connection until it clicked into place.

"Excuse me?" Angel checked her rearview mirror and backed
out of her parking place.

"You're already involved, and unless I miss my guess, you're
hesitant to do much investigating because of your leave status
with the PD."

"Yeah, well, it's none of my business, and look at me. I guess
it's true what they say, once a cop, always a cop. I should leave it
alone, but here I am questioning Candace and Gracie and telling
Nick he's rushing to judgment." Angel shook her head. "Maybe
it's in my blood."

"Of course it is. You're also chomping at the bit to find out what
really happened. So do it. I'd like you to investigate Jenkins's death

as my private investigator. The Sunset Cove PD is convinced they have their man—or woman, as it turns out."

The offer surprised Angel, but she liked the idea. Liked it a lot. "But I'm not a detective."

"With a little paperwork you could be, but you can be my assistant until then. We have a lot of people to contact, and it would take me forever to do it. I have several cases right now and court dates. I need you."

Angel chewed on her lip. "Would I get paid?"

"Well, Candace has the life insurance policy, and she'll have money from the business. I'll prepare a preliminary statement of our charges in which I'll include thirty dollars an hour for your services."

"Okay," Angel said with some reluctance.

"That's great! You'll need a PI license—which is a simple certification form with a nominal fee based on your police experience. You'll have to submit an updated Private Investigator F-7 form to DPSST, Department of Public Safety Standards and Training, to get your license, at least before you can accept payment as an official PI." Rachael paused. "Piece of cake."

"If you say so." Angel drove up to Joanie's Place and parked. "Thanks. For that I'll buy you two lattes."

Rachael chuckled and slapped her thighs. "Unfortunately, I can't afford to drink two of them."

Once they'd ordered and taken seats at one of the round bistro tables, Rachael pulled out her legal pad again. "We need a plan of action."

"My first plan is to go out to the farm and feed the animals. If Nick and the lab techs are there, I'll talk to them. See if they've found any other incriminating evidence. Not that they'd tell me if they had, but you never know when something might slip."

"Good. Maybe on the way you can stop at the store and make sure the times on their registers are accurate so we can get the real time Candace checked out at the store. Also, try to locate Darryl and get a list of relatives and people Jenkins worked with. We'll want to interview all of them and find anyone with probable cause."

"Do you really think she's innocent?" Angel asked.

Rachael pressed her lips together and leaned back when Joanie's daughter, Corisa, brought their drinks. "Ooh. I didn't want the whipped cream."

"I can make you another one." Corisa reached for the drink.

"Don't bother." Rachael heaved an exaggerated sigh and smiled. "I'll suffer through it. We don't want to be wasteful, do we?" She waited until the girl left before picking up the latte. After stirring in the forbidden whipped cream, she said, "I bet you can eat anything you want and not gain weight."

"Pretty much, but I run nearly every day. That burns a lot of calories."

Rachael wrinkled her nose. "I am not a runner. These things," she glanced down at her ample bosom, "just bounce around too much."

Angel tried to swallow before the chuckle escaped but didn't quite make it. Coffee erupted from her mouth, which she'd fortunately covered with a napkin.

"Seriously. I'm afraid all that bouncing would weaken the muscles."

Angel recovered enough to tell her she could get a sports bra.

"No thanks. I'll stick with walking. I like to hike too. Just need to start doing more of it." Lifting her drink, she added, "Especially if I'm going to keep drinking these."

She leaned back in the chair and crossed her legs. "Now, what were you saying?"

"I asked if you thought Candace was innocent."

"I don't know. But my job isn't to determine her guilt or innocence. My job is to defend her in a court of law. I'm going to do everything in my power to dispute any evidence the district attorney has. Right now it doesn't look too bad."

"Nick seems to think they have her cold."

Rachael smiled. "Think about it. They know she cleaned up the murder scene. That's not uncommon. Women hate having people see their homes messy. They'll even clean before the maid comes in. I have an expert witness in Portland who will testify to that. Every woman on the jury will understand and empathize—especially with a woman in Candace's situation. She was abused, and from what you've told me, she was forced to keep her home spotless."

Angel nodded. "Rosie mentioned gun residue on her hands. She could have gotten that just by handling the gun. The gun residue and her fingerprints don't prove she killed him. It only proves she touched the gun—which she would have done when she cleaned things up."

"Exactly. The stickler is the alibi, or lack of one. She doesn't have a witness to prove she was not at the farm, but as far as we know, they don't have witnesses putting her at the crime scene either."

"So what they have is circumstantial." Angel sipped at her iced mocha frappe. "Doesn't seem like there's enough to charge her with murder."

"Mmm. Unless they know something we don't. I'll be able to look at that in the next day or two, and then I can figure out what type of defense to mount. I might just need to attack the possibility that Candace is the killer. Of course, there's always the chance she actually did kill him. In that case, we need to prepare for the possibility that the state has evidence that places the gun in Candace's hand when the victim was killed. If she did kill her husband, then she can claim self-defense as a battered wife."

Angel blew out a long breath. "Whatever you say."

"I'm going to work on getting her released on bail this afternoon."

Angel glanced at her watch. "I can't believe it's noon already. I'll have to hustle if I'm going out to the farm before I pick up Brian and Dorothy."

The waitress brought their sandwiches, and for a while they ate in silence. Angel gazed out at the water, wondering what Callen would think of her new job. Angel Delaney, Private Eye. Had a nice ring to it. Of course, he'd hate it if he was anything like other police officers she knew, and somehow the knowledge didn't set well.

After promising to keep in touch, Angel dropped Rachael off at the church and headed back to her apartment, where she changed into a pair of slacks and a tailored blouse, topping it with a black jacket. "Looking good, Delaney." She assessed her outfit in the mirror.

"Now if I can just do something with my hair." The wild array of curls made her look like a blend of Little Orphan Annie and Shirley Temple, certainly not a detective that people would take seriously. Angel brushed through the mass of curls and gathered her hair in a ponytail at the back of her head, then secured it with a decorative band. The change made her look older, though not by much. Tossing the brush down, she used a few shots of hair spray to tame the stray ends.

Before leaving, Angel checked the phone book to follow up on the information she'd gotten from Mary Johansson. She copied down the address for Johansson Electric. Greg would be a good person to start with, as he might know other people with whom Jenkins had worked.

She headed north and east along Timberline Road; about one hundred yards later she pulled into the nearly empty parking lot servicing several warehouses and offices. She parked near Johansson Electric and discovered that Phillips Jenkins's business, Coast Contracting, shared the same building. The offices were situated at either end with warehouses in between. The only other car in the lot was a black BMW, parked in front of Coast Contracting.

Nice car. Wonder who it belongs to. Climbing out of the Corvette, she smiled smugly in the car's direction. *I'll soon find out.*

The door to Johansson Electric was locked, so she walked to the other end of the building. The door to Coast Contracting was unlocked, and Angel walked in. The reception area was empty, though from the scattered papers on the desk, she could tell that someone had been working there today. "Hello?" she called out. "Anyone here?"

A middle-aged man stepped out of an adjoining office. "Can I help you?"

"Maybe. Do you work here?" He looked familiar, and Angel tried to place him.

"Yes. Barry Fitzgibbon." He ran a hand over his balding head. "And you are?"

"Angel Delaney."

He stiffened, obviously recognizing her name. The shooting death of Billy Dean Hartwell had brought her into the public eye in a not-too-positive light.

Angel realized she had met him before at Brandon's country club. The guy was chummy with Michael Lafferty, Brandon's stuffed-shirt father.

He made no move to shake her hand. "And you're here for what reason?"

"I'm working for Rachael Rastovski. Candace Jenkins's lawyer."

"Rastovski." He shook his head. "I don't believe I know the name."

"She's new in town." Angel shifted the strap of her bag higher on her shoulder. "I'm investigating Phillip's death. Actually, I came down here to talk to Greg Johansson, but no one was at his office."

"I imagine Greg's receptionist is having lunch, as is mine."

Angel wanted to ask him what he was doing there but thought better of it. "Uh, did you work with Phillip Jenkins?"

"Yes. As a matter of fact, I did. I was his partner."

Angel didn't bother to hide her surprise. "I didn't realize he had a partner."

He leaned against the receptionist's desk with his arms folded, not bothering to comment.

"Did you know that Candace was arrested this morning?" Angel asked.

"No. I didn't. But I'm not surprised. I was afraid she'd do something like that."

"Like what?"

"Kill him. I tried to warn him." He picked a piece of lint from his jacket sleeve.

"Warn him?" Angel asked. "About what?"

"The abuse. He told me he was getting counseling and that he'd stopped drinking." Mr. Fitzgibbon hesitated. "I'm not sure I should be talking to you."

"I know all about the abusive situation Candace was in. We don't believe Candace killed her husband. I was hoping to get a list of Jenkins's employees and customers, anyone who might have had reason to kill him."

"I'm sorry, but I won't be able to give you that kind of information. I can tell you that people liked Phillip's work." He glanced at his watch and moved away from the desk. "I'll do whatever I can to help his wife. Unfortunately, I have a luncheon appointment and don't have time to talk with you right now."

"Tomorrow?"

"All right. I can see you here at 10:00."

"That'll be fine," Angel agreed before he could change his mind. "I can understand you not wanting to give me the names of your customers or employees, but maybe you could be thinking about them. I need to know if Phillip had a problem with anyone."

He smiled then. "I'll see what I can do."

Angel thanked him and left. "That was interesting," she mumbled to herself as she buckled her seat belt. She dialed a familiar number on her cell phone.

"Hey, Brandon," she said when she finally got her old boyfriend on the line.

"Angel? How are you?"

"Good." Angel watched as Fitzgibbon locked the office and got into his car.

"Are you still seeing that detective . . . Cal something?"

"Callen. And yes, I am." Angel didn't want to talk about Callen—not with Brandon. "Listen, I need a favor."

"Name it."

"Isn't Barry Fitzgibbon a friend of your dad's?"

"Yeah—he's a client too. The guy plays golf with us nearly every week."

"Did you know he and Phillip Jenkins were partners?"

"Right. We represent both of them." He spoke as though it were old news.

"So you knew Phillip too?"

"Sure, but not as well. Why are you asking?"

"Curiosity." She told him about her new position but didn't give Brandon an opportunity to comment. "About Fitzgibbon and Jenkins. I just found out about the partnership. Which surprises me, with Jenkins having an alcohol problem. How did they get along?"

"They seemed to be doing fine. Jenkins was a little rough around the edges, but Barry decided to back him anyway. He does good work and came highly recommended. Barry took care of the financial end and Jenkins the contracting part. Barry landed the deals, and there have been a couple of big ones. They built those new condos out by the golf course and were negotiating for the new mall south of town."

"Wow." *Candace wasn't kidding when she said the company was doing well.*

Angel waited for Fitzgibbon to leave, then backed out of the parking space and headed for the main road. She remembered reading about the mall and the controversy surrounding it. She must have read about the partnership, but it hadn't registered.

"I think I know where you're going with this, but you won't get far," Brandon said. "Barry and Jenkins didn't always see eye to eye, but they had a good thing going. I can save you some time. Barry doesn't benefit from Jenkins's death, so don't be looking for a motive there. He stands to lose millions unless he's able to come up with another contractor by next week."

"Hmm." Angel wasn't ready to drop the idea just yet. "Fitzgibbon doesn't benefit at all from Phillip's death? Seems like he would have had some kind of backup plan. An insurance policy or something in case Jenkins was hurt."

Brandon's silence gave Angel the answer she was looking for. "How much was it for?" she asked.

"I can't divulge that kind of information, and you know it. You shouldn't even be asking."

"Come on, Brandon, at least give me the name of the insurance company."

"I've said too much already." Brandon sounded hurt. "Friends shouldn't use friends to ferret out information."

"I'm sorry. I didn't mean to take advantage of our friendship. I'm just trying to do my job."

"Right. And I'm trying to do mine." He chuckled. "Just for the record, I think you'll make a great PI."

92

"You do?"

"Are you kidding? You are one of the nosiest people I know."

"Gee, thanks a lot. Speaking of nosiness, how are you and Michelle Kelsey getting along?"

"Great. Although my parents are horrified that I'm dating her. They keep asking me why I don't get back together with you."

"Ha! You're kidding."

"No, seriously. I guess they figure you're the lesser of two evils."

"Tsk, tsk, Brandon. You and your bad girls," Angel teased. "What a rebellious son you are."

"Yep. That's me." A click indicated another caller on the line. "I have to go, Angel. Let's have lunch together one of these days."

"Sounds good. Call me." Angel hung up and made another quick call to Nick to let him know she was on her way out to the Jenkins's farm.

"I'm about to leave," Nick told her.

"Could you hold up a few minutes? I'd really like to talk to you."

"All right." He sighed. "I'll wait for you. You'll need the key to get in anyway."

"I should be there in ten minutes max."

She had a little over an hour to get to the farm and back to the school to pick up Brian and Dorothy. Fortunately, traffic was light on the main road that led through the historic town. On her way to the farm, she stopped at the market to verify the accuracy of the time on the cash register tapes. Except for a few seconds here and there, they were all in sync.

Nick was leaning against his car when she arrived at the farm, his arms folded and legs crossed at the ankles.

"Well?" he said when she stepped out of her car.

"Well what?" *Is he still mad about last night?*

"Aren't you going to ask? You want to know why I arrested Candace so soon?"

"I suppose you have your reasons. You told me last night you thought she did it."

"Darn right. I still do."

"Do you really have enough evidence to hold her?"

"Try obstructing justice for openers. Fingerprints on the weapon and gun residue on her hands. She had motive, means, and opportunity. She tried to get rid of the evidence. Not that any of that is your business."

"Actually, it is. I'm working as a PI for Rachael Rastovski, who, by the way, is Candace's attorney."

"So she lawyered up. Why am I not surprised?" Nick glared at her. "What does surprise me is that you'd sink that low."

"There's nothing wrong with being a private investigator."

"Humph. There is when you're working for the enemy."

"I don't get it. I mean, you act like Candace is public enemy number one."

"She's got everyone feeling sorry for her. Poor little abused spouse. She comes home and finds her husband dead and she's so upset she destroys most of the evidence." He unfolded his arms and stepped away from the car. "Get real, Angel. She's not stupid. Everyone knows you don't mess with a crime scene. We're going to go for murder here. Straight-out premeditated murder."

Why are you being such a jerk? "Candace thought it was suicide. And she isn't the first woman to clean up a crime scene."

"And you believe her?"

"I guess I do." In all honesty, Angel wasn't sure about Candace, but she did take exception to Nick's bullying tactics.

"Then you're out of your mind. But hey, if you think you can do better, go ahead and snoop around. Be my guest."

"I don't think I can do better, Nick. And I'm not criticizing you. I just don't think there's enough evidence to prove she did it."

"Well, I do." He started to walk away.

"Nick? What's going on with you? Why are you being like this? I thought we were friends."

"We are." He raked a hand through his dark hair. "Nothing's going on that a good night's sleep won't fix. I'm sorry I got irritated with you."

"Apology accepted." Angel placed a restraining hand on his arm. "Can I ask you something?"

"Sure."

"I noticed that the gun was in Jenkins's left hand."

"That's the side his wound was on."

Angel bit her lip, wanting to be careful not to offend him. "He had his food and his beer on the right."

Nick settled his hands on his hips and closed his eyes. "I noticed that too. So tell me what you found out, detective."

"Candace said he was right-handed."

"Your point?"

"Like you said, she's smart. Don't you think that if she was staging a suicide, she'd have put the gun in his right hand?"

"Not necessarily. She may not have thought about it."

"Okay. There's something else."

"What?"

"Do you think there might be a connection between the Kelsey murder and this one?"

Nick groaned. "Come on, Angel."

"They were both abusers and—"

"And that's where the similarity ends. Give it a rest. We've got our killer, and Joe can't see spending a ton of money on this when we need it in other areas. Like hiring someone to take your place."

So that's where the animosity and the rush to judgment were coming from. Angel bit her tongue in an effort not to argue. She could understand tired. She could understand a budget stretched beyond the limits. But she could not understand dropping an investigation this early in the game. "I'd like to go through the house if you don't mind."

"Go ahead." Nick handed her a key. "We don't need this one anymore; you can lock it in the house when you're done. If you come up with anything, let me know."

"I will."

She started toward the house.

"Hey, Angel." Nick had one foot in his car.

"Yeah?"

"Congratulations on the new job."

"Thanks."

95

"Does this mean you won't be coming back to the department when your leave is up?"

"I don't know, I'm looking at my options. At the moment, I kind of like the idea of being a PI. Pay is good—or will be."

"Humph." He started the engine, closed the door, and rolled down the window. "Just be careful."

His words rang in her ears as she hurried toward the empty house.

FIFTEEN

Angel stood on the porch and watched Nick leave. Realizing she was now alone, she had a sudden chill. She glanced toward the barn. Not really alone—there were half a dozen animals in there waiting to be watered and fed. She strode to the barn and shoved the door wide open. The animals greeted her with their baas and moos and whinnies.

She heard a scraping sound in the loft above and froze.

"Hello?" she called out. "Is someone up there?"

No one answered, and Angel decided her mind was playing tricks on her. The sound had probably come from one of the stalls.

Angel had considered waiting for Brian and Dorothy and letting them take care of the chores but decided she'd better at least water the animals. Seeing a hose lying snakelike on the floor, she followed it to a spigot and turned it on. As she moved toward the stall where she'd seen the baby goat the day before, she noticed the water container had already been filled.

Her heart ripped into overdrive again, and she told herself to stop being silly. Maybe Nick had taken care of the animals. Or a neighbor. She'd have to find out who and thank them.

Angel threw off the trepidation she felt and jogged from the barn to the house. She started to insert the key in the door and stopped, choosing instead to explore the exterior of the house. From what she'd seen the day before, there didn't seem to be a way to enter the house that Phillip Jenkins couldn't see an intruder coming. They had seen no signs of forced entry, which probably meant Jenkins knew his killer.

Angel walked all the way around the house, peeking in windows and getting a better idea of the layout. Besides the entry into the kitchen, which was closest to the driveway and appeared to be the entrance most used, Angel found three others. Two were at the back or south end of the house, one of which looked like a root cellar with two boards lying at an angle and secured with a two-by-four shoved through two handles.

The third was the formal entry on the west side. Angel decided to try the various entrances to determine accessibility to the living room and hopefully come up with some idea of how the killer, presuming it wasn't Candace or Gracie, had gotten into the house without being seen. Of course, that was an assumption as well. Jenkins may have known his killer and made the mistake of turning his back on him—or her. The cousin Gracie had mentioned may have come to visit. There were any number of possibilities. Rachael needed options, and there seemed to be plenty.

Since she found herself at the front entrance, Angel opted to go in that way first. The true front of the house faced west and had a scant view of the ocean. A decorative stone walkway led from the parking area on the north to wide wooden steps. Candace had decorated this entrance as beautifully as she had the back with wicker furniture, colorful cushions, and plants.

Using the key Nick had given her, Angel let herself in. The door creaked as it swung open. She stepped inside and found herself in a wide entry. To her right were the stairs leading to the second floor, and just ahead, the living room, where Phillip Jenkins had been shot. Her breath caught. The snacks and beer still sat on the table beside the recliner.

"Well," Angel said aloud. "We know one thing. There's no way anyone could have sneaked up on him. If Jenkins's killer had come in this door, he'd have heard the squeak." Angel opened and shut the door several times. It needed a healthy dose of WD-40.

Of course, the game noise could have muffled the squeak. She walked over to turn on the set, aware of the fact that she had not taken off her shoes and feeling guilty about it. The sound came on at about the same level he'd had it. Going back to the door she let the breeze swing it open while she went back to the recliner. She could still hear the squeak, but maybe it was one of those noises Jenkins would tune out. Of course, the door could have been left open to air the place out. Even so, Jenkins would have seen someone coming in.

She imagined Jenkins sitting in the chair, intent on the game, the killer coming behind him and stepping to his side long enough to pull the trigger.

"Who are you?" Angel asked the faceless image. "How did you get the gun?"

Candace had easy access to the gun case and to her husband. No wonder Nick seemed so intent on charging her.

"There has to be somebody else," Angel mumbled. "Someone who had ample opportunity." Gracie? Darryl? Another family member? A good friend? A partner? Angel tucked an errant strand of hair behind her ear. She needed a lot more information than she had.

It would also help if you knew what you were doing. Angel ignored the self-inflicted jab, choosing instead to believe she could unearth sufficient evidence to show that Candace wasn't the only person with motive, means, and opportunity. Maybe in all the unearthing, she'd actually find the real killer.

Once again, she walked around the living room looking at the photos. She wished Candace were here to tell her who the people in the photos were. She assumed the older couples to be parents and grandparents. Using the process of elimination, Angel managed to figure out which parents belonged to Candace and which to Phillip. Candace looked a lot like her mother.

In one of the photos, a wide shot of a dozen or so people, Angel recognized Phillip standing off to one side at the back, with Candace in front of him. His parents sat in the center front.

After perusing the photos, she wandered down the hall and into a room that had been set up as an office. A look around confirmed that Phillip used it for his business. Maybe she wouldn't need Barry Fitzgibbon's help in getting that client list after all.

Phillip had a number of files lying on top of the desk. One held information on the new mall. Angel wondered if Phillip and his partner had hit a snag on it. The development was controversial, as a lot of people in the area resisted this kind of growth. They liked Sunset Cove just as it was. They didn't mind the tourists but wanted the town to maintain its beachy flavor.

Flipping through the pages revealed nothing incriminating or out of the ordinary. There was a note clipped to a short stack of papers for someone named Becky, asking her to cut a check to Johansson Electric.

That should make Mary happy. Angel wondered what to do with the note. Who was Becky, and had Jenkins let her know what he was doing before he died? Would anyone come here to pick up his papers? Maybe tomorrow she could find out what kind of working situation he had. She could mention to Fitzgibbon that she'd seen the note.

Angel sat down at the computer and turned it on. She wondered if Nick had checked it out. Remembering Callen's question about a suicide note, she settled in to peruse his files.

Dead end. Without a password she couldn't access anything. Frustrated, Angel turned the computer off and went back to exploring the house. She left via the front door and went to the south side and the door she'd seen there. It opened into a combination mudroom/laundry room/bathroom. Opening the door at the other end of the room, Angel found herself in the kitchen, opposite the door she'd used the day before. The pristine white linoleum was now mottled with dozens of muddy footprints.

The place seemed eerily silent, and Angel did an about-face, heading back into the laundry room. There she noticed another door and discovered it led to the basement. She peered down into the darkness and thought she heard a faint rustling sound. Hair pricked the back of her neck, and she hurriedly shut the door and went back out on the porch, telling herself the noise she'd heard had to be mice or squirrels.

It was almost time to pick up the children, but she wanted to check the root cellar. Since it didn't have a lock like the other doors, the intruder—supposing there was one—may have gained entry there. Angel went back outside, climbed down the steps, and followed the short gravel path to the slanted boards. She removed the two-by-four and tugged at the rope handles, surprised at how easily the panels opened. She lifted both sides, letting the heavy two-inch reinforced plywood doors drop to the ground. Concrete steps led to a dark, musty-smelling basement. Angel descended a half dozen stairs and looked for a light. She found one at the center of the stairs and pulled the string. The light came on, illuminating an unfinished root cellar where old wooden bins lined the walls. She spotted potatoes and carrots, beets, some apples and pears, along with several plants.

At the end of the room was another door, with most of its white paint peeled off. Opening it put her into the main basement. She found a light switch just inside the door and flipped it on. The basement housed a furnace and a number of floor-to-ceiling shelves stocked with canned tomatoes, peaches, plums, cherries, and other foods she didn't recognize. Everything had been organized and labeled. No surprise there.

The musty smell permeated this room as well but mingled with the scent of freshly cut wood and herbs that hung in bunches from the rafters. The ceiling was unfinished, exposing old wires and pipes, but someone, probably Phillip, had recently Sheetrocked the walls. She could see the new wiring as well, compliments of Johansson Electric.

Jenkins had confiscated a good-sized area in the corner for his workshop. A long, wide cabinet pressed against the wall held an assortment of tools neatly stored in drawers and hanging on pegs. In the center of the workshop sat a table saw. A gadget for every occasion. Everything a carpenter would want.

She climbed the stairs, thinking she'd exit that way, but remembered that she'd locked it from the other side. Descending the stairs, she noticed a large wooden cabinet to her left that sat against a wall in another alcove. A glass front displayed Phillip's gun collection. Phillip had been shot with one of his own guns. Odd that the exterior doors to the basement were unlocked. Anyone could have had easy access to the gun case. The gun case, however, was padlocked.

Two loud bangs jump-started her heart. Holding her hand on her chest, she ducked and crept the rest of the way down the stairs, trying to figure out what had made the noise.

Gunfire? No, that wasn't right. It didn't take too long to discover the source. Someone had dropped the doors to the root cellar and apparently shoved the two-by-four into the handles, trapping her inside.

SIXTEEN

A ngel walked back into the main part of the basement, dropped down on the second step, and stretched her legs out in front of her. "Now what?" She had left her bag and her cell phone in the car. She probably wouldn't be missed until she failed to pick up the children.

Angel had no intention of staying in the cellar that long. If only she hadn't locked the basement door.

"That's it!" She bounced up and ran into the workshop. Scrounging through the drawers, she found a long thin nail and hurried up to the door. As with many interior doors, this one had a hole in the center of the knob as a safety feature. She inserted the nail into the hole, and within seconds it opened. Slipping the nail into her pocket, Angel eased open the door.

Whoever had closed up the root cellar might still be there, and that someone could be Phillip Jenkins's killer. Angel crossed the kitchen floor when she heard the distinct roar of a motorcycle. She ran to the kitchen door and flung it open. Someone was racing down the driveway and raising too much dust for Angel to identify them.

She raced out to her car and tore down the driveway, hoping to catch up with the intruder. As she drove, she put in a call to Nick. He wasn't sympathetic.

"Serves you right, sneaking around out there by yourself. It was probably just a neighbor who noticed the cellar doors were open."

"You think?" Angel said. "Come on, Nick. My car was parked in the driveway, and in case you hadn't noticed, that cherry red is pretty hard to miss."

"Okay, so somebody else was snooping around out there. They're gone now, right?"

By the time she reached the main road, there was no sign of the motorcycle or its driver. "Yes, and I lost him. It's weird. I didn't hear anyone drive up, and I would have. You don't suppose he was here the entire time, do you?"

"You mean while we were there? That's impossible, Angel. Someone has been out there since you got there yesterday afternoon."

"True, but why didn't I hear the guy drive up?"

"I don't know what to tell you."

Angel sighed. "Forget I called."

"Consider it done."

Angel headed to town to pick up Brian and Dorothy. As she drove back into town, she wondered about the wisdom of accepting Rachael's job offer. She'd never investigated a murder before and really didn't know if she should start now. Her experience was minimal, and she doubted watching *CSI* counted for much.

How can you not investigate? The case deserves much more than the Sunset PD and Nick are apt to give it.

Callen should have been in on this one. Next time she talked to him, she'd ask him to . . .

No, you won't. Callen is up to his earlobes in work. She certainly didn't need to increase his workload.

But helping Candace was the right thing to do. Angel just hoped she would be able to do it.

After changing cars again, she picked up Brian and Dorothy from school and headed back out to the farm. On the way, she told the kids about seeing the motorcycle. Not wanting to frighten them, she didn't mention that the driver had locked her in the basement.

"Oh, that was probably Darryl's Harley," Brian said. "He stays here sometimes and keeps it in the barn."

"I see." Angel eyed him in the rearview mirror. "Was he staying here yesterday?"

"No," Brian said, "but his bike was here."

"We saw it when we were playing," Dorothy added.

"He probably just came back to get it," Brian said.

"Why would he do that?"

"Sometimes he goes places with his friends and he doesn't want to leave it at his place. He's afraid it will get stolen."

"So his bike was here yesterday. How would he get here, and why didn't anyone see him?"

"Hitched a ride, I guess." Brian shrugged. "Or he might have had a friend drop him off."

Strange. As Nick had said, the house had been watched continuously from the time she'd arrived until she'd left to pick up the kids this afternoon. Had Nick or the lab techs thought to look in the barn? She'd have to ask Nick.

When had Darryl come, and how long had he been there? Had Darryl come while Candace was gone? Had he killed Phillip? Suppose he had and was leaving when Candace drove in. He wouldn't have wanted to be seen leaving the farm. He may have hidden in the barn with plans to sneak away as soon as he had a chance, only he didn't get that chance until Angel went into the basement. Could he have hidden in the barn the entire time? She remembered the noise she'd heard in the loft earlier and how someone had watered the animals.

Had he been watching her? If so, he'd seen her go down into the basement via the root cellar. It was clearly visible from the barn. She said none of this to the children. Angel thought it best to keep the mood as light as possible.

Brian and Dorothy were happy to be able to help with the animals and took pride in showing Angel what to do. While they worked Angel asked Brian about the computer. Unfortunately, he had no idea how to access it. The office equipment was off limits to the younger children, but Gracie used it for reports and such. Angel made a mental note to ask her about the password.

105

While the children fed the animals, Angel climbed to the upper level of the barn and stood at the partly open sliding door. The intruder could have seen everything that was going on from up here with no one knowing or seeing him. She found several cigarette butts and gum wrappers off to one side along with the wrapper from a granola bar. Stacks of hay bales provided a perfect hiding place.

Angel moved Darryl up to number one on her suspect list. He'd locked her in the basement to give himself time to escape. It made perfect sense. Darryl knew about the gun collection, and Gracie had told her that Darryl had stolen one of them. Candace refuted that, but Darryl knew how to get in and out of the house undetected. Phillip wouldn't be at all concerned for his safety if his nephew had walked in.

"What's your cousin Darryl like?" Angel asked the children on the way back into town.

Dorothy grinned. "He's nice. Darryl plays pony with us in the barn and helps us swing from the rope in the loft and land in the hay. Daddy let him take us for a ride on his Harley."

"Mama didn't want us to go," Brian said. "But Dad told her it was okay and to quit babying us."

"Hmm. What's his last name?"

"Jenkins, like us."

"So you guys like Darryl?"

"He's okay." Brian shrugged. "Gracie hates him."

"She thinks he's disgusting, but that's because he smokes," Dorothy put in.

"Do you know where he lives?"

"No, but Gracie might." Brian shrugged.

"Did Darryl and your dad get along okay?"

He pursed his lips and thought for a moment. "I guess. Him and my dad were buds. Dad would drink beer with him and take him hunting. He even let Darryl shoot his guns."

Maybe he shot off one too many.

Angel drove Brian and Dorothy straight back to her parents' place and went in with them.

106

The kids settled in to do their homework, and Angel wandered into the kitchen, where her mother put her to work. Side by side they butterflied chicken breasts and pounded them to one-fourth-inch thickness. "This is a great way to relieve stress," Angel commented as she brought the flat mallet down on the thicker part of the chicken breast.

"Maybe that's why I like to cook." Anna chuckled. "Banging pots and pans around can be therapeutic."

"Funny, I never thought of you as having much stress, but now that I think about it, you would. Raising five kids couldn't have been easy. I'm glad you took your hostilities out on the food and not on us."

"My mama used to tell me all the time, 'Children are for loving, not for hurting.'"

Angel and her mother placed the chicken pieces in a large plastic bag with marinade so the chicken would absorb the spicy mixture for an hour or two. "Later we'll dredge them in a flour mixture and fry them in olive oil." She'd serve the chicken topped with a mixture of mushrooms, scallions, onions, garlic, and marsala and cream to make a sumptuous gravy. Angel's mouth watered just thinking about it.

After the brief cooking lesson, Angel poured them both a cup of coffee and sat at the table.

"Anything new?" Anna asked. "With Candace, I mean."

"I talked to her this morning. Rachael is representing her." Angel filled her mother in on the day's events.

"Sounds like you have several possible suspects."

"I'm curious about Jenkins's partner. Do you know him?"

"Of course. Everyone knows everyone in this town. Barry is nice enough. Goes to the Baptist church north of town. His wife volunteers at the shelter. A wonderful woman. Lorraine. Have you met her?"

Angel shook her head. "I don't think so. I've seen her around, though."

"I should talk to her. Or you could. You might get a lot more information from her than from her husband. Men can be close-mouthed. Barry Fitzgibbon does a lot of charity work as well. They have money, but they're not snooty, if you know what I mean. Not like the Laffertys," she sniffed. "That woman wouldn't set foot in the shelter. Barely talks to me."

"We're at least ten steps down on the social ladder, Ma. She doesn't need to talk to us."

"Still, this is the beach—there shouldn't be a class distinction."

"There isn't. The Laffertys like to think there is. They're delusional." Angel smiled. "Brandon used to say that, usually just after telling me I was in a class by myself."

"He's absolutely right."

"I have an appointment with Mr. Fitzgibbon in the morning."

Anna nodded and sipped at her tea.

Angel hauled in a deep breath. "Do we know when Gracie gets out of school today?"

"Six, I think. Yes, I'm sure she said she had cheerleading practice until six. Can you pick her up?"

"Sure." Angel drained the last few swallows of her coffee and took the cup to the sink.

"Good. I'll have dinner ready when you get back. Will you want to eat with us?"

"Are you kidding? You're making one of my favorites."

"They're all your favorites, Angel."

Dorothy ran into the kitchen and climbed into Anna's lap. Wrapping her thin little arms around Anna's neck, she turned to Angel and asked, "When are you going to bring my mommy home?"

"I don't know," Angel replied. "Soon, I hope." To Anna she said, "Rachael was going to see about getting her out on bail."

Dorothy pouted. "Brian says she's in jail because the police think she killed my daddy."

"Oh, sweetie," Anna cooed. "The police have made a mistake, that's all. And our Angel is going to find out who really did it."

"Today?"

"Probably not today," Angel said. "But soon."

"Tomorrow?"

"Maybe." Anna hugged her. "As soon as she can."

Angel cleared her throat. "Listen, Ma, I need to run over to Callen's to check on Mutt. I'll feed him then go pick up Gracie."

108

"Who's Mutt?" Dorothy asked.

"Callen's dog."

"Who's Callen?"

"My friend."

"Can I go see Mutt?" Dorothy slid off Anna's lap.

Angel glanced at her mother. "Can she?"

"Of course you can. Take Brian too. They'd enjoy it. Let them run on the beach for a while."

"Okay, guys." Angel didn't especially want the company, but her mother had her hands full. It was the least she could do.

They took Mutt for a walk, with Brian handling the leash. After an hour of running and playing, it was time to head over to pick up Gracie. As promised, dinner was ready when they got back to the house.

Despite pleas from her mother and the younger kids to stay, Angel went home after dinner. Her answering machine was blinking. Four messages—one from Callen saying he missed her and would call back later, one from Lorraine Fitzgibbon wanting to talk with her. Angel expected a disconnect, but the woman hesitated then added, "I just got off the phone with your mother, and she said to call. Several of the women at the shelter are worried their husbands might be next. Do you think there's a pattern? Well, it was a thought. Please call when you can."

The next message was from Rachael, who wanted a report and would come by after her dinner date with Paul.

The last message was from Tim telling her he'd been to the jail to see Candace. "The funeral will be next Monday. Hopefully Candace will be released by then."

Opting to make her phone calls later, Angel kicked off her shoes, shrugged out of her clothes, and stepped into the shower. By the time she'd gotten dressed again, the day's activities had caught up with her. She stretched out on the bed, thinking to rest a few minutes, but she ended up falling asleep until 9:00. She'd have slept longer if someone hadn't been persistently ringing her doorbell.

She dragged herself to the door, swinging it open after looking through the peephole and seeing her new partner. "Whoa. You look gorgeous." Angel stepped back to let her in. "My poor brother doesn't have a chance."

Rachael's cheeks brightened. "Thanks. I hope you're right." She squeezed in past Angel. "You look . . . tired. Cute, but definitely rumpled."

Angel ran a hand through her tousled curls and caught several snags. "I fell asleep."

"Well, wake up and tell me what happened. Would you like me to make you some coffee?"

"No, but you can pour me a diet Coke. There's a bottle in the fridge. Help yourself."

"Thanks, but I'm stuffed. Paul took me out to the resort. That is some posh place."

"You're telling me." Peter and Paul—their mother was into biblical names big time—were twins. They'd done well for themselves and owned several resorts in some of the hottest vacation spots in the world. They'd recently built a five-star resort on the Oregon coast.

"Paul is so sweet. You know what he did?"

"Proposed?"

Rachael rolled her eyes. "We've only been going out for two months." She cleared her throat and fished around in the freezer for some ice. "He offered to let me use an office in their complex. Rent free."

"Wow. Are you going to take him up on it?"

She smiled. Ice clinked into the empty glass, and the Coke foamed and fizzed as she poured it. "I'd have to give up my conference room. I kind of like operating out of the church. It suits me. Besides, if I had a nicer office with the use of their fancy conference room, I might attract a more sophisticated clientele."

"And that's a problem?" Angel took the drink when Rachael finished topping it off.

Rachael reached into the cupboard for another glass. "You probably think I'm nuts, but I've been there. I've had the big bucks and the palatial office with legal secretaries." She shook her head. "I want to be free to defend people who don't have the big bucks."

"Ouch. Don't remind me." Angel figured she still owed at least three thousand dollars in legal fees. Fees that her brothers had paid for and fees that she had every intention of paying back.

Rachael chuckled. "Call me quirky, but I actually enjoy working at the church. Maybe I feel like I'm closer to doing what God wants me to do. Helping people."

"So what did you tell Paul?"

"I said no." She filled her glass with water from the tap and took a sip. "I don't think he was too happy. Correct me if I'm wrong, but I get the impression not too many women turn him or Peter down."

Angel rubbed her eyes and yawned. "They can be pretty convincing." She recalled the conversation they'd had about loaning her money for legal fees, insisting that it wouldn't be fair to make Rachael wait until Angel was able to pay her. They certainly didn't feel that Rachael should take the case pro bono.

"I think the real reason he offered was so I'd be closer and he could keep an eye on me." She frowned. "I thought that was being manipulative and controlling, and I told him so."

"So you two had a fight?"

"Sort of. But we made up when he apologized. He insisted he hadn't meant to sound manipulative but could understand how I felt that way. I believed him. I think he was just being kind."

"I think so too. Peter and Paul are like that. They see a need and try to meet it. Maybe that's why their resorts do so well. They cater to people's needs."

"Hmm." Rachael sipped thoughtfully as she took her drink to the living room and lowered herself onto the couch. "So, tell me what your day was like."

Angel joined her, settling in the chair and stretching her legs out on the ottoman. She told Rachael about her afternoon, from her brief contact with Jenkins's partner to being locked in the basement. "You wanted suspects, I'm looking at three, and I'm just getting started. They're slithering out of every rock I turn over."

"Good. The more the merrier."

"My money is on the creep who locked me in the basement. That's where I'll start tomorrow. Maybe Rosie will get me an address through the DMV. If the kids are right and the motorcycle belonged to their cousin, we may be able to put him at the scene."

Rachael slipped off her black heels. "That may or may not work for Candace."

"What do you mean?"

"He may turn out to be the killer or he may end up being a witness against her. Did you tell the police about him?"

"I told Nick someone had locked me in the basement and that I thought the guy must have been there the whole time. Of course, that went over well. Nick insisted that he'd have known if someone was there. He told me it served me right and that it was probably a neighbor who saw that the cellar was open and took it upon himself to close it. Since I'm not dead or injured, I doubt he'll bother with it. I haven't told him that it might be Phillip's nephew, and I'm not sure that I will."

"You wouldn't have to unless you find something incriminating. We don't want to be accused of withholding evidence."

Angel smiled. "Not to worry. I'll keep them informed every step of the way. I don't need them any more upset with me than they already are."

"They're giving you a bad time about the leave?"

Angel nodded. "On one hand they are all really supportive, but I get the feeling they're mad at me. Nick seems to be blaming me for his long hours. He's not too happy with my becoming a PI, either."

"I think I can understand where they're coming from. I'm not a psychologist, but what happened to you hit a little too close to home. I doubt they're angry with you. They're upset about the system and how vulnerable they are. It's easier to be mad at you than to face their fears."

"Maybe you should have been a psychologist instead of an attorney."

Rachael tucked her stocking feet up under her. "There are a lot of similarities between the jobs. In both, you have to learn how to read people."

112

"Easier than it sounds. Some people are tough to read, while others, like Nick, let you know exactly what they're thinking. You should have seen his face when I told him about working for you. Sheesh. You'd have thought I told him I was a spy for Saddam Hussein."

"That bad?"

"Nearly."

They talked until 10:00 about life in general and their lives in particular. Rachael had Angel fill out the necessary forms for making her a bonafide detective and handed her a small silver gift bag.

"What's this?" Angel pulled out the tissue paper and a box. "Business cards?"

"Just a little present to congratulate you and welcome you to the firm. I didn't think you'd have made up your own yet."

ANGEL DELANEY, PRIVATE INVESTIGATOR. The cards listed her cell phone number and the name and phone number of the attorney's office.

Angel took out several cards and placed them in the leather holder that had come with them. "Thanks. That was really thoughtful of you."

After Rachael left, Angel slipped on a sweater and stepped outside onto her patio. The wind rushed in from the north and left her shivering. Still, she stood there looking into the inky darkness past the lighted waves of high tide.

Tomorrow she'd track down Darryl Jenkins. Wouldn't it be interesting if he turned out to be Phillip's killer? She imagined the satisfaction she'd get from confronting him, or better, getting a confession and turning him over to the police.

It's not going to be that easy.

She remembered the call from Lorraine Fitzgibbon. Suppose they weren't looking for someone with a grudge against Phillip Jenkins. Supposing, as Lorraine had suggested, they were looking for a serial killer seeking to rid the world of abusive men?

113

SEVENTEEN

Before going to bed, Angel turned on her laptop and clicked on the icon taking her to her home page. There she located the white pages and typed in Darryl Jenkins, Sunset Cove. No luck there. She'd have to call Rosie in the morning and hope she'd be willing to access the information for her.

The following morning Angel turned off the alarm at 6:00, threw on her sweats, and dragged her tired body outside, down the back steps, and out onto the beach. Within a few minutes her brain began to clear. She jogged to Callen's place, took care of Mutt, and ran back. This time she didn't linger. She felt bad about not spending the night with the dog, but even with the nap, she'd been too tired after Rachael left to pack a bag and drive over.

By 8:00 she'd had two cups of coffee, eaten a power bar, showered, and dressed. Then she called the PD. Her efforts were rewarded with a voice mail saying, "If this is an emergency, call 911. If you need to speak with an officer, call . . ."

Angel hung up, cutting off Rosie's recorded voice. She tried the number again a few minutes later and got a temp who was filling in for Rosie and had no idea how to access the files. "I can check with Chief Brady," she offered.

"No, thanks." Joe was the last person she'd ask.

After much deliberation, she called Nick. "Remember that guy with the motorcycle I told you about yesterday?"

"Yeah."

"I have his name. I'll trade you that for his address."

"You want me to check DMV records for you?"

"I'd do it myself, but the computer isn't available to me right now. Rosie is off today, and Joe would blow a gasket, which leaves you. Please."

"Why do I need his name?"

"Because he's Phillip Jenkins's nephew and he was at the farm before Candace got there."

"Do you expect me to believe that?"

"He was there the entire time you were. I'm sure of it." When Nick didn't respond, she said, "Look, you don't have to believe me. The guy may not have done anything, but you need his name in the case file. He's a potential witness."

"I can get his name from Candace. If you want to get hold of this guy so bad, why don't you call her?"

"I asked, but she didn't have an address."

"Humph. Phone book?"

"No luck there either." Angel sighed. "Look, I already know he lives in an old trailer. I could probably find him, but it would take me all day."

"So do it."

"Come on, Nick, I just want to talk to him. I'd be doing you a favor, all right? If he's clean, you won't need to interview him. If he's dirty, I'll let you know."

"Okay. I'll get the address and call you back in a few minutes." His tone indicated that he still didn't think much of the idea, but that he appreciated being able to pad his files with more information on Jenkins.

True to his word, Nick called back a few minutes later. The DMV records revealed an address, which Angel jotted down on a Post-it. She'd pay Darryl a visit before her appointment with Fitzgibbon—providing Darryl still lived at his last known address. She knew exactly where it was—a dilapidated trailer park northeast of town.

"I owe you one, Nick. Thanks."

"Right, just don't tell anyone where you got the info, okay?"

"Promise." Angel rang off and tossed the phone into her bag, then headed out.

Driving through town, Angel passed the pharmacy and the old cannery. While her mind tried to speed past the place and the memories, her body had other ideas. She gripped the steering wheel as panic seeped into her veins. Her breathing quickened along with her pulse. Scenes flashed across her mind like a bad movie. She and her partner getting the call, a burglary in progress. Pulling up in front of the pharmacy. Automatic weapons hitting the plate glass window from the inside, spraying glass shards all over the sidewalk. All over her. Bergman lying on the floor in a pool of blood, hanging on to life only to have it slip away later in the hospital. Billy stepping into the aisle, pretending to give himself up. Two gunmen jumping out, waving their weapons back and forth as bullets sprayed the place she'd been standing.

Angel took several slow, deep breaths, willing the scenes to fade out. She concentrated on her hands, forcing them to relax, flexing, then straightening her fingers.

Oh, God, when will it stop? When will I stop thinking about it? The flashbacks ended as quickly as they'd begun, but her body took a bit longer to adjust. Heart still hammering, she continued the drive out to Camper's Hideaway, a trailer resort that had been past its prime twenty years ago.

She passed by Darryl's place. His Harley, a fairly new model, was parked in the driveway. The bike was similar to one she'd ridden on patrol in Florida. The rundown trailer looked to be about a 1960 vintage, eight feet wide and maybe fifteen long.

The flashbacks she'd just suffered had quickened her senses and knocked her trust level to a minus ten. Even so, she forced herself to drive back around and pull up in front of the place, then exit the car and walk up the wooden steps. After knocking several times Angel gave up, deciding she'd wait for a while and try again. Maybe Darryl had been out late. *Maybe he's hiding inside with a gun.*

You really shouldn't be out here alone. Angel chided herself

116

for being a coward as she retraced her steps to the car and folded herself in. She sat there a moment trying to decide what to do next. She still had that appointment with Barry Fitzgibbon. Unfortunately, she had two hours to kill before then.

Angel drove over to her parents' place. When she walked in, she almost wished she hadn't. Her father was up and sitting in his chair, napkin around his neck, and her mother was helping him guide his left hand. Angel forced herself to greet them with a cheerful hello, forced herself to kiss his cheek and act like everything was normal and right.

But it wasn't right. It wasn't right at all. *How could this happen? He's always been so healthy and strong.*

Angel avoided his watery eyes and glanced down the hallway. "Where are the kids?"

"In school. Tim came by, and I asked him to take them."

Angel nodded. "You should have called."

"It worked out fine."

Noting the eggs and waffle on her father's plate, Angel asked if there was more.

"I can make you some. The waffle batter is in the fridge."

"No, that's okay. I'll just get some coffee."

"You should eat." Anna dabbed at a dribble of syrup as it escaped the corner of her husband's mouth.

Frank dropped his fork and leaned back.

"You need to eat too," she chided. "You need your strength."

Frank pulled the bib off and banged it on the tray.

"All right. I get the point." Anna picked up the dishes. After taking them to the kitchen, she grabbed a washcloth and took it back to him, waiting while he took it from her and clumsily washed his face.

"Where is Tom?" Angel asked when her mother came back into the kitchen. *How are you going to manage him by yourself?* Frank was still in his pajamas. Her petite mother had somehow gotten him into his wheelchair.

"He's off the rest of today and tomorrow. Another aide is supposed to come, but he's not here yet."

"You're not lifting him, are you?"

117

"Not too much. Tom has worked wonders with your father. He's learning how to use his left hand more. He managed to get himself into the wheelchair. All I had to do was stand there and help guide him."

"Good." Angel smiled, hopeful that her father might regain some of what he had lost.

Anna poured a cup of coffee for herself and set it on the counter while she plugged in the waffle maker and settled a frying pan on the stove. "How do you want your eggs?"

"Mom, you don't have to . . ." Angel shook her head, knowing the objection wouldn't wash. "Over easy."

Anna pulled the carton of eggs out of the refrigerator and cracked two in a bowl. "I got an interesting phone call this morning."

"Oh?" Angel set her cup down and went to the cupboard to retrieve two place settings.

"Candace's parents called. They flew into Portland yesterday. They're renting a car and should be here around noon."

"Why did they call you?"

"Actually, they called Candace first, and she told them we had the children."

"Hmm." Angel wasn't certain what to say.

"Ester and George Michaels—they seem very nice. They, well, Ester, actually, thanked me for taking care of the children for them. She and George plan to take them out to the farm and care for them until Candace is released."

"That could be a while."

"They're aware of all that." She glanced at Angel.

"How do you feel about the kids leaving? You seemed to be getting kind of attached."

"Oh, honey, relieved. Thankful. The children are wonderful, but they need to be with family."

"But you're disappointed too. I can see it in your face."

Anna dropped batter onto the waffle iron. It sizzled briefly before she closed it. "Well, I have to admit it was nice having them here. Seemed like old times. But . . ." She shrugged and turned on the burner under the pan, then lowered the gas flame. "When

118

you get to be my age, there are limitations. I'm not near as agile as I used to be. And your father . . ."

I know how it is. "Taking care of kids is a big responsibility. I'm not even thirty yet, but I couldn't begin to take care of three of them."

Anna laughed. "Motherhood is something you grow into. And besides, you do—"

"What you have to do," Angel finished the well-worn phrase.

"And don't forget it."

Minutes later Angel and her mother sat at the table enjoying breakfast together for the second time in two days. Angel took a sip of the fresh coffee her mother had poured, wondering what her next step should be regarding Candace.

"What are you thinking, Angel?"

"About my new job. I think I'm in over my head. I'm getting all sorts of information, but I'm not sure what to do with it. I haven't found anything to prove she didn't do it."

"Maybe you need to keep digging." Anna cut her waffle in half and reached for the blackberry freezer jam. "Have you talked to the women at the shelter? If nothing else, they'd be good character witnesses. They've all called to see how they can help. One of them, Debra, even said that of all the women there, Candace was the least likely to resort to violence."

Angel smashed up her eggs and sprinkled on salt and pepper before taking a bite. "When Candace stayed here Tuesday night, did she say anything to you? Did she have any ideas about who might have killed her husband?"

"I asked her if Phillip had any enemies—someone who'd want him dead."

Angel paused, her fork in midair. "You did?"

Her mother gave Angel a knowing smile. "I haven't been married to a police officer for forty years without having picked up something."

"What did she say?"

"She couldn't think of anyone but said he owed a lot of people money—the usual stuff that goes on with contractors. One couple was threatening to sue because Phillip didn't tell them the cliff he'd built their house on was in danger of falling into the ocean. Apparently he didn't know it either, so he was suing the previous owner and the realtor."

"Funny she didn't mention that to Rachael and me. Losing a cliff house might be motive enough for murder. Those homes go for around half a million and up."

"I thought so too. I told her to come up with a list of people to check out. And to give it to you."

Angel took a sip of her now lukewarm coffee. "Well, she didn't give us a list of any kind and said she couldn't think of anyone. Of course, getting arrested may have thrown her off a little."

"You think so?" Anna's voice held a light hint of sarcasm.

Angel smiled and glanced at her watch. "I have some time before I meet Fitzgibbon. Do you have the names of the women from the shelter? I could start calling them."

Eyeing the kitchen clock, Anna nodded. "I think they have a support group from 9:00 to 10:00 today. If you head over there now, you might be able to sit in on the meeting. Do you want me to call and ask?"

"Sure." Angel took her empty cup and plate to the sink and rinsed them off. "Do you think they'll let me come even if I'm not being abused by anyone?"

"They let me come."

"Well, you work there."

"Go. I'll call them. They'll welcome you with open arms—especially when I tell them you're there to help Candace."

Angel tiptoed past her sleeping father and several minutes later pulled into the gravel parking lot adjacent to the women's shelter. There were only three cars there, and one belonged to Janet Campbell. Angel's watch indicated she was three minutes late.

The shelter was a large older boardinghouse that had been remodeled. The grounds weren't immaculate but adequate, seeing as how the women themselves did most of the work. Various churches and businesses in town donated funds that allowed the shelter to house women who needed to take advantage of the temporary respite. The shelter was clean and neat with lots of space. There were ten bedrooms, a super-sized kitchen, a dining room, and a large living room in which they held their meetings. The building housed up to ten women and their children, and each room held three or four bunk beds. The home had the kind of eclectic decor you'd expect to find in a place furnished with donations.

Angel went in the side door and was directed down the hall into the living room. The living room held two sofas and three armchairs, all in mismatched fabrics. Three faux fur beanbag chairs lay in misshapen pods. She recognized three of the five women.

Janet stood when she came in and greeted her with a friendly smile. "Hi, Angel. Your mother called, and we've already voted to let you stay. Ordinarily we don't let people just walk in without some preliminary counseling, but for you, we'll make an exception. All we ask is that you keep what we say confidential."

"Sure—unless someone confesses to a murder or something."

The women laughed. "Like that's going to happen," one of them said.

Janet turned back to the group. "Everybody, this is Angel." Pointing to the woman closest, she said, "This is Lorraine."

"Hi." Angel offered her hand. "Lorraine and I have met. Sorry I didn't call you back last night." Angel was surprised to see Lorraine in the group. Her mother hadn't said anything about Barry Fitzgibbon being an abuser.

"No problem. I wasn't really looking for a call back, just wanted to let you know what I was thinking."

"I appreciate that."

She glanced down at her hands. "I'm really not a member of the support group," she said, answering Angel's question. "I'm a volunteer, but . . . well, since you're here about Candace, I asked Janet if I could sit in."

Janet gestured toward the youngest and thinnest of the group. "This is Heather."

Angel greeted her, thinking the woman looked anorexic. Heather couldn't have been much older than twenty; she had streaked blonde hair and was rail thin and holding an unlit cigarette. She had a black eye and bruised cheek, not quite obscured by her makeup.

"And Debra." Angel guessed Debra to be in her midforties.

121

She had long burgundy hair secured loosely at the back of her head with a scrunchie and was dressed in an expensive-looking top and slacks.

"You've met my assistant, Claire." Janet nodded toward one of two remaining beanbags. "Have a seat."

Angel settled onto the one nearest the counselor.

"What can we do for you?" Lorraine asked.

"Um . . . are you sure you don't mind? I hate to interrupt your group."

"Nonsense," Debra said. "We're all yours this morning. Janet told us you'd want to question us about Candace and Phillip."

"Okay." Angel set her purse on the floor and pulled out a small pad and pen. "Is there anything you can tell me that will help Candace? Did any of you see her the day Phillip was killed?"

No one had.

Heather shook her head. "It's just so sad. I can't say I'm surprised, though. I just wish she'd called us."

Beans within the sealed bag shushed as Angel shifted. "Does that mean you think she did it?"

Heather shrugged her shoulders and offered a lopsided smile. "Maybe when she gets out I can have her get rid of my old man."

Angel sat in stunned silence as the words sank in. She glanced around at the others. Claire had a pad and was taking notes, her glasses on, the beaded rope swaying slightly. Lorraine looked like she wanted to say something as her gaze swung from Janet to Angel.

Heather laughed at Angel's reaction. "I'm kidding. We do that sometimes, you know. Make jokes about it. Wasn't more than a week ago we were all sitting here and Debra pipes up, 'I have a solution to all our troubles. Why don't we hire a hit man to get rid of all of them?'"

Angel frowned and turned to Debra. "You actually said that?"

"Yeah." Debra rolled her eyes. "Like Heather said, it was a joke. We all had a good laugh, but we wouldn't actually do anything."

Janet shook her head. "We have an open forum, Angel. The

women can say anything they want. Expressing their anger is a way of letting off steam."

Heather waved her Virginia Slim cigarette in the air. "You won't tell anyone I said anything, will you?"

"I don't intend to." Angel hoped they wouldn't be scared away.

"Good, 'cause we weren't serious," Heather said.

Angel nodded. "I'll keep that in mind, but I hope you all have alibis for Tuesday afternoon."

"Whatever." Heather waved her skinny arms again and stood up. "I gotta have a smoke. Be back in three minutes."

The other women seemed to take Heather's personal break in stride, using the time to refill their coffee cups. Turning to Janet, Angel said, "I was surprised to hear you were counseling here. The last I heard, the counselor was a woman from Lincoln City."

"Yes. Marcia is dealing with some personal problems right now. She's taking the next four months off, so I volunteered to step in."

"Is what Heather said true? Do they actually talk about killing their husbands or having someone kill them?"

"Not usually, although the subject has come up a time or two. We talk about options and agree that murder isn't one of them."

Angel nodded, not entirely convinced. "Has Candace been in any of your groups?"

"She's been coming on Monday nights," Debra volunteered. She crossed her legs. "Candace is not a killer. In fact, when we were talking about it, she got really upset. Told us we shouldn't be talking that way. She actually thought we meant it. She was pretty upset, but by the end of the session she was okay."

"How long ago was that?"

"Mid-April," Claire said. She flushed then as everyone's gazes slid to her. "It's my job to keep track of who comes and when and what we talk about."

"Has she been in group since?"

"Yes," Claire answered. "She's one of our regulars."

"How did Candace seem to you last time she was with you?"

"The same as always." Debra tucked strands of chestnut hair

123

behind her ear. "She told us she was glad she'd decided to stick it out with Phillip. Listening to her talk, I think she really believed he was improving. He was going to counseling."

"Do you know who he was seeing?"

"Janet." Debra glanced at the counselor. "Isn't that right?"

"I can't really say." Janet seemed hesitant to reveal that information, but Angel could tell it was true.

"Well," Debra went on, "she told us Phillip was seeing a counselor and that he wanted to make some changes."

"Humph." Lorraine apparently disagreed. "Which means nothing to an abuser. They can be all apologetic and sincere and sweet one minute and then the cycle starts again. They're like Jekyll and Hyde."

Lorraine sounded as though she spoke from experience, yet she had said she wasn't one of the group. Was Barry Fitzgibbon an abuser as well? She'd have to talk to Lorraine about that later. "Are you saying there's no hope for these guys?" Angel asked.

"There's always hope." Janet spoke in a tone so soft Angel barely heard her.

Angel sensed a deep sadness in her answer. As though she didn't really believe what she was saying. Something was definitely wrong here.

"Phillip wanted to keep his family together," Janet said. "I can't give you any details, of course, but he was making progress."

"So, he was pretty up front with you?" Angel asked. "Did he talk about problems he was having?" When Janet didn't answer, Angel said, "He's dead. I don't think confidentiality extends beyond the grave. Besides, maybe he told you something that could help Candace."

She folded her hands across her chest. "I suppose. Phillip Jenkins was like a lot of men who abuse. He came out of an abusive background with a poor father figure, if there was one at all. His father abused his mother. Phillip didn't want to be like that." She bit her lower lip. "Too bad he didn't have a chance to prove himself."

Heather came back in and sat down in the beanbag she'd occupied earlier, noisily scooting herself into a comfortable position. "Did I miss anything?"

"Tons," Debra answered. "I'll fill you in later."

"I wonder," Angel said, thinking again of Jim Kelsey, "do any of you know Michelle Kelsey?"

"Yes," Lorraine said. The others nodded in affirmation. "Michelle came to meetings here before Jim died. Odd, isn't it, that both women would be suspect in their husbands' deaths?"

"Weird," Debra said. "But wives are usually suspects. Isn't that right, Angel?"

"Not suspects, necessarily, but they are always investigated."

Lorraine pursed her lips. "Do you think it's possible that someone really did hire a hit man?"

"Don't look at me," Heather said.

"Me either." Debra rubbed her neck and tipped her head back. "None of us would have done it, especially not after we talked about it."

Claire looked up, concern clouding her features. "Or maybe it isn't a hit man at all. Maybe there's a serial killer out there somewhere."

Debra's hand flew to her chest, her lips curling in an evil smirk. "A psycho killing off abusive men? Now that's a novel idea. Maybe mine is next on the list."

"Or mine." Heather cast her friend a conspiratorial wink.

A shiver made its way up Angel's spine, causing the hair on the nape of her neck to rise. Didn't jokes often reflect truth? Were these women angry enough to kill?

EIGHTEEN

Ladies, this is serious," Janet said. "What do you think, Angel?"

"I suppose either case is possible. The police have yet to find Kelsey's killer or Phillip's. Remember, they've arrested Candace, and they don't do that without having compelling evidence."

"She didn't kill Phillip." Debra bit her lower lip. "And Michelle certainly didn't kill Jim."

"How can you be sure?" Angel asked. "Maybe Candace killed both of them. Maybe that's why your comments upset her. Or maybe Michelle . . ."

"Honey." Lorraine slid a nicely manicured hand along her jeans as if to smooth a wrinkle. "I know these women. They're weak and ineffective, which is why they kept going back to their men. They held on to some kind of pipe dream that if they did all the right things, their husbands would change their ways. God forbid they'd have the backbone to just walk away. I know the type all too well." She fixed her gaze on the floor, as if she'd run out of steam. "I keep going back to my husband too, hoping he'll change."

So Barry Fitzgibbon was abusive. Interesting.

The others offered looks of compassion.

"Oh, Lorraine," Janet said. "I didn't know."

"It's not something I talk about. When a husband is as wealthy as mine, you tend to overlook things." She sighed. "Maybe it's time I did something about it." Looking at Angel she said, "Please don't say anything about this. Your mother . . ."

"I won't," Angel reassured her. Going back to the discussion, Angel picked up the thread. "I understand what you're saying about Candace and Michelle hoping that things will change, but anyone can reach a breaking point. It happens way too often where the woman ends up feeling trapped and feels like the only way out is to kill her husband."

"Or herself. I know." Janet tugged at her skirt. "But talking about the issues and finding alternatives to deal with the problems—even meeting together once a week—keeps the women sane. They'd call me or the shelter before they did something so drastic."

"Are you sure?" Angel asked.

"There are no absolutes, of course, but—"

"Hey, Angel," Heather interrupted. "I thought you were on Candace's side. You said you wanted to help her."

"I do," Angel assured them. "But the police are going to be looking at all the angles. I'm trying to do that too."

Debra stood up. "I need some coffee. Can I get some for anyone else?"

"I'll come with you," Lorraine said. "We need to get the cookies out. This might be a good time for a break."

"Good idea." Janet stood as well.

Heather grabbed another cigarette and lighter out of her purse and headed back outside.

Claire removed her glasses, letting the beaded chain catch them as she stretched, then walked over to the fireplace. Angel figured Claire to be about her own age. An attractive woman.

"Do you have an abusive husband too?" Angel asked.

"Me?" Claire shook her head. "I'm not married. After being around these women, I'm not sure I want to be."

Angel glanced toward the kitchen, where the other women had gone. "I know what you mean. Makes you wonder if there are any nonabusive men out there. I mean, I know there are. But it is kind of scary."

127

"Hmm. My father was—abusive, that is. I didn't have much to do with him while I was growing up. He died when I was around twelve."

Angel didn't know how to respond. "How sad," she said lamely.

"That he died? I guess it was sad, but mostly I felt relieved." She sighed. "He wasn't mean all the time, and in some ways I miss him." She folded her arms. "I suffered a lot of guilt over the way I felt about his death. My counselor helped me through a lot of rough spots."

"Are you still in counseling?"

"No, haven't been for a while. I've gotten past the guilt, and now I'm just doing what I can to help the women here at the shelter."

"So you volunteer here too?"

She nodded. "I answer phones and stay over a couple nights a week. Take notes for Janet. Gives me something to do on my time off."

"That's nice." Angel appreciated Claire's candor and thoughtfulness but wondered if her helping other women went beyond the norm. Angel dismissed the thought—she'd begun to suspect everyone, even Janet.

"We could use another volunteer around here." Claire came back to her chair.

"You're recruiting me?" Angel grinned.

"Sure."

"I'll think about it." From time to time Angel had considered volunteer work, outside the programs involving the police department.

"Think about what?" Janet came back in and sat down. Rather than coffee she had a glass of ice water.

"Coming to work at the shelter." Claire stretched before sitting back down.

"That's wonderful, Angel. When can you start?"

"Whoa." Angel held her hands up. "I said I'd think about it."

"Claire is very good at recruiting people."

"I'll bet."

"Seriously, Angel," Claire said. "You should try it. Feels good

128

to help these families. We give them a safe place until they can figure out what to do. We babysit sometimes while the women look for work. I like that part."

"Like I said, I'll think about it." And she would. She could certainly afford to give up one weekend a month or an evening a week.

Claire reached into her bag for a diet Coke and popped the cap. One by one the women filtered back in and settled down, looking to Angel to continue.

Angel felt uncomfortable for some reason. Maybe because of their openness. Checking her watch, she said. "I should be going soon, but I do have some questions. These are a little more personal. Feel free to tell me if you think I'm out of line, but I wanted to get a little better idea of who all of you are and, well, I'd like to know what you were doing on Tuesday between noon and 3:00."

Debra laughed. "I can see you're not buying the joke bit."

"Not entirely." Angel smiled to ease the tension.

"I'll go first," Heather said. "I was at the casino. Spirit Mountain gives out coupon books on Tuesdays and . . ." She bit her lip and glanced around the room. "You can get a buffet for three dollars off."

"Tuesday." Janet pulled out her Daytimer and flipped back. "I would have been in the office all day."

"I think that's the day Claire and I went to Lincoln City to the factory outlet store," Debra said.

"It was," Claire agreed. "We were there from noon to around 3:00."

Debra dug around in her purse and pulled out a wallet. "I should have a receipt in here somewhere." After a moment she produced a receipt and handed it to Angel.

Angel studied it and handed it back. The receipt, from Coldwater Creek, put Debra Stanton there at 2:10. "Stanton?"

"That's right."

"As in Mrs. Douglas Stanton?" Angel asked. "Your husband is the president of the Sunset Cove Bank?"

"One and the same." She offered an almost apologetic smile.

"I thought you looked familiar, but . . ." Angel had met Mrs.

Stanton at a reception honoring a retiring police officer several months ago. This was not the same person.

"It's the hair," Debra admitted. "I used to be a mousy gray."

"It's . . . different. Very nice."

"Thank you." She brought her coffee mug to her lips and took a sip. "I changed my hair and I'm working on my lifestyle."

What surprised Angel more than the woman's appearance was learning that Doug Stanton was abusive. He didn't seem at all like Phillip Jenkins or Jim Kelsey, or like Barry Fitzgibbon, for that matter. He was a soft-spoken man, a deacon in the church, and a member of the city council. Of course, all the trappings in the world didn't mean much, but she'd always liked Mr. Stanton. Angel remembered meeting him as a kid when she first opened a savings account for the money she earned babysitting and running errands.

"Don't look so surprised, Angel." Debra raised an eyebrow, as though she knew what Angel was thinking.

"But your husband seems like such a nice man," Angel blurted out.

"He is, to his customers. And to people who matter. He was nice to me too—the perfect gentleman until after I married him."

"You're saying you didn't know he was abusive before?"

"Are you kidding? I didn't have a clue. Oh, I know better now. There were signs, but I was too young and inexperienced to read them."

Janet set her glass on an end table. "Men who abuse often don't show their true colors until after you've known them a while. Unfortunately, you can't always tell if someone will turn out to be an abuser. There are signs, like Debra said, but they aren't always easy to read. Especially when you're hopelessly in love."

"They say love is blind." Lorraine shook her head. "That's all too true."

"My husband treated me like a queen before we got married, and even for a while after," Debra said. "I guess I'm lucky that he doesn't abuse me physically. But the things he says and does . . ." She closed her eyes, frowning at an apparently painful memory.

"It's important to know a person well before you get married," Janet said. "It's easy to get caught in an abusive relationship."

"How do you know?" Angel asked, thinking now of her own budding relationship with Callen. "What are the signs?"

"Background will tell you a lot." Janet wrapped a napkin around her drink to absorb the condensation before picking it up. "How they handle anger. How they treat you. Sometimes the abuser will go out of his way to be kind."

"Almost too nice," Lorraine concurred.

Too nice? That was how she'd classified Callen when she'd first met him. He'd come out of an unhappy childhood. His father had been an alcoholic. He and his sister, Katherine, had lived with their grandparents.

Angel's stomach crunched into a tight knot. Callen had told her about an incident in which he'd almost lost his job. After his wife died, he'd had a hard time and turned to alcohol. He admitted to losing control while making an arrest, thankful that a fellow officer had restrained him. When she'd been attacked after Billy Dean Hartwell's funeral, he'd nearly come unglued. Callen had said it was out of concern for her. At another time, he'd been furious with her for getting involved with the investigation.

Could Callen be a potential abuser? How well did she know him? In some ways he fit the pattern.

Callen is not an abuser. Denial coursed through her. Angel pictured his kind smile, the way he'd treated her when she'd given her statement after the shooting of the twelve-year-old boy. She imagined his kisses and how sweet they were.

Too nice.

She'd have to be very careful not to let love blind her as it had apparently blinded these women.

"Abusers aren't all bad," Janet went on, drawing Angel's errant thoughts back into the conversation. "They often have some good traits, which is why their spouses stay with them for years. Abuse also takes many forms. While our group and the shelter focus on abused women, there are a growing number of men whose wives abuse them."

Angel noted the time and announced that she had to leave

for an appointment but wanted to get a statement from each of the women regarding their whereabouts during the time Phillip had been murdered. To save time she had each of them write the information down and hand them to her. She thanked them for their help and insights and tucked the notes into the side pocket of her bag.

Janet walked her to the door. "Are we still on for 4:30?"

"Today?" Angel grimaced. "I'd forgotten."

"We can change it if you want," Janet said.

"Um, no. I'll be there. I want to talk to you about something."

"Good. See you this afternoon then." Janet waited until Angel got into her car before closing the door.

Angel had just enough time to get to Coast Contracting and her appointment with Lorraine's abusive husband, Barry Fitzgibbon. In a way she was glad to have the information, but she also felt more wariness about meeting him again.

Angel walked into the office three minutes early and was greeted by the secretary, who stared at her for several seconds.

"Hi," Angel said. "I'm here to see Mr. Fitzgibbon."

"Right. I'm sorry, it's just . . . um . . . you must be Angel Delaney. I thought I recognized your name. I just didn't make the connection until this minute. You're the police officer who got into all that trouble for shooting that kid. I saw you on television. Mr. Fitzgibbon said you'd be coming in. I'm sorry, I'm babbling. I'm Becky Reed." She held out a hand, and Angel shook it. Her hand felt cool, clammy, and limp.

The tall, slender blonde wore her shiny long hair straight. She kept tucking the strands behind her ears.

"Mr. Fitzgibbon is in his office—said to send you in as soon as you came."

"Thanks." Angel eased open the door to the office.

Barry Fitzgibbon stood as she walked in, then came around his desk to shake her hand. Polite, posed, but not glad to see her. His eyes told her that—cool as they had been the day before, calculating. Hazel, she decided, neither brown or blue. They fit his personality—at least what she could see of it so far. She could see no indication of his abusive tendencies. Maybe he saved that

132

for his wife. From what she'd heard, Jenkins was nice around other people too.

Fitzgibbon went back behind his desk. "Now, what can I do for you?" His leather chair made a swishing sound as he settled into it.

She eased into the straight-back chair across from him.

"As I said yesterday," Fitzgibbon continued, "I'm not sure I have much to offer."

Angel pulled a notepad out of her bag along with a pen. "I appreciate your willingness to talk to me. As to what helps and what doesn't—well, you never know." She hadn't given a lot of thought to what she would ask the man. Primarily because she hadn't had much time to prepare. Maybe that was just as well. She'd begin with the obvious and work up. "How long had you and Jenkins worked together?"

"He built some condos for me in the San Francisco area. I liked his work and asked him if he wanted to move up this way."

"How was he to work with?"

"Good. Excellent. We got along great."

Angel noted a slight hesitation and told him so.

He frowned and worked his jaw back and forth. "Sometimes Phillip wanted to get more involved with the financial aspect of the business. We had a few arguments, but nothing serious. I occasionally had to remind him that our partnership worked because of our distinct and separate responsibilities and that we both needed to remember that."

"So you're saying he wasn't much of an expert on finances."

"Humph. That's putting it mildly. Jenkins was a spender. He liked expensive things and tended to . . . well, let's just say that Candace had to manage their finances at home or they'd have been bankrupt."

"I'll bet he liked that," she said with a sarcastic tone.

Fitzgibbon gave her a condescending look. "Actually, he preferred it. He knew his limitations. It's one of the things I liked about him."

"But you said he wanted to get involved in the financial aspect of the company."

"Yes, and when I reminded him of our deal, he would always back down."

Angel wasn't sure she believed that. "Jenkins had a temper. Did he ever threaten you?"

"No. And I never threatened him, either. Although I did tell him a while back that if he didn't go into treatment for his alcohol problem, I'd be forced to dissolve the partnership."

"Really. Seems like a threat on your part."

"I suppose so. More of an intervention, actually. I prefer to think of it as a confrontation designed to make him a better person."

Okay, I guess I could buy that. "Was Phillip doing a good job?"

"Yes. He was a very talented man. You can go to any of the people he built homes for."

"What about the cliff house?"

He raised an eyebrow and leaned back. "How did you know about that?"

"My mother, actually. Candace told her about it."

"That has nothing to do with Phillip's work. There are several lawsuits pending on it, but the owners were certainly not of a mind to kill him over it. Most people settle these things in court, and these people are doing just that. Besides, if anyone is to blame, it's the original property owners. We think there may be fraud involved."

"You mean the owners knew about the fault before selling it?"

"We're looking into the possibility, but as I said, that's not going to help Candace, and I'd just as soon not discuss it."

Angel nodded. "What happens now?"

"What do you mean?"

"Now that your partner is dead. Kind of leaves you high and dry, doesn't it?"

"Not really. I still have the crew. Our site supervisor is excellent. Despite all that's happened, we're still on schedule."

"Are you planning to replace Phillip?" Angel leaned forward in her chair.

"Eventually, but for now we'll just keep doing what we were doing."

"The show must go on, huh?"

"Something like that." Fitzgibbon slipped a paper clip off a stack of papers and began twisting it.

Her line of questioning seemed to be making him nervous. "Did Phillip have any enemies? Someone who might want him dead?"

"Not to my knowledge."

"Other than the cliff house situation, did he talk to you about any trouble he was having with clients or family?"

"He mentioned a nephew. The kid was in some trouble, and Phillip wanted to help him out by giving him a job. Trouble was, the kid worked for about two weeks, collected a paycheck, and split. We had to fire him." He pursed his lips. "You might want to look there. I haven't heard anything about the kid for a while, but I don't suppose he was too happy about being let go."

"Do you know where I can find him? Where he hangs out?" Angel didn't tell him she knew where he lived. She was having second thoughts about confronting Darryl at his place. Maybe a neutral location would be best.

"My guess would be the casino."

"You wouldn't happen to have a photo of him, would you? I could get one at the farm, but since he was an employee . . ."

Fitzgibbon seemed much more congenial now that they were talking about someone other than him and the company. "We might, at that. We get photos for security badges. At some of the construction sites, no one is allowed in without clearance. We should have a photo in his personnel file."

He got up and went to the door, asking Becky to pull Darryl's file. By the time he got back into his chair, Becky had placed the file in front of him.

Every movement sent the secretary's shimmering hair into motion. She looked Swedish, Angel decided. Her deep tan indicated that she'd recently been on vacation in some hot spot or that she frequented a tanning salon.

"Thanks." Barry's eyes warmed as he watched her leave. His cheeks flushed when he caught Angel's assessing gaze.

"She's very attractive," Angel said.

"Yes, she is."

He opened the folder and pushed it across the desk to Angel. "Take whatever you need out of it. Becky can make copies for you."

"I appreciate that." Angel perused the contents of the file. Inside was a photo of the quality you'd get on a passport or a driver's license. A half-page form caught her attention. A red "terminated" stamp had been placed diagonally across the page. Absenteeism was sited as the reason for dismissal.

Fitzgibbon folded his hands on the desk. "Is there anything else?"

"Um, I do have one question. If you were handling the finances, why was Phillip giving Becky instructions to pay the bills?"

He frowned. "What are you talking about?"

"Out at the house I found some invoices and a note telling your secretary to pay Johansson Electric."

He didn't answer right away, and when he did Angel detected more than a trace of anger. "That might have been something Johansson did for him out at the farm. They'd been remodeling out there."

Angel got the impression Phillip had committed some sort of snafu. "So, Phillip was using company money to pay for his private remodel?"

"He may have been; of course, if that were the case, the money would be deducted from his paycheck." The flush in his cheeks had deepened. If Angel were to venture a guess, this was the first Fitzgibbon had heard of it.

"Has he done that before?"

"Good question."

On the other hand, Angel thought, maybe Fitzgibbon knew about it and had confronted Phillip. Maybe they had argued and Barry had killed him. At the least, Phillip's indiscretion would have caused some conflict between the two men. "How much do you stand to gain with Phillip dead?" Angel asked outright.

His eyebrows nearly came together when he frowned. "What are you implying?"

"Just that you took out a sizeable insurance policy on him."

"Ms. Delaney . . ." Barry's face turned an even deeper shade of red. Something akin to rage contorted his features.

Angel bit into her lower lip. He wouldn't hurt her—not here in his office. Not with Becky right outside. But it made her wonder how often Lorraine had seen this side of her husband. How often had she been the brunt of his anger? No wonder the woman seemed cynical.

"This conversation is over." He went to the door, yanked it open, and held it for her. "Do yourself a favor, Ms. Delaney. Let the police handle this. I'd hate to see you get hurt."

Angel frowned. "Was that a threat?"

He shook his head and laughed. "Just looking out for your welfare. If you go around asking other people questions like you did me, you might find them not quite so accommodating."

Angel scooted past him.

Fitzgibbon stopped at Becky's desk and in a surprisingly polite tone said, "Becky, something's been brought to my attention. Do you have a few minutes?"

Angel had no doubt his request had to do with the note she'd found asking Becky to pay the bill. She'd have to catch up with the receptionist later.

It wasn't until she got to her car that she realized she'd left the personnel file on Fitzgibbon's desk. Well, no matter, she had what she needed.

NINETEEN

Feeling hungry, Angel left the warehouse area and headed toward her favorite restaurant. The Burger Shed was a little place located near the wharf. It had been there forever and still served the biggest, juiciest hamburgers on the coast. Living up to its name, the restaurant looked like a shed with weathered gray siding. A sign, made of the same gray wood, had been sloppily painted in red letters and hung haphazardly near the entrance. A porthole, salvaged from a sunken ship, adorned the front door. On warmer days people could eat outside on the dock at one of the picnic tables. Angel eyed the feathery clouds against the pale blue sky and opted for outdoor seating, but first she went inside to place her order. The place smelled like hot oil and charred meat, stirring her hunger pangs.

"Hey, Angel." The owner, Jack Cole, greeted her with his you're-welcome-anytime smile. Jack, a middle-aged man with a midsize chassis, did most of the cooking, while his wife, Minnie, waited tables and took orders.

"What'll it be, sweetie?" Minnie rested her thin freckled arms on the counter.

Angel ordered her usual fare, a Monster Burger with bacon, cheese, onions, lettuce, tomato, mayo, relish, and catsup, fries, and a Marionberry milkshake.

"You go ahead and set yourself down, hon," Minnie drawled. "I'll bring it out when it's ready."

Angel walked out to the dock, noting the half dozen or so diners seated at tables along the way, and sat down at one of the ten picnic tables that overlooked the water. A seagull swooped down, landing on the deck near a sign that asked patrons to please not feed the gulls or seals. The seagull didn't seem the least bit inhibited.

A fishing boat passed by, coming back with whatever they had caught that morning. Angel waved, and the passengers waved back. Her gaze drifted over the water as she looked for the resident seals. She wasn't disappointed. Here one came, barking and begging for a handout.

Minutes later, Minnie plunked down her food and utensils wrapped in a paper napkin.

While Angel ate, she added to her notes, deciding she'd better input all the information she'd been gathering into her laptop. She'd print it out each day or so and give Rachael a copy for her files. That way there would be tangible evidence that Angel was doing her job. She'd keep track of her hours that way as well. Going over the notes from the women at the shelter, she realized it looked as though they all had an alibi for the time Phillip was killed. Which meant they were all innocent or they were lying. Lorraine said she'd gone to Road's End to visit her daughter and grandchildren—that would be easy enough to check out.

Debra had the only tangible proof so far—the receipt from the store at the outlet mall. Claire had already filed her receipts but promised to get them to Angel later.

Not that Angel really suspected any of the women. At the moment, she was leaning more toward Fitzgibbon or Darryl. Still, she couldn't help but consider the possible connection between Kelsey and Jenkins.

When she'd finished eating, Angel drove to Callen's house to take Mutt out and let him play in the surf for a while. Mutt loved it as usual, and at 1:45, promising the dog she'd be back later, Angel closed the door and headed for Joanie's, where she planned to relax for a few minutes.

Rosie was there and seated in one of the overstuffed chairs, a tall iced latte sitting on the coffee table in front of her. She was reading a tattered *People* magazine and set it aside and waved when she noticed Angel at the counter. "Hi. Want to join me?"

"Sure." Angel placed her order, then dropped her bag beside a matching chair that sat just to the right of Rosie's.

"How's your day going?" Rosie asked.

"Great. I can't believe how much I've gotten done."

Angel paid for her drink and had Corisa punch her coffee card. One free drink with ten. She was at number six. "Go ahead and sit down, Angel," Corisa told her. "I'll bring it to you."

Angel dropped into the chair. "So, how are you doing?"

"Great." She grinned.

"You and Nick still going out?"

"Absolutely."

After they'd discussed Nick's virtues, silence loomed around them, and Angel felt at odds. Rosie looked like she wanted to say something but was taking her sweet time about it.

"You've lost weight." Angel blurted out the statement without thinking.

"I was wondering when you'd notice. Ten pounds."

"Congratulations."

Rosie offered a broad grin and tipped her head. "Angel, Nick tells me you've taken a job with Rachael—as a private investigator."

Angel nodded.

"Does that mean you're not coming back to us?"

Angel's shoulders rose and fell with a sigh. "I haven't decided yet. I'm sort of trying the job on—see how it fits."

"The guys aren't too happy about it. They don't like PIs getting in the way of their investigation."

"I don't plan on doing that."

"Nick says you already are."

"Well, Nick can go soak his head."

Rosie laughed. "Just for the record, Angel, I think it's a good thing. I want you to know that while I can't give you classified information, I'll help when I can."

140

"What brought this on?" Angel leaned back when Corisa brought her drink.

Rosie stirred her coffee and took a sip. "Nick and Mike Rawlings for starters."

Angel frowned. "What about them?"

"You know how men say women gossip? Ahem, women don't gossip nearly as bad as these guys. I overheard them in the report room this morning, and they were going on and on about how you not only gave the PD a bad name, you went to work as a PI for a lawyer—like it was the most disgusting job on the planet. I didn't say anything. Figured it wouldn't do any good."

Angel could have lived without hearing that little bit of gossip. It hurt to think her fellow officers would turn their backs on her.

"I don't know what you did to Nick," Rosie went on, "but he was really upset." She ducked her head. "You and Nick don't have a thing for each other, do you?"

Angel nearly choked on her drink. "No. Nick is an old friend. He practically grew up at our place. But he has been acting strange toward me lately, and I don't know what to make of it. It's like he dislikes me. He says he's just tired, but . . ."

Rosie rolled her dark eyes. "That's garbage. He's been perfectly nice to me. Except when I try to defend you."

"I appreciate that."

"Well, regardless of what you hear, you have at least one friend in the department."

Angel smiled. "Thanks."

They sat in companionable silence for several minutes, watching customers and admiring the decor and gifts scattered about the place.

Rosie set her empty cup down. "Oh, have you heard the latest on the Jenkins case?"

"What? Did Nick finally realize Candace is innocent?"

"No." Rosie frowned. "You haven't talked to your attorney friend today, have you?"

"No, why?"

"Candace confessed."

141

TWENTY

Angel used her cell phone to put in a call to Rachael. When the attorney didn't answer, she left a message on the answering machine. She then drove back to Darryl's and, finding his Harley gone, headed north to Lincoln City and to the Chinook Winds Casino in hopes of finding the elusive nephew.

She located Darryl's bike in the parking lot on her first pass through. After parking her Corvette, she went inside and wandered through the smoke-filled casino looking for Darryl Jenkins. She finally found him in the food service area behind the escalators. The clerk called number 762, and he got up, picked up his tray, napkins, and plastic utensils, and sat back down. He had ordered soup, a hamburger, and fries.

Darryl Jenkins reminded Angel of the kind of character one might find on skid row in downtown Portland. Sort of scruffy with a transient look about him. Darryl didn't appear to give much attention to clothes and looked as if he wasn't much into personal hygiene either. He had at least a week's worth of beard and wore baggy pants. The grunge look was popular these days, but not so much among the over-twenty set.

Angel ordered a fry bread and soup, took a deep breath, and sidled over to his table. She pulled out an empty chair at the table

142

next to his. Gazing intently at him, she waited until he caught her eye, then said, "Don't I know you from somewhere?"

She thought she might have seen a glint of recognition in his eyes, but he said, "No." Darryl wiped his mouth on a napkin and grinned at her. "I'd remember you for sure, but we could change that."

She forced a smile, not certain what to think. Had he not seen her clearly at the farm before he locked her in the basement? "Do you mind if I sit with you while I eat? I'm not much for eating alone."

"Suit yourself."

Angel pulled out the chair opposite him and slid into it, feeling a bit like she was going in for a tooth extraction rather than a conversation. He wasn't that bad up close, she noted. His clothes looked and smelled clean. At some time in her life—at fourteen, maybe—she might have thought Darryl cute and dangerous enough to be fun. He had dark hair a bit too long for her taste, but he reminded her a little of Brad Pitt and Tom Cruise all rolled into one. His gray sweatshirt bore a Tommy label.

Darryl was younger than she'd thought. At first glance she'd put his age at twenty-four or so, but looking more closely, she figured him to be eighteen, maybe nineteen, possibly underage and certainly not old enough to be gambling—not legally at least. Her assessment ended when the clerk called her number. She picked up her order and sat back down.

Buttering her fry bread, she said, "I think I know where I've seen you before. Your picture is in a photo out at the Jenkins's place."

"You know them?" He glanced warily at her.

Angel nodded and wiped a dribble of butter from the corner of her mouth. "Not real well, but yeah. So you must be related."

"Phillip Jenkins is my uncle." He bit his bottom lip and frowned. "Was my uncle."

She gave him a sympathetic look. "I'm sorry about what happened to him. Are you in town for the funeral?"

"Actually, I live here. Uncle Phil got me a job at the construction company." Darryl set down his hamburger and took a sip of his iced drink. "Don't know what I'll do now. With Uncle Phil gone I'll probably get fired."

Darryl didn't know he'd been terminated? That seemed odd. Then again, maybe he hadn't been back to work to find out. Or maybe his uncle had told him moments before he was killed.

"The foreman didn't like me much," Darryl added.

He might have liked you more if you had showed up for work. She gave him a look of genuine concern. At least she hoped it was genuine. "Why would he fire you?"

"Well, I haven't been doing a great job lately. I took a few days off and . . ." He leaned back and eyed her. "You don't want to hear about my troubles."

Angel shrugged as if she didn't care one way or the other. "I don't mind."

"I do. Tell me about yourself. You live around here?"

"Sunset Cove, actually." Angel smiled and lobbed the ball back in his court. "Were you and your uncle very close?"

"I guess. He was my dad's brother. My father took off when I was around twelve, and Uncle Phil tried to step in to fill the gap. He took me hunting and taught me survivor skills."

"Must be really sad for you to have him gone. Do you think Candace killed him? I mean . . . Candace doesn't seem the type to do anything like that, but these days anything can happen."

"Humph. Cops don't know which end of the rifle to put the bullets in. Candace wouldn't have had the guts to kill him."

"Have the police talked to you? I mean, I've watched enough cop shows to know they talk to everybody in the family."

"Not yet." He frowned. "But I'm not worried. I got nothing to hide."

"Are you sure? Do you have an alibi or something?" Angel leveled her gaze on him, hoping he'd see her question as innocent concern.

He bit into his hamburger and wiped his mouth on the napkin, chewing thoughtfully before he answered. "You think I'm gonna need one?"

"Everybody who knew him will. Even me. See, I'm the one

Candace called to come out to the farm. When I got there he was dead, so I called the cops."

His Adam's apple bobbed up and down, and Angel felt certain he remembered seeing her there. She leaned forward, elbows on the table. "I'm just glad my mother can vouch for me. I was at her place making soup when he was killed."

He took another swallow of whatever he was drinking. "I was on the road."

She sighed. "I don't think so, Darryl. I think you were in the barn when Candace came home that day. In fact, I'm surprised you didn't recognize me, since you were there."

"I wasn't there. What makes you think that?"

"I think you went inside the house to say hi when you came to pick up your Harley. Maybe you even saw your uncle. Was he alive when you got there?"

"No way, man. Who are you, anyway? You a cop or something?"

"Or something." She leaned back, hoping the gesture would lessen his anxiety. "Look. I'm a friend, and I'm just trying to figure out what went down so we can get Candace off the hook and out of jail. Candace and the kids told me about you. She said she hadn't seen you for a few days. But you had to have been in the barn when she came home. You couldn't possibly have left there without someone seeing you."

He glanced toward the exit, his fist gripping a paper napkin.

"I was just out there yesterday, and you locked me in the basement," Angel went on. "See, Darryl, I saw you take off on your bike. Brian told me you sometimes leave your Harley in the barn. My theory is that you went out to the farm the day Phillip was killed to get your bike. I'm thinking you hitched a ride with somebody. You saw your uncle, and maybe you killed him and maybe you didn't."

"I didn't kill him." He sucked in his bottom lip. "He was dead when I got there."

"Why didn't you call the police? An innocent person would have called the cops."

"I couldn't." His breathing escalated, and Angel thought he

145

was going to run. "Okay, you're right. I did go out to the farm to pick up my bike, but I didn't kill him. He was dead when I got there. After I saw him, I went out to the barn to get the Harley. I was gonna leave when Candace drove up, but I was afraid she'd think I killed him and would tell the police, so I just hid out in the barn. Only then you came and then the cops. Don't you see? I couldn't leave. Figured nobody would find me out there in the loft, so I just camped out there."

"Must have been rough hiding out there all that time."

"Not really. I've stayed out there before. I got kind of hungry, but I had my backpack and a couple granola bars in it, so I did okay. I was just waiting for a chance to leave. Darn cops had somebody out there all night."

"And this afternoon I showed up again."

He ducked his head. "I saw you snooping around, and when you went into the cellar, I figured that was my chance. Sorry about locking you in." He cast her a furtive grin. "How did you get out?"

Angel told him about the doorknob.

"Smart thinking. You're not gonna tell the cops about me, are you?"

Angel skirted the issue. She couldn't very well tell him she'd already talked to Nick. "Can you give me any reason why I shouldn't?"

Darryl picked up a French fry and examined it. "No, except that I didn't kill Uncle Phil. He was always real good to me."

Angel rested her arms on the table again. "Tell you what. I won't press charges against you, but I'm going to have to tell the cops what I know. If you tell them first, they might not charge you with anything. They seem bound and determined to believe Candace killed him, especially now that she's confessed. If you're telling the truth and he was dead before you got there, that means she must have killed him before she left to pick up the kids, which is what they're thinking anyway. Personally, I think someone else killed him."

"Well, it wasn't me."

"Okay. I'll take your word for it. By the way, how did you get out to the farm to pick up your bike?"

"I hitched a ride with some guy. He let me off on the highway, and I walked in."

"What time did you get there?"

"A little before 2:00."

"Did you notice anyone coming or going?"

He frowned. "Yeah, actually I did. I didn't think much about it, but I saw a truck pull out onto the highway and head into town. I thought I saw Gracie in the front seat. I waved, but she ducked out of sight."

Angel held her feelings in check. "What kind of vehicle was it?"

"A Toyota pickup—gray primer all over it."

"You think it might have been Gracie?" Angel asked.

"Wouldn't surprise me. That girl is one coldhearted—"

"Did you notice who was driving?"

"A guy. Blond hair . . . well, not blond; actually, he had dark roots. He had a tan—like he'd been to California or Florida or something."

Angel nodded. "Thanks, Darryl. I appreciate your talking to me. Like I said, I'm going to give you a chance to tell the police what you know. You could end up being the witness they need to solve the case."

"You think so?" His expression held a hint of something she couldn't quite read. She had a feeling he wasn't about to turn himself in, that he'd probably skip town the first chance he had.

"Well, I'm glad that mystery is solved." She gave him another smile. "Now, if we could just figure out who killed your uncle. We know it wasn't Candace or you . . ." Angel knew nothing of the sort, but she wanted this guy's cooperation and she definitely didn't want him to run.

"Gracie didn't much like him or me, but I never figured her for a killer."

Angel took a sip of the lukewarm, bland, greasy soup, wondering for a moment if gamblers lost their sense of taste like smokers did. Of course, a lot of people who gambled also smoked. There you go. She crumbled up a package of crackers and dumped them in, hoping to add a little flavor.

"Hmm," Angel began, "we do know that Gracie was at the house that afternoon. I wonder why. I'll have to talk to her again." She looked Darryl straight in the eye. "Are you sure you didn't see anyone else when you drove out there? Did your uncle like to invite friends over to watch the games with him?"

"Not that I know of."

"Did he talk about having problems with anyone? People he didn't get along with or who might have had some gripe with him?"

Darryl dipped a fry into some catsup and seemed more relaxed and even friendly. "Yeah, his partner. I never could figure out why they got together. Except that Fitz—whatever his name is—had a lot of money. Uncle Phil told me he had a plan to get more of it. One time when we'd been drinking, he said he knew something about Fitz . . ."

"Fitzgibbon," Angel offered.

"Yeah. Something big that the guy would pay bucks for."

"Blackmail?" Now she was getting somewhere.

"No." His tone was adamant. "He wouldn't do nothing illegal."

I'll bet. "Then what?"

"Uh, I shouldn't be telling you this. Phil was just talking. He wouldn't have done anything."

"Maybe his talking is what got him into trouble, Darryl. Maybe Fitzgibbon didn't like the idea of your uncle having something against him."

"You think?"

Angel pushed her soup aside and finished off the last bite of buttery fry bread. "It's possible. You have a lot of good information that the police are going to need if we want to clear Candace."

"Guess you're right about that, but still. I'm not too crazy about talking to the cops."

"Are you in some kind of trouble?" she asked, leaning toward him and talking low.

A flash of uncertainty swept across his face and lingered in his eyes. "Why would you say that?"

Because you look guilty. She shrugged. "Most people would

148

have come forward with that kind of information, unless they had something to hide."

"Well, I don't." He crumpled another napkin and tossed it on his tray. "I'll talk to them." His lips formed a hard line. "They won't arrest me, will they?"

"Darryl, coming forward is the smartest thing you can do." She reached into her bag for a notepad and scribbled her name and number on it. "They'll know you're innocent. But if they find out you were there . . . and if Gracie saw you, she could tell them. They'll be wondering why you didn't come forward."

He gave that some thought. "Okay, then."

"If you think of anything else, give me a call." She handed him the note. She wasn't sure she'd convinced him, but it didn't matter. She would tell Nick about him herself. Darryl being out at the farm and saying Gracie had been there opened the door to all kinds of possibilities. And that business about Fitzgibbon being a blackmail victim upped the suspect list significantly. Rachael would have no problem at all proving that there were others with motive, means, and opportunity, including Darryl.

Angel glanced at her watch. "Wow, look at the time. I have an appointment at 4:30. It was nice meeting you, Darryl."

"Real nice meeting you. Sorry about locking you in the basement."

"I'll forgive you this time. You're just lucky I got out as quickly as I did, or I might not be so magnanimous. I appreciate you taking time to talk to me." She stood up, pushed the chair in, and grabbed her bag.

Angel glanced back as she hit the set of doors. Darryl eased into a chair at one of the machines and slipped in a card along with a bill. So much for going straight to the police.

She shook her head, wondering where he got the gambling money when, from all appearances, the guy barely had enough to feed himself and keep a roof over his head. Especially since he'd lost his job. Maybe he won a jackpot. Could be blackmail. Maybe Darryl was taking over where his uncle had left off with Fitzgibbon. Something to think about.

TWENTY-ONE

A ngel called Rachael to let her know she would be in a counseling session. The session was one Angel had scheduled last week, and although she did want to talk to Janet about some personal concerns, she would use some of her time to ask more questions. When Rachael didn't answer her phone, Angel left a message. She thought about calling Nick as well, but decided to wait until she had more time. She doubted Nick would do anything about Darryl, anyway.

Janet's office was in an upscale office building near the waterfront that housed Maxwell's, Sunset Cove's most elegant restaurant. Stepping into the reception area, Angel greeted Claire. The receptionist let her glasses drop, her beaded holder catching them.

"Hi, Angel, Janet will be out in a few minutes." She put a check beside Angel's name.

The door opened, and Janet ushered one of her clients out with a reminder about next week's appointment. She turned to Angel. "Hi, sorry I ran a little over. Come on back." Angel followed her to her office and sank into the easy chair.

Angel remembered the first time she'd come and how she'd perched on the edge of the seat like a rebellious teenager planning to stay through her one required visit, then quit. She'd resented having to go, but Janet, who was an old friend, seemed like a safe person to talk with. Angel had done her six sessions and decided to stay on. These forty-five minutes provided Angel with a place to say whatever was on her mind. And, if she were completely honest with herself, she still had a lot of issues to deal with, her father being one of them.

"How is everything?" Janet asked.

"Depends." She smiled. "I didn't get a chance to tell you at the support group, but I'm keeping busy." She gave her the details of her work with Rachael.

Janet raised an eyebrow. "How do you feel about working as a private investigator?"

"Good, I think. Though I'm not sure I know what I'm doing. I'm asking questions, digging up whatever information I can."

Janet smiled. "Let me guess, you want to interrogate me in private."

"Not interrogate, but I did want to ask you more questions."

"Are you sure you want to use your time for that?"

"Part of it."

Janet shrugged. "It's your dime, but I'm not sure I can add anything to what you already have."

"I know Candace saw you in group, but did you counsel her individually too?"

"Angel, I can't talk about my clients. You know that."

"So she is a client."

Janet sighed, crossed her arms, and leaned back in the chair.

"Do you think she killed her husband?"

"No. I already indicated that."

"Any idea who might have?"

"I wish I did, Angel. I hate to see Candace suffer like this. She's a good person."

"Did she ever talk to you about anyone Phillip might have had a problem with?"

Janet picked up a pen and tapped it against her left hand. "There just isn't anything I can tell you. What has Candace told you?"

"Not much. She and Gracie both mentioned Darryl, Phillip's nephew. I'm working that angle too. I just thought you might know something that could help."

"I'm afraid not."

"What about Michelle Kelsey? I know she hasn't been coming to group lately, but are you seeing her privately?"

Janet pinched her lips together. "Angel, please don't ask me about these people. Whatever clients say is confidential, and unless they are a danger to themselves or others, I won't break that confidence. You of all people should respect that."

"I do." Angel frowned.

"Then go to the source. Talk to Michelle and Candace yourself."

"Guess I'll have to."

"Now, how about we get back on track?" Janet asked. "What do you want to work on today?"

"My father," Angel said without hesitation.

Janet made a note on her pad. Rather than ask about it, she settled back in her chair and waited for Angel to continue.

Angel wasn't sure where to start. Just envisioning her father brought tears to her eyes. "He looks so frail and . . . old. I guess I never really thought of him as getting older. He's always been my dad—the guy who could do anything. Now someone has to do everything for him."

Janet nodded. "Must be hard."

"I can hardly stand to be around him. He looks at me as though it's all my fault."

"Your fault? You mean the stroke?"

"That and the heart attack. I can't blame him for thinking that. If I hadn't argued with him that day my place was broken into . . . He wanted me to go home, and I refused." Angel used the tissue Janet handed her to dry her eyes and blow her nose, then tipped her head back against the chair. "I should've listened to him and just gone along. Maybe things would have been different."

"Do you really think his medical condition is a result of what you did or didn't do?"

"No, not in my head. The doctor told us he had coronary artery disease and that he'd had a heart condition for years."

"You say he's angry with you. Has he told you that?"

"Not in so many words. He can't talk, but the way he looks at

152

me . . . I feel so guilty and he treats me differently than he treats everyone else."

"Maybe you've been treating him differently."

"Well, yeah. He is different." Angel picked up a throw pillow and hugged it.

"We've talked before about putting your feelings on the table. What kind of feelings does being around your father evoke?"

"Guilt, mostly. My mother says I don't visit with him enough."

"Do you agree with that?"

"No." She sighed. "Yes. I don't want to be around him. I know it sounds crazy, but I feel angry and resentful." She pinched the bridge of her nose. "And that makes me feel even more guilty."

"Angel, some of what you're describing is grief."

Angel considered that for a moment. She had and was still experiencing grief over Dani's death, and Billy's. That grief she understood. "But he didn't die."

"No, but part of him has. He's not the same now as he used to be. He's lost his health, his job, his strength. You lost the father you knew. It's not at all unusual to feel guilty and angry. That's a big part of grief. Maybe your father's anger isn't directed at you. Maybe it's directed at himself."

"What about his disappointment in me? I mean, that's pretty clear. I took time off my job, and he hates me for it."

"Are you sure? Have you asked him?"

"No, I haven't asked him. He can't talk, he . . ." Angel blinked away tears and bit on her lower lip. She hadn't asked him because she was afraid of the answer. Shaking her head she added, "I can't talk to him."

"I could be wrong, but it seems to me you are projecting your own feelings onto him. And you're not giving him a chance to let you know how he really feels."

"So you think I'm imagining those looks?"

"I didn't say that. But it's important for you to know what he's really thinking."

"I know you're right, I just don't know how to start."

"I think you do." Janet's gaze met Angel's.

153

"Tom seems to understand him. I suppose I could talk to Tom and get some pointers. I could talk to my dad more when I'm at the house. I haven't made much of an effort to communicate."

Janet smiled. "Good start."

"You think it will work?"

"Getting at the truth will help."

"Yeah, but what if I'm right, and he is disappointed in me?"

"Then it'll be his problem, not yours. You may not find the answer you're hoping for, but you'll know the truth . . ."

"And the truth shall set you free," Angel finished.

"That's true, but it's not what I had intended to say. Knowing will allow you to stop beating yourself up over it."

"Okay, if you say so." Angel folded her arms. "I'll work on it."

Janet nodded. "Sounds like some good first steps."

Angel left the office with resolve to work things out with her father. Soon. First, though, she had to check in with Rachael.

"Sorry," she said when Angel finally reached her. "I've been in court all morning, then I had to go talk to Candace."

"Yeah . . . I heard about her confession. What's up with that?"

"I could strangle the woman. Of course, she did it without my say-so. She's protecting Gracie. She hasn't been able to talk to the kids. When you talked about Gracie having been home, it really upset her."

"I'm sorry."

"Don't be. You were right. I'm sure Gracie's footprints were part of what Candace cleaned up."

"So, she thinks confessing will protect her daughter?"

"She's convinced of it, and unless we can come up with a more compelling suspect than Gracie, I'm afraid Candace won't budge."

Angel told her about her interviews with the women's group, Fitzgibbon, and Darryl.

"Wow, you've had a busy day. Interesting. So either Fitzgibbon or Darryl could have killed Phillip. Better see if Fitzgibbon has an alibi before we get too excited about him. There's a small problem with Darryl in that you're the only one who can testify to his being at the farm during the investigation. I'm surprised none of the officers checked out the barn—well, I'm not really. The guy was killed in the house, and the murder weapon was there."

"Are you telling me my say-so isn't good enough?" Angel switched the cell phone to her other ear.

"The DA would rip it apart on the stand. You didn't actually see Darryl. You saw a guy on a cycle. You called Nick and told him you hadn't gotten a good look at him."

"Right. A lot of good that did me."

"Basically, you can't prove it was Darryl," Rachael went on. "We could try to get the police to go back out to the farm and check out the barn."

"I'm not sure that will do any good. They might be able to prove he was there but probably couldn't pinpoint a time."

"Right."

"I need to tell Nick about him, anyway." Angel frowned. "I wish Callen were on the case. He, at least, might listen to me."

"I don't know, Angel. He'd likely side with the Sunset PD on this. Especially since they've got a confession. They're certain they have enough to make the arrest stick with the prints and gun residue and now the confession. In the hearing yesterday afternoon, the judge ruled against her getting out on bail. That's not a good sign, especially since I stressed her spotless record and the fact that she had three children she needed to care for. He almost found me in contempt of court because I wouldn't back down. I tried everything, but the DA convinced him that Candace is unstable enough to harm her children as well."

"That's ridiculous."

"Well, maybe not. The children were interviewed at school yesterday, and they talked about how strict their mom was and how she made them keep the house spotless. She must have been terrified of what Jenkins would do to them if they were the least bit messy."

"They're suggesting she was abusive?"

"Unfortunately, yes. The children will be going back to the farm to stay with their grandparents for now."

"Mmm. Mom told me they were in town."

"They seem nice. They called me today, and I had a good talk with them. The kids will be well cared for. What we need to do is focus on clearing Candace."

"How do the grandparents feel about our investigation?"

"They're all for it. In fact, they urged us to keep going and even offered to pay part of the bill. They want answers."

"They may not be thrilled with the outcome. If Darryl is telling the truth, Gracie was out at the farm before he arrived. He says Jenkins was already dead when he got there and Gracie and some kid were driving away. He gave me a description of the pickup she was in. I'll try to track it down at the school tomorrow."

"All right. Keep me posted."

On her way home, Angel wondered how Gracie would take the news about her mother's confession. Her thoughts drifted from the case to her session with Janet and, consequently, her father. A glance at her watch told her it was dinnertime at the Delaney household. Maybe she'd stop by to see what wonderful dishes her mother had cooked up and invite herself to dinner.

When she reached the house, Angel knocked and at the same time turned the doorknob. There were no familiar smells emanating from the kitchen. No sign of her mother or father. Had something happened?

"Ma?" Angel called.

A muffled sound came from the back of the house. Angel hurried through the living room and down the hall to her parents' bedroom. "Angel, is that you?" her mother cried out.

"Where are you?" Angel pushed open the door but didn't see anyone. The bedcovers had been tossed back.

Anna grunted. "Over here. Help me."

Angel crossed the carpeted floor to the other side of the bed. Anna lay on the floor, pinned down by Frank's bulky form.

"What happened?" Angel scrambled over the bed and knelt beside them.

"Call an ambulance," Anna gasped. "I was helping him get

into bed, and he fell on top of me. I hurt my arm and I can't move him."

Angel placed the call and at the same time dragged and rolled her father onto his back and away from Anna. She wasn't certain who to attend to first.

"He blacked out. I'm afraid he may have had another stroke. He's still breathing, isn't he?" Anna tried to sit up but cried out in pain.

"Don't try to move, Ma. Just lie still."

Anna whimpered. "I think I may have broken my arm."

Angel checked her father's carotid artery for a pulse. Nothing. She pressed deeper, desperately feeling for the familiar beat, watching his chest and praying for it to rise. There was no movement. Angel leaned down, putting her ear to his chest. Nothing.

No, God, no. Please. Angel rose up on her knees and started CPR, knowing as she did that her efforts were too late. Frank Delaney was dead.

"Angel?"

She leaned back on her heels. "He's gone, Ma. He's gone."

A strangled cry escaped her mother's lips, mingling with the screaming sirens of the emergency vehicles. Anna closed her eyes, and Angel crawled over to her side, placed a pillow under her head, and grasped her hand. The sirens increased in intensity as the strobing lights flashed across the bedroom walls. Anna gripped her hand.

"I need to let them in, Ma. I'll be right back."

How she managed to survive the next few hours, Angel would never know. She moved robotlike through the house to let in the EMTs and explain what had happened. She watched silently as they loaded her mother onto the stretcher and wheeled her out to the waiting ambulance. At her mother's insistence, Angel stayed behind. "See to your father," she'd said. "Call Tim."

"I will, Ma. I'll come to the hospital as soon as I can." She called Tim, arranging to meet him at the hospital. He would call their brothers and the funeral home. "Go be with Mom, Angel," he said. "She needs you."

Numb, Angel followed in her car as EMTs transported her

father's body to the hospital, where he was pronounced dead on arrival.

You do what you have to do. Anna's oft-spoken words drifted over her. Angel stayed at the hospital while her mother was examined and x-rayed and told she had a fractured radius and ulna in her right arm.

It was 10:00 p.m. when Angel and Tim finally left the hospital. The doctor opted to admit Anna for observation, more because of her age and what she had been through than the extent of her injury. She'd been pinned under Frank for two hours. If Angel hadn't come by when she had, Anna might have been trapped all night.

Pain medication dulled the pain and Anna's senses, acting as a sedative and allowing her to sleep. Tomorrow she'd awake to find she was a widow.

Angel sat in the darkened room for a long time, watching over her mother's sleeping form. Silent tears slipped down her cheeks as reality dawned. Frank Delaney was gone, and she would never have an opportunity to make her peace with him. She would never know how he really felt about her, because she had never asked. Now it was too late.

Couldn't you have waited, Dad? Not even for a day?

TWENTY-TWO

———

The next morning, as students were settling into their classes, Angel drove over to the high school and up and down the rows of cars in the parking lot, looking for the pickup Darryl had reportedly seen.

She had awakened at 6:00 a.m., dazed and disoriented. She'd talked to Anna at 7:00 and arranged to come to the hospital around 10:00 to take her home. Neither spoke of their loss.

Perhaps because her emotions were too raw, Angel kept thoughts of her father at bay. When thoughts of him came to mind, she shoved them aside. She could not bear to think of his passing, or face the reality of his death or the fact that the troubles that had divided them would never be resolved.

You should call Callen. The thought came unbidden and settled in among the others. Angel knew very well what would happen. He'd rush back to Sunset Cove to be with her, to comfort her. Angel didn't want comfort. She didn't want tears. She'd have to tell him eventually, but not now and not over the phone.

Her only escape was to focus on work. So here she was, scanning the parking lot for the gray, primer-coated pickup that Darryl

159

claimed to have seen Gracie in shortly before he had supposedly found his uncle's body.

She found the pickup parked in an end space under a maple tree and wrote down the license plate number. With students in class and no one around, she parked behind the vehicle and walked around it. On a whim, she tried the driver's side door, surprised to find it unlocked. She found the registration form and insurance card in the glove box. The owner's name was Justin Bailey, the auto repairman's son.

Small world. Too small.

Callen would be questioning Mitch Bailey about the cheerleader from Florence. The mechanic's car had apparently been stolen, but maybe it hadn't been stolen after all. Maybe his son had taken it? The thought churned around in her stomach like spoiled milk. Angel didn't like drawing a correlation between the two cases. Didn't like that Gracie had been out at the farm with this kid. Her stomach knotted and her heart tripped along a little faster.

She was going to have to talk with Justin and Gracie soon. Maybe she'd try to catch them after school.

Angel got into her car and headed for the Jenkins place to interview the neighbors. As she drove, she ruminated over her progress so far. The information she'd gathered jumbled around in an incoherent mess—like puzzle pieces that refused to fit together to make a picture. Which meant she was nowhere near finished with her so-called investigation. How did Callen manage to keep all the details of his cases straight in his head?

Guilt gnawed at her as she drove. *Who do you think you are, playing detective? You should be at the hospital, sitting with your mother.* She brushed the negative thoughts away, but they kept coming back and lighting in her mind like pesky flies on rotting fruit.

Dad had a massive stroke, she told herself. *There was nothing you could do.*

Several times she thought about turning around and going back into town but didn't. Part of her wanted to give up, to go straight

160

home and crawl into bed. Part of her resisted the urge, determined to stay on task as her father had taught her.

When the going gets tough, the tough get going. She could almost hear her father's voice reciting the old saying. He had a lot of them. He wasn't a quitter and never allowed his children to quit either, not even his little girl.

She hauled in a deep, determined breath and turned onto Cayman Road.

Officers usually interviewed neighbors when a crime took place, and she felt certain Nick had done that. She doubted, however, that he'd share his findings with her. Which meant she'd have to talk to them on her own.

Though Candace and Phillip had no close neighbors, maybe one of them had heard or seen something. Plus, Angel wanted to verify Darryl's story and find out if anyone else had been out at the farm. She drove into the driveway opposite the one leading to the Jenkins's farm. And after a short drive along a tree-lined paved lane, she found herself parked in front of a beautiful home with a horse barn and several well-cared-for thoroughbreds.

Angel pulled up to the house and started up the walk. A German shepherd bounded around the corner of the house, barking and snarling. Angel started back to her car when she heard someone ordering the dog to stop. "Sit!" The dog backed off immediately and obeyed the order. A woman in a wide-brimmed hat, coveralls, and a long, loose overshirt came around the corner of the house. In her hand she carried a weed puller.

"Can I help you?"

"Possibly. I'm Angel Delaney."

"Oh, of course. I thought I recognized you."

Everyone seems to these days. "You look familiar too."

The woman tipped back her head and laughed. "Well, I should think so. I'm Elsie Moore, Brandon's aunt—Beverly's sister? We met at a Christmas party at the Lafferty's last year."

Oops. The party Angel couldn't wait to leave so she could get back to the Christmas Eve celebration at her parents' home. Beverly, Brandon's mother, clearly hadn't wanted her there. "I'm sorry. I met so many people . . ."

161

"No apology needed. I couldn't wait to get out of there myself. My husband can't stand her. Don't get me wrong. I love my sister." She sighed. "Beverly seems rather haughty, but it's just a facade. Inside she's an insecure woman desperately trying to maintain the lifestyle she married into."

"Beverly insecure? Are we talking about the same person?"

"Hard to believe, I know. We came from a very poor family. In fact, our father spent ten years in prison for embezzling funds from the company he worked for. Our mother divorced him, and we moved here to escape the embarrassment he caused us, but the damage was done. Beverly was mortified by it. She suffered much more than I did."

"Why's that?"

"She was still in grade school, and the kids teased her unmercifully."

"And they didn't tease you?"

"They did, but I have a more resilient personality. I was five years older and able to understand that what my father did was not a reflection on my character." A deep, throaty chuckle escaped Elsie's lips. "I shouldn't be telling you all this. Beverly would be mortified. She tries so hard to keep all those sordid details a secret and keep up appearances." She tilted her head, a frown wrinkling her forehead. "I'm not sure why I'm telling you. Guess I just wanted to apologize for any grief she may have caused you."

Angel didn't know what to do with this new information. "Well, it doesn't matter much anymore, because Brandon and I broke up."

"I know, and I'm terribly disappointed." She smiled. "You were good for Brandon. I'm not certain about Michelle. Do you know her at all?"

"Um . . . not really." Angel didn't feel it appropriate to go into Michelle's history with her abusive husband. "She seems nice, though."

"Hmm. I'm worried that Brandon's infatuation for her is misguided."

"Meaning that he feels sorry for her?"

She nodded and brushed a sleeve across her brow. "Time will tell, I suppose. But you didn't come all the way out here to talk about Brandon, did you?"

"Actually, no. I'm checking in with the Jenkins's neighbors."

"Does this have something to do with Phillip's death? That poor man. I understand his wife killed him." She shook her head. "Hard to believe. She seemed so sweet."

"She's been arrested, but that doesn't mean she did it. I'm investigating for her lawyer. How well did you know them?"

"I spoke with Candace once or twice and the children a few times—lovely children. We knew Phillip quite well. He built our house, and we couldn't be happier. He actually took over for the man we fired . . ."

Fired? "Who would that be?"

"Jack Savage." Elsie clucked. "The man was impossible. He refused to change his building plans to accommodate us. I had specific measurements for my kitchen and pantry along with some changes in the master bath. Come on in and I'll show you."

Angel walked into a high-ceilinged entryway that opened into an elegant open area containing a kitchen, dining area, and family room.

"I wanted all of my cupboards done with pull-out drawers that were custom made to fit my various appliances."

The kitchen was huge with a long bar—a little too austere for her tastes, but nice.

"We entertain a lot, and I needed shelves and cupboards to accommodate our lifestyle. After arguing with Jack for about a week, with him telling me why what I wanted couldn't be done and treating me as if I didn't have a brain in my head, I fired him. I heard about Phillip through a friend—do you know the Fitzgibbons?"

"Yes."

"Lorraine and Barry recommended him. I invited Phillip over, and he seemed genuinely impressed with my design skills and was happy to incorporate the changes I wanted. He even came up with some ideas I hadn't thought of. He suggested the private patio off the bathroom. It made the bathroom seem twice as large and gives us a private Jacuzzi. We love it."

It was Angel's turn to be impressed. Fitzgibbon had said Phillip was talented, and this house proved him right. "How did Jack Savage handle the rejection?"

"Not well, I'm afraid. He threatened us with a lawsuit. Our lawyers are still battling it out."

"Is Savage the kind of guy who might want revenge?"

"You're not suggesting . . ." She placed a hand over her heart. "Oh, dear. I hope not."

"Did you notice anyone coming or going the day Phillip was killed?"

"I'm afraid not. I was here all day." She waved her arm. "As you can see, we're rather remote. I can't see the road from the house, which is the way we like it."

"Did you hear anything—a gunshot, maybe?"

She moved her head from side to side. "I don't believe so. I wish I could help, but I get involved in my gardens and tune out the rest of the world."

"My mother is like that." Angel wondered what her mother would do now. Would she find her garden a respite from her grief? Angel dragged her thoughts back. "Thanks for talking with me." She headed for the front door. "I'd like you to give me a call if you think of anything." She handed Elsie one of the cards Rachael had given her and thanked her. Once in the car, she added another name to her suspect list. Jack Savage.

From Elsie's place, Angel headed over to the Jenkins's farm. Someone's blue Ford Taurus was parked in the driveway. Angel recognized it from the parking lot at Coast Contracting and assumed it belonged to the receptionist.

The door was unlocked, and Angel slipped inside. "Hello!" she shouted from just inside the door. "Anyone here?"

Becky, the receptionist, stepped into the kitchen. "Oh, hi, I . . . um . . . I was just getting some files. Phillip used to work here sometimes, and Mr. Fitzgibbon asked me to pick up whatever belonged to the company." Her gaze darted to the door. "I got permission from the police and from Candace's parents. They stayed in a hotel last night and were planning to come out here after school today."

"I'm glad you're here." Angel smiled. "I wanted to talk to you earlier, but your boss seemed upset—probably something I said."

Becky flipped her long hair back and tucked it behind her ears. "Can you blame him? You practically accused him of killing Phillip."

"Do you know that he didn't?" Angel asked.

"No, but . . . What did you want to talk to me about?"

"How long have you known Phillip?"

"Three years. Since they moved here. He advertised in the paper for office help, and I applied. I got the job."

"Did you like working for him?"

"I loved my job." Tears pooled in her eyes, and she looked away. "I'm going to miss him."

"Did you come out here often to get work he may have done?"

"Sometimes. He brought stuff with him into the office too."

"Can you get into his computer files?"

She frowned. "Yes, why?"

"I'd like to take a look at his files." Angel glanced at the screen, which displayed a screen saver of a howling wolf under a blue moon.

"Do you have a court order?"

"No. I'm trying to find out who might've killed him."

"Candace did. I mean, she's been arrested and she's admitted to doing it. No one else had any reason to."

"Why would you think that?"

"Phillip and Candace didn't get along. He was planning to ask her for a divorce."

"A divorce?" Angel ran a hand through her hair. Great. Becky had just given Candace another motive.

"He told me he didn't love her anymore."

"Whoa." Becky's tears and her expression left no doubt in Angel's mind. "Let me guess—you and Phillip were having an affair."

Becky pinched her lips together. "It's not what you think. I'm not a home wrecker, it's just that we fell in love not long after I

165

started working for him. We tried to resist, but . . ." Her voice broke into a sob.

Angel waited for the crying to subside, feeling sad for the woman and at the same time wondering how she could have fallen for a man like Phillip Jenkins.

"I'm sorry," Becky finally said. "It just hurts so much."

"I'm sure it does," Angel said. "Were you out here the day he was killed?"

She nodded. "Yes, but he was alive when I left."

"When did you get here?"

Becky shrugged. "A little after noon. I was only here for half an hour—Phillip wanted to get back to the game."

"Was Candace here?"

"No. She'd gone shopping. My coming here made her uncomfortable—so I always waited until she'd gone to pick up the kids or run errands."

"How convenient."

"It was the only time we could . . . be together."

"Right."

"Don't look at me like that. I wasn't doing anything wrong. Their marriage was over a long time ago."

"I can't believe you fell for that line. You know what I think? I don't think Phillip ever meant to divorce Candace to marry you. I think you called his bluff and when he said no, you picked up his gun and shot him, then tried to make it look like a suicide."

"You're out of your mind." She picked up her purse. "I would never kill him. We loved each other. Candace must have found out about us and . . ." The tears flowed more freely now, as if admitting their affair compounded her grief. She fumbled in her purse for a tissue and found one.

Had Becky killed the man? Phillip's failure to get a divorce told Angel the guy was one of those have-your-cake-and-eat-it-too types. She doubted he'd ever asked Candace for a divorce. Angel made a mental note to ask Candace about it later.

When she'd finished crying, Becky gathered up the paperwork

166

Phillip had left for her. "His password is Becky," she said with undeniable pride.

"Thanks. Um, before you go, I have a couple more questions. Mr. Fitzgibbon didn't seem too happy to hear about the payment to Johansson Electric. Did Phillip often use business money to pay for personal jobs?"

"Barry took far more than his share out of the business, and Phillip was only taking what rightfully belonged to him."

"And you were helping him do it."

"I worked for Phillip before Fitzgibbon came into the picture. Just because Barry has the money to back the big projects . . ."

"What happens now? Will you keep your job?"

"I convinced Barry that I didn't know anything about it and that I thought it was part of my job. He agreed to let me stay."

"Lucky you." Angel pursed her lips. "Did Fitzgibbon have any reason to want Phillip dead?"

Becky shook her head and answered almost too quickly. "No, not at all."

"Did he know about the relationship you had with Phillip?"

"No. No one knew, unless Candace found out . . . Phillip told me he was going to talk to her that day. I still think she killed him."

"When would she have had a chance?" Angel asked. "She went shopping. You said he was alive after she left. Candace said she didn't come home until after she picked up the kids. That means he died between the time she left and came back. And if you didn't kill him, who did?" Angel opted not to mention that Candace's alibi had an hour-long hole in it. Or that Darryl and Gracie had both been there.

"I have no idea."

"You know what I think, Becky? I think you found out he wasn't going to ask Candace for a divorce now or ever."

"That's ridiculous."

"You were furious with him," Angel pressed on. "Maybe you realized he'd been using you, and you couldn't handle it. I think you shot him."

Tears watered Becky's eyes again. "I didn't kill him. He was alive when I left, I swear. Candace must have come back home before she picked up the kids."

"It'll be interesting to hear what the police have to say."

"You're going to tell them?"

"Of course I am. They think they have an ironclad case against Candace, but the list of suspects is getting longer by the minute, and you're right up there at the top."

Becky put her purse over her shoulder. "I'll deny everything I've said to you."

"That's fine."

Becky swung around in a huff and headed for the door. She stood in the open doorway and turned around, acting as if she wanted to say more. She didn't. Angel heard the door slam and the Taurus start. As soon as she saw Becky's car turn toward town, she reached for the phone and called dispatch, asking for Nick.

"Sorry, Angel, he's out of town today—some seminar in Portland. I think it's part of his detective training. Can someone else help you?"

"No, just let him know I called and that I have information for him about the Jenkins's case." Angel frowned. Nick hadn't said anything about a seminar. Detective training? Why hadn't he mentioned that earlier? Before she'd left the department, they had talked about taking some classes together. Looked like Nick was going ahead without her. Angel pushed the thought from her mind, not certain as to why she found the idea annoying.

She thought briefly about telling Joe what she'd uncovered, but opted not to. He probably wouldn't want her opinion any more than Nick did. Besides that, he might ask her about her father, and Angel couldn't deal with that. Not yet.

Forcing her thoughts back on the case again, Angel went over her interview with Becky. Phillip Jenkins was scum on life's pond. No wonder Gracie felt as she did. Had Gracie come home and found her father with Becky?

Angel noted pieces of her conversation with Becky in her notepad, then headed for Phillip Jenkins's office and his computer. After thirty minutes of exploring files filled with blueprints, bids, measurements, and business letters, she turned it off. She had found nothing incriminating in his business files or in his emails. In fact, there were no current emails, which caused Angel to think maybe Becky had erased them.

Of much more interest were the people in Jenkins's life. Gracie, Darryl, Jack Savage, Fitzgibbon, Becky, and Candace. It was beginning to look like they all might have had motive to kill him.

TWENTY-THREE

C allen flipped open his cell phone and, noting the caller, said, "Gretchen, what do you have for me?"

"Doing great, Callen. Thanks for asking. Family's fine." Gretchen Davis was the supervisor at the state crime lab in Portland and a longtime friend.

Callen chuckled. "Point taken. Sorry about that. I tend to get tunnel vision when I'm on a case."

"No joke. I think we all do. Especially with one like this." She sighed. "The ME found defense wounds on her hands and arms. What that guy did to that little girl . . . 'Course it doesn't help when you got kids her age."

Callen knew what she meant. Christy was a stranger, but she could have been one of his nieces, or one of Gretchen's girls.

"As you know, the guy wiped down the steering wheel and console. We got some good prints just the same, but I'm not sure how much good they'll do. The Sunset PD supplied prints from the car's owner and his family. We're in the process of ruling them out. There's a single thumbprint on the underside of the trunk that doesn't seem to match any of the others. We're running the print through AFIS. No match so far."

"I was hoping for a name." Callen reached for his bottle of orange juice. "Make my job much easier." AFIS was in Salem, and Callen had a friend in the office of Latent Print Identification. He'd call him personally.

Gretchen snorted. "Dreamer."

"Tell me more."

"We're certain the victim was transported in the trunk, but the blood we found in the vehicle and at the body dump wasn't consistent with the amount of blood loss she must have had from her wounds."

No surprise there. "So, we're still looking for a primary crime scene."

"Judging from the amount of blood we found in the trunk, we know she was still alive when he put her in there but she'd already been stabbed. Where he actually committed the deed is anybody's guess. Why would he transport Christy after he'd stabbed her? What was he planning to do?"

"Bury her, maybe. I don't know. We'll have to ask him," Callen said. "Looks like his plans were thwarted when the car broke down. He had to get rid of the body in case someone came along. So he dumped her and covered her with brush. Apparently he gave up on the car and walked home. Wherever that is."

"Whoever killed that girl did a decent job of destroying his fingerprints, but we have that partial thumbprint, hair, fibers, and semen, so you find the creep and we'll nail him."

"That's something. I'm heading up to Sunset Cove now. Hopefully we can get some DNA samples from the vehicle's owner and anyone who might have had access to it."

"Are you thinking the vehicle wasn't stolen like the guy reported?"

"I'll know more when I interview the owner," Callen said.

"Well, there's one more thing I think you'll find interesting. There were some grease smudges on a piece of duct tape we found in the trunk. Looks like the stuff he used when he bound and gagged the victim. I think we're looking for someone who works on cars."

"A mechanic." Callen thanked Gretchen and hung up, grateful that the forensic lieutenant had approved the overtime hours so they could work through the weekend.

Things were moving too slowly to suit Callen, but Gretchen's comment sounded promising. He had the local PD and Coos County sheriff's office in the Florence area checking out leads they'd gotten from family and friends and following up on tips phoned in by people responding to the media. Most of those tips were vague and misleading. There had been several callers who'd reported seeing Christy the day she was found. Nonetheless, these tips were important, and every once in a while they'd strike gold, like in the case in which a motorist called in to report seeing the car belonging to a man accused of killing his wife and children.

The suspect in this case had apparently struck out on foot, cutting through brush and walking along streams to cover his path. While Callen still had people combing the woods, he doubted they'd turn up anything. The guy was long gone. He'd zigzagged to throw them off the trail but was headed in a northerly direction. Maybe toward home—toward Sunset Cove where he'd stolen the vehicle. Callen suspected he may have hitched a ride, and the police had let the media know they were looking for anyone in the area who might have given their suspect a lift. So far, nothing.

Callen liked following the evidence better than he liked following his gut, but in this case he felt like he needed to do both. He'd question the owner of the car and get DNA samples from him and his sons and the mechanics—anyone who might have had access to the car. Someone who had been out of town for a few days.

It would all take time, but as long as nothing earth-shattering happened, he promised himself a few hours off tonight. He'd pick up a few groceries and make dinner for Angel. Hopefully she'd be available. He needed a night at home to unwind and get his bearings. He needed Angel by his side and in his arms. That need still surprised him. For a long time he'd been numb, longing for his Karen, talking to her as if she were still with him. Lately when he talked to her, it was to reassure her that no one, not even Angel, could take her place in his heart. Funny how he felt like he needed to apologize for his feelings. Karen had been dead for two years. Two long and lonely years.

He called Angel's cell phone and got a busy signal. He hung up. The last few times he'd called, the line had been busy. Remembering their last conversation, his concern grew. She hadn't been happy with Nick's investigation of Phillip Jenkins's death. It wouldn't surprise him a bit to find she'd been doing some investigating on her own.

He knew all too well how tenacious she could be. He'd butted heads with her on more than one occasion when he'd been investigating a string of deaths in Sunset Cove. True, she'd been caught in the middle and wanted to clear her name, but she should have stayed out of it entirely. She should have trusted him. He'd been furious with her for handling evidence. On the other hand, her quick thinking helped them nail the killer in record time.

As Callen neared Sunset Cove, he checked the address of the owner of the car in which the victim had been transported. It was hard not to speculate, especially since Gretchen had said they were looking for someone with automotive grease on their hands. Most guys fixed cars from time to time, but this was a mechanic's car. What were the odds?

While he drove, he admired the rugged coastline stretching out ahead of him. The Oregon coast was one of the most beautiful places in the world. It still had huge undeveloped wilderness areas and virgin forests where a man could easily get lost. Where a man could kill a teenage girl and then disappear.

"Not if I can help it." Callen's mouth clamped in a determined scowl. He called the deputy medical examiner for Coos County for a full autopsy report. The report was every bit as gruesome as Callen suspected it would be. The victim had been raped, beaten, and stabbed and had her hands and feet bound and duct tape put over her mouth.

A painful lump stuck in his throat. He'd seen far too many killings and still could not comprehend how someone could treat another human in such an inhumane way.

Callen went back over the details of the case. He'd already talked to family members. No real leads there, other than that Christy, like a lot of kids, had a troubled home life. Her family consisted of a mother, stepfather, and an older stepbrother. Callen had a photo of the two men, as well as DNA samples. Both of them had alibis, or so they said. Callen had interviewed students at the school as well—three boys who had been absent the day Christy went missing. He had officers checking out the alibis for all of them.

Callen had a strong suspicion the killer was from Sunset Cove, since the car had been taken from there. Their killer may well be connected to the man who owned it.

Then again the killer may have been passing through. It may have been a random act or even part of a series of murders in the Northwest. They certainly were not without their serial killers. If it had been random, the chances of finding the killer grew slimmer with every hour.

A phone call came in from the chief of police in Florence. "We may have something," he said with a slight drawl. "We got a salesman who says he picked up a hitchhiker five miles north of where we found Christy."

"Must be our lucky day. What did he have to say?"

"Name's Stanley Harrison. He sells and distributes bottled water. Described the kid as a long-haired, unkempt teenager. He'd been watching the news this morning and saw where we were looking for someone who'd been walking through the woods and may have gone through some water. This guy says that clued him in right away. This kid had wet shoes—like really wet, not just from the rain, 'cause they were leaking all over his floor mat. He also said the kid had some twigs in his hair. Harrison asked him about it, and he said he and some friends had gone camping and he'd gotten lost in the woods and his friends had gone home without him."

Callen shook his head, surprised the salesman hadn't come forward earlier. "Make sure we get prints and DNA on the guy. He's probably okay, but if there's the slightest chance the two men were working together . . ."

"You got it. We'll do a polygraph on him too."

"Did he give us anything else? Do we have a description?"

"The guy's here now, talking to an artist. We're trying to get a composite. Here's what we have so far: young, eighteen to nineteen, maybe twenty. The kid had several days' growth of a beard,

174

possibly to make himself look older. Blue eyes and a thin face. That's about it. We'll keep you posted."

Callen thanked him for the update and told him to fax the composite to the Sunset PD as soon as they got it.

The preliminary check he'd done on the car's owner showed the guy had no record. Mitch Bailey operated a body shop and employed six guys—three of them were between seventeen and twenty. He had three sons, one married and living in Portland, one in junior college who'd done some time on a possession charge last year, and one at home and still in high school.

High school. Something niggled at his brain, finally surfacing. Christy had been a high school cheerleader. Adrenalin surged through him as he thought about the possible link. Had there been a connection? High schools battled it out with each other over football, basketball, wrestling. Right now it would be track season. Had there been a sporting event recently between the Sunset Cove and Florence schools?

He called the police chief back and asked him about it. Turned out there had been a track meet between the schools just three days before Christy was abducted. Was it relevant? Had their killer known the victim—or wanted to? Maybe. Callen jotted down some notes on his pad. He didn't want to get ahead of himself or get his hopes up, but he had a feeling he was getting close.

He tried Angel again; this time she answered.

"Hey," she said in a voice that started a longing deep in his chest. Would he ever get used to the idea of loving someone other than Karen? There were differences, of course. Karen had been an artist, easygoing, quiet, a homemaker, and a great cook. He smiled, thinking that Angel's idea of a good meal was a hamburger and fries and a milk shake at the Burger Shed. But she'd made him soup, which could only mean there was hope for her.

"How would you like to have dinner with a tired old cop tonight?"

"Seriously?" There was an edge to her voice.

"Absolutely."

"Does that mean you're in town?"

"About half an hour away."

"That's great." She didn't sound as excited as he'd hoped.

Callen made the arrangements and told her he'd do the cooking. They had a lot of catching up to do. He had a feeling she wanted to tell him something, but he hadn't asked.

When he got into town he'd stop at Andy's Market to pick up some salmon and other perishable items he'd need. He'd make sautéed salmon pieces with tomatoes, mushrooms, scallions, capers, and hollandaise sauce with rice and asparagus. His mouth watered just thinking about it.

His cell phone rang again; it was Nick Caldwell. "Hey, Riley, how goes the investigation on that girl from Florence?"

"Slow. Lots of leads, nothing substantial yet. I heard you were running the Jenkins case."

"Yeah, not very exciting. We've got the wife dead to rights. Just one thing. Reason I'm calling is to ask you if you're going to be talking to Angel anytime soon."

"Yeah, tonight. Why?"

"I want you to call her off."

"What do you mean?" Callen hoped Angel hadn't gotten herself into trouble.

"She hasn't told you?" Nick sounded almost angry.

"Told me what?" Whatever it was, Callen didn't like Nick's tone or his attitude.

"Well, buddy, Angel has flown the coop. She's taken a job with your lawyer friend, Rastovski."

"And that's a problem because . . . ?"

"Angel is working as a PI."

"No kidding." Callen shoved his sunglasses back against the bridge of his nose. The news hit him like a fist to the stomach. For most cops, being a PI for a defense attorney ranked somewhere between being a stripper and a circus clown.

"She's driving me nuts. Wants me to keep the investigation open and keeps calling me with these little hints to follow up on."

"Hints. As in leads?"

"That's what she's calling them."

"And has anything she's told you panned out?" Callen hoped

the PD wasn't dismissing her completely. Angel may have flown the coop, but she still had good instincts.

"Like I've had time to go on her wild goose chases."

"What if they're not wild?"

"Are you kidding? She's convinced the wife didn't do it and is just trying to complicate things."

Callen sighed. This was beginning to sound like a case of sibling rivalry. "That doesn't sound like Angel."

"Don't get me wrong," Nick said. "I love Angel—she's like family, you know? But I gotta tell you, she's driving me nuts. She's bound and determined to prove me wrong."

Callen was tempted to ask him what he'd done so far and to get more details about the information Angel had been feeding him, but it wasn't his call. He had his own investigation.

Besides, he was more concerned about Angel's new career. What in the world did she think she was doing going to work as a PI? He didn't much like most of the PIs he'd met or the way they got in the way, begged for information, walked on the edge, snooped in places they didn't belong.

"I don't know what I can do to help, Nick," Callen finally said. "I have a feeling Angel isn't going to want me telling her to back off. Is she obstructing justice?"

"Not yet, but it's only a matter of time. She's just finding all kinds of what she calls 'important' information on the case and is making sure she lets me know about it. The other day she called to tell me some guy on a motorcycle had locked her in the cellar out at the Jenkins's place."

"And you didn't check it out?" Callen's heart had dropped to the vicinity of his feet. Angel locked in a basement by some pervert on a motorcycle?

"Of course I did, but there was nothing to go on. The guy was long gone, she didn't have a description, and I didn't have time to go chasing after him. Like I told her, it was probably a neighbor who saw that the cellar was open and thought they'd better close it. Anyway, she's fine—got out right away."

Callen breathed a little easier. He was overreacting, and he knew it.

"What's the deal?" Nick asked. "Are you on her side?"

"I don't think it's a matter of taking sides."

"Well, we've got the killer, and that's it for us. We're too busy to follow rabbit trails."

"I hear you, Nick, and I don't like the idea of her being a PI any more than you do, but if she's coming up with good information, you owe it to her and the PD to check it out."

Callen was new to the area and had worked only briefly with Nick, but he knew Nick was hoping to make detective soon. He was a fast learner and seemed like a good cop. On the phone the other night, Angel said she felt Nick had rushed the investigation. She had little experience in investigating homicides, but she had a good mind for it.

But a PI? Angel, what are you thinking?

Callen didn't know what to say. Was the Sunset Cove PD wrapping things up too quickly? Budget cuts could push officers to make arrests before getting all the evidence. When that happened, they fried in the courts. "I'll talk to her," he said.

"That's all I'm asking."

Callen pulled into the parking lot at the grocery store. Inside the store he snagged a cart and headed for the produce section. He tossed a head of romaine lettuce and examined the vine-ripened tomatoes. His euphoria of a few moments ago had subdued. The last thing he wanted to do was confront Angel. Anger flared up inside him along with an uneasy feeling. He hated that Nick Caldwell had put him in this position. If Nick had a problem with Angel, he should deal with it himself. Callen frowned at a bunch of grapes, more angry with himself than Nick for getting caught in the middle.

TWENTY-FOUR

———

Angel turned into Callen's driveway, feeling giddy as a teenager at a prom on one hand and heavyhearted on the other. Callen had called earlier asking her to meet him there, and she'd been more than ready for the distraction. Guilt nagged at her for being with Callen instead of taking care of her mother. For not yet having told Callen about her father.

Tim had insisted Anna stay with him and his family for a few days so his wife, Susan, could care for her. He'd also insisted Angel spend time with Callen. She needed the respite. Anna agreed with him, patting her on the arm and telling her to go.

Callen opened the door and pulled her into his arms. Apparently, he'd missed her as much as she had him. After several minutes they broke apart. He seemed almost embarrassed. "I've missed you, but then you probably gathered that."

She hugged him around the waist and leaned back to admire his features. "I missed you more than I should have." Thoughts she'd harbored earlier surfaced. How well did she know Callen? He frightened her in a way. Or maybe it was the feeling she had just being near him. Was it fear, anticipation, or both?

The timer on his stove went off. He let her go. "Are you hungry?"

"Starved." She hadn't eaten much and hadn't wanted to.

"Good. I'm doing salmon."

"Can I help?" Angel still had no appetite. A rock-sized lump sat in her stomach. She needed to tell Callen about her father, but knowing it would be her undoing and wanting the moment to be right, she avoided the task. She hadn't told him on the phone because it didn't seem the right thing to do. He was tired, and she didn't want to saddle him with her problems.

You have to tell him.

Later, she promised. *After dinner.*

"Yeah," Callen answered. "You can have a seat out on the deck."

Minutes later, they were sitting on Callen's new patio furniture, eating the most delicious, melt-in-your-mouth salmon Angel had ever tasted. She just wished her stomach would stop churning so she could enjoy it.

"How's the case going?" She pierced another chunk of fish.

"It's okay. We think the killer might be up in this area."

"No kidding?" Angel thought about Justin Bailey but didn't mention the possible connection.

"We have a description, but it's not doing us much good." Callen talked more about the connection with the stolen vehicle. "You said you knew this Bailey guy?"

"I know Mitch. He takes care of the Sunset PD's vehicles, and we've taken our personal cars to him for as long as I remember."

"He reported one of his cars stolen the day after Christy disappeared."

She chewed on her lower lip. "Mitch is a really nice guy. He has three sons—but then you probably already know all this."

Callen nodded. "Do you know them?"

"Not well. I do know Jimmy is in junior college and Justin is still in high school."

"I don't suppose you know where I can find them."

"Not Jimmy, but Justin was in school today. His pickup was parked in the lot there this morning."

Callen frowned. "And you know this because . . . ?"

Angel sighed. "It's a long story."

"Hmm." He put down his fork, apparently not wanting to hear it. "That reminds me. I got a call from Nick tonight."

180

"And?"

"And he's worried about you."

"Worried? About what? That I'll find out who really murdered Jenkins? That I'll make him look bad?"

Callen leaned back. "Okay, maybe worried isn't the right word. Concerned, then. He said you were working as a PI for Rachael."

Something in his tone raised her defenses. "So what if I am?" She hadn't really given much thought to how Callen would feel about her new job. Did he share Nick's animosity? Probably. Most cops didn't think much of private investigators. Though he hadn't said the words, she saw disapproval in his eyes.

"Nick tells me you're investigating the Jenkins murder on your own."

"And I'm finding all kinds of people with motive, whom Nick, at least as far as I know, hasn't even talked to. All I've done is tell him he might want to look into a few things."

"Such as?"

"People besides his wife who had a motive. Jenkins's nephew for one. He was at the house that afternoon and admits to seeing his uncle's body, but he didn't call it in. He was hiding in the barn the entire time Nick and the CSI team were out there. No one bothered checking out the barn, Callen. Doesn't that seem odd to you?"

"Not necessarily. If the guy was killed in the house, and there was nothing to indicate the barn was used at all . . ."

"Don't try to cover for Nick. At least be honest with me. You would have gone over the barn, wouldn't you?"

"I don't know. I wasn't there. And how do you know he was in there at the time?"

"I found evidence in the barn, and the timing is right. Nick was just leaving as I came to check over some things for Rachael. Darryl, the nephew, locked me in the basement—or tried to."

Callen frowned. "Nick said you couldn't identify him."

"I saw him leave—at first I didn't know who it was, but the kids helped me figure it out. I talked to him today, and he admitted—"

"You talked to him?" Callen's voice rose at least an octave. "What do you mean, you talked to him? Alone?"

"Of course, alone. Well, not really. We were in a public place."

"Are you telling me you went to interview a potential killer without backup?"

"Backup?" Angel's angry tone matched his. "I'm on leave, remember? I couldn't very well call in for backup."

"You should've called Nick."

"Oh, right, and have him blow me off." Angel rolled her eyes. "Besides, I don't think Darryl killed his uncle."

"But he could have, right?"

"I haven't completely ruled him out."

Callen ran a hand down his face. "This is unbelievable. I want you to quit. You have no business interviewing potential suspects."

"You think I should leave this to Nick? He's made up his mind that Candace is the killer. I'm telling you, Callen, he's wrong."

"And I'm telling you it's not safe."

Angel threw her napkin down and stood, tipping her chair in the process. It clattered against the wooden deck. Not bothering to right it, she went around to the front of the house and got into her car. Callen stormed after her.

"Angel, wait!" Callen rounded the corner as she yanked open the car door and slipped inside.

"What for? So you can tell me how inept I am? That I'm not cut out for the job?"

"You're not making sense. Angel, please—let's talk about this."

She slammed the door and jammed her keys into the ignition. Callen gripped the door handle, then jerked his hand out of the way as she started to back out.

"Angel, please!" Callen doubled his fist and struck his car.

More upset with himself than with Angel, Callen stood there holding his hand and watching her back out of his driveway. He wanted to go after her, but he wouldn't. Best to let her cool down. He certainly needed to. He turned back and headed into the house.

"That went well." He knelt down to scoop up his bewildered dog.

Mutt wriggled down and ran around to the back of the house. By the time Callen got there, Mutt had devoured most of what was left on Angel's plate. Callen shooed him down and put him inside.

He lowered himself into his chair and pushed the once-warm dinner around on his plate. Their argument had left him raw and empty inside. He should have known better than to try to mediate between Nick and Angel. Nick should have been covering his bases. He had a hunch some of this was the department's doing. Callen could almost hear Joe Brady telling his people that the investigation was over, they had their killer, case closed.

He blew out a long, deep breath. Angel had said she'd found several people with motives. What if she was right and the wife was innocent? That would mean the killer was still out there. He wished now he'd heard her out and talked with her about the suspects she'd uncovered. It sounded as though she had more than the nephew. What had Angel called him? Darryl?

He should stay out of it. This wasn't his investigation. He should never have told Nick he'd talk to Angel. Callen tipped his head back and was rewarded by pellet-sized raindrops.

He didn't think he could feel much worse, but then the phone rang. It was for Angel. "Sorry, Tim, you just missed her."

Tim sounded so dejected that Callen asked him what was wrong.

"I just called to ask about the funeral."

"Funeral?"

"You mean she didn't tell you?"

"I guess not."

"Dad died last night," Tim said. "Angel and Mom were both there."

Angel drove straight home and let herself into her apartment. The encounter with Callen had left her shaken. She'd seen this side of him before—the anger flashing in his eyes when she'd been involved in another murder case. But this time was different. He'd been rude and obnoxious, and he was taking Nick's side.

She locked the door behind her and sank onto the couch, pulling her feet up and hugging her knees. She was hurt that Callen wouldn't take her seriously. Hurt and angry. Obviously he wouldn't be advising her about anything. How foolish of her to even hope he might. And she couldn't count on help from Nick or the other officers either. Except for maybe Rosie.

Well, fine. She'd do it without them.

The phone rang, and Angel let the answering machine pick up.

"Angel, it's me, Callen. I'm sorry about what happened. I need to talk to you. Please call me."

She could hear the sadness in his voice and wanted more than anything to make things right. Remembering what the women in the support group had said, she resisted the urge to answer the phone. She didn't want to talk to him. What would be the point?

Someone else had left a message as well. Angel listened as her brother's voice filled the room, telling her he'd tried to call and asking why hadn't she told Callen about their father. The funeral was set for Sunday after church.

Funerals. Death. It all seemed surreal, like something in a strange and terrible dream.

Angel showered and got ready for bed. It was only 9:00, far too early to sleep—not that she could, anyway. She curled up on the couch with a copy of *Physical Evidence*, a manual for detectives. She sighed and started reading, determined not to think about her father's death, determined not to think about Callen, determined not to think at all.

At 10:00, the phone rang again. This time it was Janet Campbell. She sounded strained and frightened. Angel picked up before Janet finished her message.

"Hi, Janet. What's wrong?"

"I—I need to talk to you."

"Sure. Want to come over?" Angel got up and headed toward her bedroom. She'd need to get dressed.

"No, not there. You'll have to come to my apartment."

"Tonight?"

"Please. I was just going online and . . . Phillip Jenkins's killer just sent me an email."

TWENTY-FIVE

J anet lived in one of the upscale condominiums on the bay. Angel had never been in them but heard they were now selling for around a quarter to half a million dollars depending on the size. Angel maneuvered the curves on Bayside Drive, then wound down toward the waterfront. Curiosity caused her to drive a little faster than she should have, but fortunately Sunset Cove's few officers on duty were somewhere else.

Why had Janet called her? Why not the police? This could be the break they were looking for. Angel thought about calling Nick and decided against it. It was too soon to go running to the police, and she couldn't tell Callen. Her bridge with the PD may not be burned, but she could sure smell the smoke. Besides, she wanted to talk to Janet first.

Angel's mind spun with possibilities. How had Janet known it was the killer? Why had the killer contacted her? Angel settled her thoughts into some kind of order as she paused at the security gate and punched in the numbers Janet had given her. The gate slid open, and Angel drove through, then made a left, winding through the individual homes, finally reaching the condos. She parked in the driveway and took a deep breath to settle her jangled nerves.

Janet looked terrible. Bags drooped under her red, watery eyes as she opened the door to let Angel in.

"Thanks so much for coming. I'm sorry to bother you so late at night, but . . ."

"I'm glad you called me." Angel stepped inside, hesitating in the entry. "Why did you call me and not the police?"

"Several reasons. I'll get to those in a minute, but you need to read these emails."

Seeing the champagne carpet and Janet's bare feet, Angel slipped her own shoes off at the door. "Lead the way."

Angel followed Janet into a nicely decorated living room with a vaulted ceiling. The house had double sliding glass doors on the side overlooking the water. It was dark beyond the doors now, but Angel could imagine the view. Her feet glided over the cool slate tiles in the entry and kitchen.

Janet paused at the kitchen island. "Can I get you anything? Coffee, tea, water, juice, wine?"

"I'm fine. Thanks."

"I hope you don't mind if I indulge. This thing has me creeped out."

"Go ahead."

Janet grabbed a glass of wine she'd already poured for herself and ascended the carpeted stairs to a roomy loft with its own small bathroom. A daybed sat against one wall and against the other was a desk and computer. "Nice office," Angel commented as she looked over the railing toward the open living area.

"Thanks." She sat down in her leather ergonomic office chair and moved the mouse to eliminate the scenic screen saver—a sunset. Janet clicked Outlook Express and got into her mailbox and waited for the new mail to come in.

"I had probably twenty emails. Most of them I deleted. Like I need Viagra and a new line of credit. I get so tired of all this stuff."

"I know what you mean." Angel moved impatiently from one foot to the other.

Janet groaned. "That jerk."

"Who?"

"My ex-husband."

Angel read the note over Janet's shoulder. The email from C. Campbell read: *"It's that time again. I hear things have been going well for you. Lucky me."*

"What does he mean, lucky him?"

Janet sighed. "I really shouldn't be talking to you about this. You're still my client and . . ."

"Come on, Janet. We're friends first. If it makes you feel any better, I'll fire you as my counselor. So talk to me. Is there a problem?"

"Oh yes." She turned back to the computer. "I do know why I told you. I keep hoping he'll go away. Um . . . I'm sorry. You didn't come here to hear about my woes."

As much as Angel wanted to see the emails in question, she felt the dread in Janet's demeanor. "No, but you might as well tell me about it. I have plenty of time. The only thing I was planning to do tonight was sleep." And there wasn't much chance of that.

Janet smiled. "In that case, you'd better sit down. This could take a few minutes. I'll print out the emails, and we can talk while they're printing."

Angel dropped onto the bed.

"My ex," Janet said as she continued to type in commands, "is blackmailing me."

Angel wasn't sure what she had been expecting, but it wasn't this. "Did I hear you right?"

Janet nodded and turned her chair around to face her. The printer began making noises as it readied itself for the task Janet had given it.

"Why don't you go to the police?"

"What good would it do?" She ran both hands through her hair. It was down now and fell in large, soft curls on her shoulders. "He's very subtle. He's never threatened me with anything more than coming to Sunset Cove. I don't want him coming here. I don't want him back in my life."

"I don't understand. Why would his coming here be a threat?"

"He'd come here for one reason. To ruin my life."

Janet wasn't making sense. "Can't you get a restraining order?"

"Yes, but it wouldn't do any good. I doubt he'll actually come here anyway. But that won't stop him from going to the police." Janet closed her eyes and hauled in a deep breath.

Angel hardly dared to breathe. What did this man have on her that was so terrible? What was Janet hiding?

"Okay." Angel chose her words carefully. "You decided to tell me about it. I take it that means you're tired of living with this—whatever it is you've done—over your head. Are you in some kind of trouble with the law?"

"I suppose in a way I am. I came so close to killing that man. In a way I wish I had."

Angel pulled her legs up, sitting cross-legged on the bed, and urged Janet to continue.

"I still couldn't believe the rage I felt that day. I had lost my baby—a miscarriage. She died because of him. He hit me and pushed me down the stairs. I ended up in the hospital. They released me the same day. My baby was gone, and all I wanted to do was end my own life. I stayed in bed for five days. I hated him so much, but I didn't think I could do anything about it."

"Why didn't you go to the police? Why didn't you go to a shelter?"

"I don't know. It's easier to look back and make judgments. Maybe I felt like I had no alternative but to kill myself. He'd convinced me that I was the problem. He wouldn't get angry if I didn't do things that upset him."

"And you fell for it?"

"What can I say? I was young and fresh out of school. One day he came in and pulled me out of bed by the hair. Told me I'd had enough time to lay around. He wanted breakfast. He needed clean clothes."

Angel covered her mouth. "How awful."

"He said he was glad I had miscarried. He didn't want a brat running around anyway. I started crying and yelling at him. I pushed him away. He pushed back and sent me sprawling across the bed. Something inside me snapped. I can't remember ever being really angry in my entire life. But the rage . . ." She covered her face. "In that moment I realized I wanted him dead. I watched

188

him leave the room, and I flew out after him. He was at the top of the stairs, and I hit him from behind. He fell all the way down. Ended up with a concussion and broken back."

Angel moved her head from side to side. How could a man be so cruel? "What happened then?"

"I thought I'd killed him. I called 911 and told them he'd fallen down the stairs. I was terrified. He wasn't dead. He ended up in a wheelchair, partially paralyzed. I was devastated. Charles never told anyone about my pushing him. He told everyone that he'd slipped on the stairs and fallen. I was thankful for that. For a while I thought it was my responsibility to care for him. I kept working as a counselor and hired a nurse. After all, I had caused the accident, and he had lied to protect me. I had to stand by him.

"For a while guilt paralyzed me as much as the accident had paralyzed him. I was terrified that if I didn't do everything exactly right, he'd go to the police and tell them what really happened. I'd lose my license and never be able to practice again. The physical abuse stopped, but not the verbal. Not the emotional. When he was finally able to manage on his own, I filed for divorce. I thought I'd be safe in Sunset Cove, but he hired a detective and found me. That's when the emails started. Pleas for money that I owed him. I'd ruined his life and needed to pay. So I did. Every time he asked."

"I'm in shock. Here I thought you had everything together. I'd never have guessed."

"I thought I had everything together too. I've been paying him for three years now, and I want it to stop, but short of having him killed, I don't know what to do."

"You're serious? You'd have him killed?"

"No. But I've thought about it."

"There's a better way. It'll take some courage on your part, but in the long run, you'll come out way ahead."

"What should I do?"

"Talk to Rachael. Tell her what happened to you. She can help you go through the right channels. You'll eventually have to tell the police and get it all out in the open. Expose the jerk for what he is."

189

She sighed. "I suppose you're right. It may mean giving up my practice here in Sunset Cove, but at least I can hopefully put it all to rest."

"It may not even go to trial or get into the papers," Angel assured her. "Even if it does, no jury in the world would convict you for doing what you did. Janet, it was a crime of passion, and there were extenuating circumstances."

"I hope you're right." She lifted her chin and turned slightly to grasp the papers the printer had spit out. "I'm sorry. I didn't ask you here to talk about Charles. You need to read these." Janet handed the pages to Angel.

Dear Dr. Campbell,

For obvious reasons, I can't tell you who I am. For now, consider me a guardian, an avenger, an angel of death—your alter ego. I think that if you were not constrained by your position, you would do the same. You talk against violence, but deep down, you know it's the only way.

The police are calling what I did to Jim Kelsey a murder. That's far too strong a word. I didn't murder the man, I simply disposed of a piece of garbage. Men like Jim Kelsey deserve to die. Don't you agree?

Angel read the rest of the letter and those that followed in stunned disbelief. Dragonslayer had murdered Phillip Jenkins and was planning to kill again. When she finished reading the letters, Angel glanced over at Janet. "This is unreal. Evil. Talking about a murder as if it were nothing more serious than picking out paint to redo a bathroom. Whoever wrote this is . . . psychotic. Dangerous."

"The women in group may have been right. Remember when we talked about the possibility of a serial killer?"

Angel nodded. "Which means there may be other men on the list. Why would the killer send these to you?"

"I don't know. The notes indicate that he or she might have been a client." Janet picked up a pen and wove her fingers over and under it. "It's not unusual for a serial killer to confide in someone. Maybe they feel validated somehow."

"And maybe the killer is still a client." Angel shifted, freeing her legs and letting them dangle from the bed. "What's your take on the gender?"

"A man, I think. It sounds like a business letter, and I thought it was a man when I first read it. I don't know why. There's something so cold and calculating about it all. And the way the men were killed—Phillip with a gun out of his own collection. Kelsey was also shot, then pushed over an embankment in his car. Both methods sound more masculine."

"That was my first impression too. But now that I think about it, I'm not so sure. Suppose one of the women in the group decided to take things into her own hands?"

"I find that hard to believe. One of the things we stress is that you can't fight violence with violence."

"You can stress it all you want," Angel argued, "but you know as well as I do that people can't always control their emotions. And whoever wrote this obviously has a lot of anger."

Janet's shoulders sagged. "I just can't believe any of those women would kill someone. Talk, yes, but act on it, no."

"Can you think of anyone you've been seeing who might have written these? Someone with a vendetta against these men?"

"The only link is the abuse." She closed her eyes and sighed. "I'm sorry. I can't think of anyone. I'll go over my files. It's possible someone may have said something. Even then, there's the confidentiality matter."

"If this pans out, the police can get a subpoena."

"We'll have to deal with that if and when the time comes."

Angel acquiesced. "I should go. I'll take these with me."

"That's fine." Janet licked her lips. "I . . . I'd rather you didn't talk to the police just yet. I was hoping you'd investigate on your own before . . ."

"Why did you call me and not the police?" Angel asked again.

"I didn't know what else to do. I tried to find the source of the email . . ." She hesitated. "Angel, the account is in my name, but I swear to you I didn't write them."

"How could that be unless they were sent from your computer? Are you suggesting someone broke into your house and wrote these and mailed them to you?"

She shook her head. "I don't know. I have three computers— here, at my office, and my laptop. I carry my laptop in my car, and all I have to do is find a phone hookup. But anyone could have set up an account using my name."

"Something like identity theft," Angel mused. "Develop an account in your name, using your address and maybe even your credit card to set it up. Maybe it was the killer's way of making certain you didn't go to the police. They wouldn't have to use your computers at all."

"It worked." She hugged herself. "The police would take one look and decide I'd written them myself. The situation with my ex doesn't help. That's why I had to call you."

"What makes you think I won't go to the police? This may be proof that Candace didn't kill her husband. We have to let them know."

"Could we take my name off them? We could fax them in as anonymous letters."

Angel rubbed her forehead and began pacing. "I almost wish I hadn't seen them."

Leaning forward, Janet cradled her head in her hands. "What am I going to do?"

"I wish I knew." Angel read through the emails again. "Dragonslayer said he or she wouldn't send these. Why the change of heart?"

"I wondered that too. Maybe they went out by mistake."

"I doubt it," Angel said. "On my email program I can save emails as drafts. They don't go out unless I want them to."

"Right." Janet's eyes registered genuine fear.

"Of course, there is another possibility. Maybe whoever sent these hasn't killed anyone at all. Maybe they just want to draw fire away from Candace."

"Do you think so?"

The computer dinged, indicating another message had come in. Janet turned back around. "Another one." She clicked on the message, and it popped onto the screen.

Angel read it over her shoulder. The words chilled her to the bone.

Friday, May 9

Dear Dr. Campbell,

Angel Delaney is getting to be a major problem. I don't want Candace in jail, but I don't want Angel snooping around either. If she gets too close, she might discover my secret, and I can't have that. I don't want to hurt her, but I may have to do something to get her out of the way.

Dragonslayer

Angel swallowed hard.

"You're right, Angel," Janet said. "You do need to go to the police. This isn't about me—maybe it never was."

Seconds later another message appeared on the screen.

Friday, May 9

Dear Dr. Campbell,

You'll be happy to know I've chosen my next victim. It's someone I've wanted to dispose of for a long time. I just never had the nerve until now.

Dragonslayer

TWENTY-SIX

D etective Riley." Janet said his name as if it were the answer
to all her problems. "We can show these to Callen. He'll
know what to do."

"I don't think that's a good idea. I'd rather not involve him."

Janet frowned. "What happened? I thought you and he . . ."

"I think he may have an anger problem. And the way he yelled
at me tonight . . . I don't know."

"Did he hit you?"

"No." Angel didn't want to talk about Callen. She wasn't ready
to deal with her feelings. Yet suddenly she found herself telling
Janet about the argument they'd had.

Janet frowned and seemed to be having difficulty accepting the
concept. "Callen Riley? Abusive?"

"I don't know for certain that he is."

"I'd never have pegged him as the abusive sort, and I should
know. I'm a pretty good judge of character these days."

"You know him?"

"Yes, he interviewed me regarding the Jim Kelsey case. He was
very kind. I suppose I could be wrong, but I don't think so."

Angel felt as if she were gossiping about a good friend—as
though she were betraying him. "I didn't realize you knew him. I
shouldn't have said anything." She remembered his kindness in

the interview room shortly after she'd first met him. He'd listened intently, been protective. And after she'd been attacked after Billy Dean's funeral . . . *Protective. Maybe that's what it is.*

His anger had been because of the way she'd endangered herself. Those were the only times she'd seen him angry—at least with her. But how healthy was that? Angel needed to rethink things. Callen had been upset when she'd told him about Darryl. He didn't want to see her in a job in which she could be hurt. But what did he think being a police officer was all about?

She had gotten angry with him as well. In fact, she was the one who'd run away from their conversation, acting like an adolescent instead of a responsible adult. She should have stayed and talked the issue through.

"Please don't say anything to anyone." Angel focused back on Janet. "I mean, I've only seen him angry a couple of times. I may be overreacting."

"Of course not. You know what you tell me is confidential. And I hope you'll keep what I've told you confidential as well. I will talk to Rachael and see where things lead. Hopefully I won't have to leave town over it."

"I doubt you will."

"If you have the slightest doubt about Callen, give it time." Janet took a deep breath and moved to the kitchen. "Wait until you're sure one way or the other before you commit to anything. I married after only three months, and look where it got me."

"You may be right. I need to talk to him. I owe him an apology anyway." *And you need to talk to him about your father.*

"Let me know how things go." Janet walked Angel to the door. She frowned. "I should have said something earlier. I heard about your dad. I'm so sorry."

"Thanks." Angel nodded. "Looks like I'll never get to talk with him—find out what he really thought about me."

Janet bit into her lower lip. "Sometimes it helps to write a letter or go to the grave. Talk to him and think about what he might say. You might be surprised at the answers that come to you."

Angel doubted it would help but thought it might be worth a try. "Thank you." She ducked out, closing the door behind her.

As she got into her car, she thought about the emails again. Dragonslayer had threatened to keep her out of the way. *I don't want to hurt her, but . . .* She'd been threatened before, but as frightening as that was, she needed to keep her wits about her. She'd have to be more aware of her surroundings and try not to be alone too much—like she was right now.

Angel drove fear from her mind with a prayer of protection, then forced her thoughts back to Janet. Angel now saw the competent counselor in a different light. Janet had counseled both of the abused women whose husbands were now dead. She had been abused herself. Could her rage run so deep that she would kill abusive husbands to save their wives from further pain? Janet had claimed that she'd received the emails, but what if she had written them and sent them to herself to confuse the authorities? It had certainly confused Angel.

Angel had to admit the idea made no sense at all. Why would Janet use her own name?

Then again, the therapist could have a multiple personality. Angel had only a superficial knowledge of psychiatry, but she wondered if Janet had suffered severe enough abuse to send her over the edge. Psychopaths often played mind games with the police and others, sometimes wanting to get caught, sometimes setting traps. But Janet couldn't have written the last two as they had come in while Angel was there with her. Unless Janet had found a way to time their arrival or had a partner.

Of course, the emails could be bogus—an attempt to get Candace and Michelle off the hook. The mysterious Dragonslayer could be nothing more than a farce. Still, she had to go to someone in authority. She was too upset with Nick to take the information to him. As much as she hated to admit it, Janet was right. Callen seemed the obvious choice.

Angel got home at 11:30. Her answering machine was blinking, and when she pressed play, it said she had three new calls, all from Callen issuing an apology and urging her to call him back. She picked up the phone and punched in his number, then almost hung up before it could ring. It was late and he'd probably be in bed. But Angel needed to talk to him, more for her own peace of mind than because of the emails.

Callen picked up on the first ring. His first inclination was to ask Angel where the heck she'd been for the last four hours. He held back, realizing he'd been way out of line in telling her to quit her job. He would be even more out of line grilling her about her whereabouts. Especially now that he knew about her father. No wonder she'd been so upset.

"I'm glad you called," he said in as calm a voice as he could muster.

"I wanted to apologize for flying off the handle," she said. "I should've stayed and talked to you about how I felt."

"It was my fault. I knew talking to you about Nick's issues was wrong. And then I had to add my two cents. Angel, please forgive me." The only excuse he had for his behavior was that he cared far more than he was willing to admit. He wanted to keep her safe. He'd felt that way since he'd first met her. Angel was anything but vulnerable. He hadn't liked her working as a cop and liked her working as a detective even less. He'd handled the whole situation with Nick in the worst possible way.

"You lost your temper. You hit your car," Angel said.

"I know. I let my frustration get the best of me." After a long pause he said, "Angel, Tim told me about your dad. I'm sorry."

"Yeah, me too."

He heard the distress in her voice and wished he could be there to hold her.

Silence again. "I need to talk to you about something," she finally said. "I should probably call Nick, but I'm not sure I trust him to handle it right now. I wanted you to see it first."

It was Callen's turn to hesitate. The call was about the Jenkins's murder investigation, not their relationship. No matter. He'd take what he could get. He thanked God she was still talking to him. He had a lot of damage to repair. He only hoped it was repairable.

"Do you want me to come over?" He was still in his jeans and

T-shirt. He'd gotten as far as taking off his shoes and sweatshirt but hadn't wanted to give up hope.

"Please."

Callen tapped on her door at 11:45. It was all Angel could do not to throw herself at him, hold him, and smother him with kisses. He looked rugged and weary, and Angel wanted to soothe away the worry lines on his forehead and tell him everything was going to work out.

Is love so blind it makes you stupid? Their argument and his reaction had caused a rift between them, and she was not about to close it without some degree of analysis.

She let him in and handed him a cup of coffee, then poured one for herself.

"I'm sorry for getting you out this late. I probably should've waited till morning."

"I'm glad you called. What can I help you with?" He took his coffee and eased onto the sofa.

My heart. Tell me you would never hurt me. Tell me you don't have an abusive bone in your body. Tell me everything will be all right.

Angel set her cup on the counter and picked up the email letters she'd brought from Janet's. "You know Janet Campbell?"

"We've met."

"Well, she called me tonight and asked me to come over. She'd gotten some disturbing emails." Angel handed them to Callen and watched his face grow pale as he read them. He looked up at her with an expression she couldn't read, then picked up his coffee and took a sip. She wasn't certain what to expect—and didn't know what to say next.

"You need to give these to the Sunset Cove PD," Callen told her.

"I know. I wanted you to see them because . . . I guess because I wanted you to know I was right. It's very possible that someone other than Candace killed Phillip Jenkins and Jim Kelsey and may kill again."

She told him why Janet had called her—that the therapist's name had been at the source of the emails. "I don't think she wrote them. She got two more messages just before I left, and I know she didn't type them while I was there. Even if she had, there's no reason I can think of that she'd send them from her own account. The last thing she needs is that kind of attention."

"Where are those last two messages?"

"I didn't get a printout. One said he'd picked another victim. The other was a threat." She swallowed hard before finishing. "Against me."

Callen closed his eyes for a moment, his lips clamped shut. When he opened them again, he went to her and without a word wrapped her in his arms and held her. Angel stiffened at first, then melted against him, tears tumbling down her cheeks and onto his shirt. The fear that had ridden her all the way from Janet's broke over her. She cried for herself and for her father and mother.

She clung to him, not wanting to let go. Being with him felt right and safe. As the tears subsided, the comfortable feeling passed. She moved back. "I'm sorry."

"There's no need to be." He used his knuckle to sweep away the last of her tears. He led her to the sofa. When she sat down, he lowered himself beside her and settled his arm around her shoulder and tucked her into him.

She let her head rest on his shoulder.

"You're on to something, Angel," he finally said.

"What?" She lifted her head to look into his eyes.

"This investigation. Looks like you were right all along about Jenkins's wife. Nick may not have been as thorough as he should have been. I'm not saying I think it's a good idea for you to put yourself in danger." He guided her head back to his shoulder and kissed her forehead. "But you've gotten too close for someone's comfort."

"And you want me to back off?" Angel's fists tightened at the implication.

He rubbed his chin. "I'd be lying if I said no. I want you safe, but I know better than to redirect you." He smiled. "At least I hope I've learned that much. I'll go in tomorrow and talk to Joe and Nick. Do you mind if I take these with me?"

"No. I thought you might." Angel sighed. "I don't think it will do much good."

"Why's that?"

"They'll think someone wrote the notes to get them off track. I wouldn't be surprised if they accuse Janet of writing them—just like she was afraid they would."

"But you said she couldn't have written the last two."

"My say-so, which doesn't account for much these days."

"I believe you." And his eyes told her he did.

"They'll check into Janet's background and find out she was abused too."

"Oh?"

"I can't tell you the details. All I can say is that it won't look good for her. You'll probably hear about it soon. She's going to see Rachael tomorrow." Angel glanced at her watch. "Today."

"Sounds ominous." Callen laced her fingers in his. "You seem to be sending a lot of business Rachael's way."

"There may be more."

"Tell me about your other suspects. Whose cages have you rattled?"

Angel went through the list—Darryl Jenkins, Barry Fitzgibbon, Becky Reed, and the women at the shelter.

When she'd finished Callen removed his arm from her shoulder and rubbed his chin. "You've been busy. Are you sure you don't want to get back on at the PD? Maybe with the idea of becoming detective? At least there you'd have someone watching your back."

Angel pursed her lips. "I have my cell phone. If there's a problem, I can call for help."

Callen frowned. "Sounds as though you've stirred up several hornets' nests. Does any one of them stick out for you? Can you put a face to those notes?"

Angel shook her head and pushed herself off the couch. "I've been trying to. I can't even tell if it's a man or a woman."

Callen read through them again. "A woman," he said. "There's a vindictiveness there—a hatred for men, and I don't think it's just abusive men."

"Janet thought they sounded more male oriented because of the way the men were killed." Angel shuddered as she thought again about the language used in the messages. "If the letters are genuine and came from the killer, this person sees it as their job to destroy men like Kelsey and Jenkins. He—or she—sees them as animals who deserve to die."

He deserves to die. Gracie had used those exact words that first night after her stepfather's death. Angel hadn't mentioned Gracie in her list of possible suspects. She didn't want the girl exposed. Maybe that was a mistake.

TWENTY-SEVEN

_____

Saturday morning brought sunshine and far too many questions. Angel's weary mind swept to the night before and the time she'd spent with Callen. He'd listened to her—taken her seriously. Though she suspected he wanted to, he hadn't even told her to be careful. Concern for her had shone in his eyes and in his demeanor. He hadn't wanted to leave her alone and had made certain she'd bolted the door when he left.

He hadn't kissed her good night when he left either, except for the brotherly peck on her cheek. He hadn't wanted to upset her, nor she him. He'd said very little after she told him about the evidence she'd turned up, other than to say he'd talk to the local police, which translated to Nick and Joe. It hadn't taken him long to notify the local authorities regarding the threat she'd received. Before going to bed, she'd taken a look outside and had seen a police car drive into the parking lot, linger for about ten minutes, and leave.

Angel had half expected Callen to tell her he'd take over the case, but he didn't. He wouldn't unless Joe asked for his help, and even then he would probably only come in as a consultant. She seemed to remember the OSP detectives being assigned one case at a time. Besides, Callen was too wrapped up in the investigation surrounding the murdered teenager.

Admittedly, she was a bit nervous about the fallout from Callen's talk with Joe Brady and Nick Caldwell. Would Nick be even more upset with her than he already was? To his way of thinking, Angel had been a nuisance; now she'd be stabbing him in the back. Callen didn't seem to think there would be a problem. He suspected most of the lack of thoroughness came from having what they saw as adequate evidence and a confession.

The entire day went by in a blur as Angel stayed at the house with her mother and brothers, talking, making arrangements, and answering phone calls from well-wishers. Nick came by around 3:00 to offer consolation to his second family. He'd hugged her and Anna and then spent the next hour with Peter, Paul, and Tim. He'd said nothing about the Jenkins case or Callen or the letters, and Angel wondered if Callen had talked with him.

Angel didn't ask, nor would she—not today at any rate. She was exhausted, and her eyes felt as if they were full of sand—probably from all the crying. She was hardly able to talk to anyone without tearing up. She finally went home at 10:00 and fell into bed, sleep hitting at about the same time her head hit the pillow.

The morning sun woke her at 7:00, and she dragged herself out of bed, snatched the Sunday paper off the porch, and made coffee. Normal Sunday morning events on a not-so-normal Sunday. Frank Delaney had been gone for three days, and Angel still could not absorb the reality of it. All her tears from the day before left her eyes feeling gritty and unfocused.

She thought briefly about the threatening note from Dragonslayer. Maybe he or she didn't see her as a threat at the moment. Maybe he was biding his time.

You can't afford to be paranoid about it, she told herself. *There's a good chance it was just a warning to stay away.* Angel didn't much like to listen to warnings. She took the threat seriously but wouldn't allow it to stand in her way. She'd just have to watch her back.

After a cursory glance at the paper and a cup of coffee, Angel showered and got ready for church. Angel planned to spend most of the day with her mother and the rest of the family. Church at St. Matthew's started at 10:00. Angel entered the sanctuary at 9:59 and walked up to the second row from the front, easing into the space between Callen and her mother.

Callen's tentative smile warmed her and disturbed her at the same time. He looked so right sitting there as though he were already part of the family. Her mother had no doubt talked to him before the service, asking him to sit with them.

How awkward things would be if she and Callen split up. It would be hard on Anna, maybe on the entire family. Funny how family, her family, anyway, merged a boyfriend or girlfriend into the fold so quickly. Rachael and Paul sat at the other end of the pew. Next to Rachael sat Tim's daughter Heidi and Susan, Tim's wife. Then Peter and Abby, Tim's second daughter. When Abby saw Angel, she made her way over laps until she found Angel's.

The organ music started, and they all stood to sing the first hymn. The bulletin held news of Frank Delaney's death and the funeral. There would be a luncheon served by the women's group after the funeral, which would be held after the service.

Tim went on to preach his prepared sermon—the second in a series on marriage. The sermon was on relationships. He began with the verse that talked about wives being obedient to their husbands. That verse had always given Angel trouble. Probably because she'd seen too many men use it as a reason to abuse their wives. Jenkins had done that.

Her brother surprised her by turning the tables and making obedience the responsibility of both partners. Husbands were to love their wives as Christ loved the church. Husbands and wives were to obey one another, but in order to achieve that obedience, there had to be sacrificial love on both sides. Both partners were to undergird one another and offer support in a way that each would become the best at whatever he or she was meant to do. Tim gave an example in his own life in which he wanted Susan to quit working after their first child was born.

"I thought she should do what I wanted because I, after all, was the head of the house. I made the rules. I wanted a traditional pastor's wife who would head up the women's ministry team and hostess our get-togethers. Susan came to me one day and told me that if I really wanted her to be a homemaker, she would. She loved staying home with the baby. But she also wanted me to understand that the choice would be costly. She loved nursing, and by taking it away I would be diminishing her as well as our relationship.

"You see, nursing is Susan's ministry," he went on. "It's part of who she is." Tim glanced at Susan, his eyes tearing. With difficulty he managed to end his sermon, saying, "God showed me that day that what Susan chose to do was between him and Susan. My job was not to tell her what to do but to support her in whatever God wanted for her."

Angel's admiration for her brother went up several notches that morning, and at family dinner she told him so.

Callen came to the house after the funeral, insisting on taking over the kitchen so Anna could rest. Surprisingly she didn't argue. Angel made her mother comfortable on the sofa and helped Callen prepare a simple meal of oven-fried chicken, mashed potatoes and gravy, fresh green beans, and a tossed salad. Callen was strangely quiet during the meal preparation and through dinner.

After the meal, the women cleaned the kitchen while the guys set up the volleyball net on the beach. Guys against the girls. Angel played hard, but her competitive spirit was missing. She guessed they all felt that way, because they gave it up after forty-five minutes.

Callen went home after offering his condolences again. He hadn't asked Angel over, and she hadn't asked him to stay. She couldn't say why and didn't really want to know. Had Tim's message on marriage scared him off? He hadn't commented on it. Had she shown him too much of her own temper, her own stubbornness? Maybe it was for the best. No need to break things off. Just let whatever it was they felt for each other fade into oblivion. *That suits me.*

Liar.

Angel offered to spend the night, but her mother said she didn't want to stay in the house just yet. She'd be staying with Tim for a few more days. Angel didn't blame her. Besides, Susan would do a much better job of taking care of her than Angel could. That settled, Angel said her good-byes and went back to her empty apartment.

Feeling restless and lonely, she did her run that evening an hour before sunset. She ran past Callen's home, thinking to at least say hello to Mutt. She cleared the dune enough to see Callen's porch and stopped. A woman stood at the railing, smiling into the wind as she watched the setting sun.

Getting up on Monday morning was always hard, but today the task seemed monumental. Amid the aching muscles from the volleyball game was the heartache of seeing a woman standing on Callen's deck as though she belonged there. She might have been a model, sleek and trim, all dressed in white, with a red mane tossing in the wind. No wonder Callen hadn't invited her over. He'd apparently had other plans.

Angel didn't know what to make of it. Didn't really want to think about it. They hadn't made any kind of commitment. Still, it hurt far more than it should have that he would be seeing someone else.

She got up and made coffee, showered while it perked, and tried to keep the woman's image out of her mind. Hurt melded into anger. He could have at least told her he was seeing someone else.

You're beyond all that, she tried to tell herself. *Jealousy is for those who care.*

Okay. She cared, and she was jealous and angry and hurt.

And you don't have time for it.

Angel swept the turmoil under a rug in the corner of her mind, determined to concentrate on her job. Once dressed in her PI uniform—jeans, a light blue V-neck T-shirt, and a plaid wool blazer—she fixed herself a piece of whole grain toast with crunchy peanut butter, drank her second cup of coffee, and picked up the phone. It was 9:30.

"Rachael," she said when the attorney answered. "We need to talk."

"Right. I was hoping you'd call. I just had the most interesting conversation with a new client." She cleared her throat with deliberation and disapproval. "Why didn't you tell me about this email business yesterday? You're supposed to keep me informed."

"When did I have time? You were hanging on to my brother all day. And you two took off right after the game. Besides, no one seemed very talkative yesterday."

"I know. Paul was having a hard time—all of you are. Um, I don't mean to be insensitive, Angel. If you need some time . . ."

"No. I need to keep busy."

"I wish I'd known about Janet before you told Callen."

"Sorry, my priorities were a little out of line. The point is, what do we do now? Will the emails make a difference for Candace?"

"I'm not sure. It hasn't so far. Listen, I haven't eaten breakfast yet. Pick me up at my office, and we'll go to Joanie's."

Once they'd ordered and received their coffee and bagels, Angel filled Rachael in on what she'd discovered so far. "Do you think they'll drop the charges and let Candace out?" Angel bit a piece off her cinnamon raisin bagel. "Phillip's funeral is today."

"I doubt she'll be able to go. The police aren't buying it. I have a call in to the DA, but I don't expect him to change his mind. They're saying Janet may have written the notes to protect her client and that she's somehow all involved in this diabolical plan to free Candace."

"The DA told you that?"

"Joe told me. Janet has an alibi for the afternoon Jenkins was killed. According to her assistant, she was in the office all afternoon."

"I'm glad to hear that." Angel licked cream cheese off her knuckle. Something Rachael had said clung to her mind like a magnet. "Diabolical plan," she said aloud. "This may sound really far-fetched, but what if several women devised a plot to kill off their husbands? Maybe they establish an alibi for themselves while another woman from their group kills the husband. Candace has her alibi, but the timing didn't work out the way it was supposed to."

"Whoa. That's some imagination you've got there." Rachael was quiet for a moment. "It sounds pretty crazy, like all those government conspiracy theories, but . . . it's possible, and that scares me."

"What's really scary is that they aren't finished yet." Angel sighed. "At least that's what the last email indicated."

"Or the police might be right. Maybe Janet did manufacture this Dragonslayer to take the attention off Candace." Rachael picked red onion strings off her bagel and set them on her plate. "Might have worked too, if she hadn't confessed."

"Hmm. It does seem a bit contrived that someone would come forward now, especially with the letters appearing on Janet's computer and Dragonslayer using her account."

They continued eating and after a few bites, Angel asked, "Have you talked to Candace about her confession?"

"She's sticking by it. Says she still wants me to defend her. Guilty by reason of insanity." Rachael picked up her lox and cream cheese bagel and looked at it, opened her mouth, and closed it again.

"She's lying," Angel said. "I know it and you know it, but she won't back down."

"Thanks to your little confrontation. I wish you hadn't told her Gracie had been there. But like you said, she already knew."

"Like I said before, I'm sorry."

"Well, it's not really your fault. I'm working up a good defense, but it won't be easy."

Angel stared into her drink before taking a sip. "If the emails are bogus, what about the threat against me? Was that bogus as well?"

Rachael frowned. "What threat?"

"Dragonslayer wants me out of the way."

Angel's cell phone rang. It was her mother. "Where are you?"

"At Joanie's, why? What's wrong? Are you okay? Do you need me to come over to Tim's?"

"I'm at home." She sighed. "Where I belong."

"Alone?"

"No, Susan brought me. At any rate, Debra Stanton just called. She's frantic. Her husband is missing."

Angel dropped what was left of her bagel and rummaged in her bag for a pen. "Has she called the police?" Her heart picked up tempo. Was Douglas Stanton Dragonslayer's next victim?

"Yes, but they're not really doing much at this point. You know that twenty-four-hours thing. She's afraid he's been murdered like the others. She called me hoping I could talk you into looking for him. I gave her your number."

"All right, but I'm not sure there's anything I can do."

Angel rang off, and her phone rang again. This time it was Debra, and she sounded far more distressed than her mother had indicated.

"Calm down," Angel told the woman. "Tell me what's going on."

"Doug didn't show up at the office this morning. I called and he wasn't there and no one knows where he is. I've called the nursing home where his mother lives and he wasn't there. This isn't like him. The police are giving me the runaround. Please, your mother said you'd help."

"Hold on a minute." Angel covered the mouthpiece and turned to Rachael to explain the situation.

"Debra is in the support group, right?"

Angel nodded.

She whistled. "Tell her we'll check it out."

"Debra, I'm with Rachael, and we're going to look for him."

"Thank you," she sobbed. "I know I've said some hateful things about Doug, but I love him."

"I need to ask you a few questions." Angel pulled out a pad and began writing. "I imagine you checked, but is anything missing, like an overnight case, any of his clothes . . . ?"

"No, nothing. He left at 8:00 like he usually does to open the bank, and apparently never got there. Laura Ostrander, the vice president, called me at 8:30 asking if he was okay. Fortunately she has keys, but he wasn't there and there was no note or anything."

"What kind of car was he driving?" Angel began making notes to herself.

"The Mercedes. Black with black leather interior."

Angel asked for the license plate number and got a description of what he was wearing. She had met the bank president and knew him by sight. He was around fifty with dishwater blond hair graying at the temples. About five-ten to his wife's five-six. Thin but muscular and in good shape. Angel had often seen him running on the beach when she did her own runs, and he went to the same gym. Of course, everyone in Sunset Cove went to the same gym, since it was the only one they had.

Angel dropped off Rachael at the church and headed toward the bank. She was just getting out when she heard a gunshot. It thunked into the flower box above her head. She dove to the sidewalk as another shot bit into her arm.

In utter disbelief, Angel rolled to her side and grabbed for her arm, pressing against the searing pain. Someone nearby revved up an engine and sped away. An eerie silence followed the gunshots. Angel fought off the all-too-familiar images and ensuing panic and struggled to her knees.

Then voices. And in the distance, sirens. A young man ran out of the bank and knelt beside her. "Are you all right?"

"Yes." Angel ran a shaking hand through her hair. "I think so."

The man had dark hair and kind blue eyes. He wore a denim shirt and jeans and cowboy boots. "You're bleeding."

Angel glanced at her hand still pressed against the wound. She held the hand out in front of her, watching the blood drip to her jeans. She lifted her blurred gaze to the stranger. "I guess I am."

"Don't try to get up. The police are on the way; so is an ambulance."

The last thing Angel remembered before losing consciousness was Nick's concerned face. "Why couldn't you have listened to me? You just had to go and get yourself shot, didn't you?"

As if getting shot was her idea. "Thanks, Nick. I love you too," she murmured as the EMTs strapped her onto the stretcher.

TWENTY-EIGHT

S he awoke in the emergency room, smelling anesthetic and seeing bright lights that hurt her eyes.

"Welcome back." The same man from in front of the bank stood over her, only he was wearing a white coat and smiling. A stethoscope hung around his neck. His hands were hidden by a green paper. "I hear you're an Angel. I've never stitched up an Angel before."

"Just my name." She must have already gotten something for pain, as her words slurred and her mouth didn't seem capable of following orders.

He chuckled. "I'm Doctor McMahon. Thought I'd finish what I started."

"So I really got hit?" She couldn't feel the pain any longer, only a slight tug.

"It's not as bad as it looks," he said. "The bullet took a nice little chunk out of your deltoid. Skimmed off some muscle, but it looks clean. You lost a fair amount of blood—nicked an artery, but you'll live."

His bloodied, gloved hand rose up over the green paper, along with the curved needle he was holding.

"How many stitches?"

"Oh, a dozen or so."

"Did you see who shot me?"

"Sorry. I was in the bank. Thought for a while we were being held up. The first shot had everybody on the floor. I don't think anybody actually saw anything, but the police are questioning people up and down the street. I heard a car take off, and when I got up I saw you. Told everyone else to stay put, and I ran out to check on you."

Angel closed her eyes. "Thanks."

"You're more than welcome." He held up the needle again and snipped the thread. Looking past her he said, "A couple four-by-fours and some cling wrap should do it."

Angel tipped her head back. A woman in green scrubs tore open the bandages and held the package open so he could take them. She gave Angel a smile.

"So tell me, who'd want to shoot a nice girl like you?" the doctor asked.

"Humph. I wish I knew."

After dressing the wound, Dr. McMahon stripped off his gloves and went to the sink to wash his hands. Looking over his shoulder, he told the nurse, "Go ahead and get her cleaned up."

To Angel he said, "You can go home, but no pull-ups for a few days. I want to see you in my office in a week to ten days to take out the stitches. You can shower if you cover the dressing with cling wrap and promise not to get it wet. You'll get an instruction sheet and a prescription for pain pills if you need them. Take it easy today. Rest." He smiled. "Of course, I doubt that will be a problem. Your boyfriend told me he wasn't letting you out of his sight."

"Boyfriend?"

"Detective Riley. At least I assumed he was your boyfriend. He's waiting outside."

Angel didn't comment one way or the other. She thanked the doctor and nurse and let them assist her into the wheelchair. When the nurse wheeled her through the automatic doors into the waiting room, Callen stopped pacing.

"I'm taking you home," he said. "To my place."

The look on Callen's face told Angel he wasn't taking no for an answer, and Angel had no energy to argue.

Callen blamed himself for not taking the threat more seriously. Blamed himself for leaving it to the shorthanded Sunset Cove police to deal with the mysterious Dragonslayer. He'd been interviewing the mechanics at Mitch's Auto Body regarding the supposed stolen car when he got the call from Nick. "Angel's been shot," Caldwell had said. "Thought you'd want to know."

He'd practically flown to the hospital, even after Nick had told him it wasn't life threatening. "A few stitches and she'll be fine."

Thank God for that. What upset him most was that the shots could have been fatal. He'd beaten himself up over and over again, but the moment the doors opened and the nurse pushed Angel through, Callen's heart turned to mush. He had no time for ruminations and self-loathing. He had to focus on one thing—keeping Angel safe. On the drive to the hospital and in the waiting room, he'd made all the arrangements. He'd reassured Anna that Angel was fine and he'd be taking her home. Anna blessed him and said she'd let the others know. They'd be over later in the afternoon to see her.

It was all settled, and he was more than pleased with his efficiency until he saw Angel's face. Something had changed. Her obvious displeasure at seeing him may have just been the pain medication and loss of blood, but he didn't think so. Of course there was the argument, but he thought they'd resolved that.

She was in his car now, and still she hadn't said anything. She'd tilted the seat back and had fallen asleep. Maybe that was best for now. He drove her home and parked beside a Lexus.

"New car?" Angel asked as they pulled in the driveway.

"My sister's. She's here for a few days."

"Oh." Angel reached for the car door and winced. The pain medication must have been wearing off.

"Hold on." Callen jumped out and ran around to the passenger side of his SUV and pulled open the door. "You're supposed to be resting that arm."

She bit into her lower lip. "Thanks for the reminder."

The door opened to Callen's house, and Mutt shot out, followed by the redhead. She was even prettier up close. The beautiful woman who had given her so much grief was his sister. Angel felt ridiculous, glad she hadn't made a complete fool out of herself by confronting Callen about his mysterious woman.

"Mutt, you come back here." Kath ran after him.

Her command fell on deaf ears as Mutt made a beeline for Angel.

"Hey, boy," Angel crooned down at him. "Did you miss me?"

"Obviously." Kath sidled up to the car and scooped the dog into her arms. "I'm Kath. It's so nice to meet you." She stepped back. "Wish it were under different circumstances, though."

"Nice to meet you too," Angel managed to say.

"Let's get you inside." Callen slid his arms around Angel's back and under her legs, lifting her out of the car and into his arms.

"I can walk."

"You're weak. You've lost a lot of blood."

Angel didn't argue. Truth be told, she doubted her legs would hold out for more than a few seconds.

Callen deposited her on the bed in his room. "Kath's using the guest room. I'm sleeping on the couch," he said before she could even protest.

"This isn't necessary. I can just go home."

"Yes, it is. You can't be home alone. You can't stay at your mother's. She's in no condition to help you. Kath volunteered to help me take care of you and—"

"That's that." Kath squeezed in front of her brother. "No arguments, young lady." She turned around and poked a finger in Callen's chest. "You, go back to work. Catch that killer before he abducts another victim."

"But—"

"Angel will be fine."

Callen frowned. "I'm sorry, Angel. She's right. I have to get back to the body shop and finish interviewing those guys." He moved in front of his sister and kissed Angel's forehead. "You'd better do as she says or she'll beat you up." He grinned and ducked away as Kath punched his shoulder. "I'll be back as soon as I can."

When he'd gone, Kath tucked Angel in and brought her a glass of water with a straw. "I'll let you sleep for a while and bring you something to eat when you're up to it."

"Hmm." Angel relaxed against the pillows. Mutt jumped up on the bed, circled once, and sat down, resting his chin on her leg.

"Come on, Mutt. Leave her alone." Kath reached for the dog.

"He's fine." Angel smiled. "Probably worried about me."

"I'm sure he is." She stroked his head. "From what Callen has told me, you've been through a lot. Losing your father and now this." Kath stood there a moment watching her. "My brother really cares about you."

"I know."

"I mean, he *really* cares."

If there was a hidden meaning behind her words and the protective expression on her face, it was probably something like, *I hope you're worth it.*

Angel slept for what seemed like two minutes; the clock indicated it had been two hours. She awoke to see her mother clucking over her and thanking Kath. Anna seemed to be moving her arm more freely and showed Angel a bright blue cast that ran from just above the elbow to the middle of her hand. "This is my fault, Angel. I shouldn't have sent you looking for Douglas. I should have told Debra you were too busy."

"Ma." Angel sighed and lifted her uninjured arm to grasp her mother's good hand. "It's not your fault or Debra's. The only person to blame is the guy who shot me."

Kath brought in a cup of chicken broth with a straw. "Thought you might want this. Your mother brought it."

"Ma, you've got a broken arm—what are you doing in the kitchen?"

"I took it from the freezer," she said. "I always make extra and store it just for times like this."

Angel moved to sit up when an unexpected wave of nausea washed over her. "I don't think I'd better eat anything right now."

215

She leaned back into the pillows. "Maybe later." Mutt whimpered as if feeling her discomfort and snuggled a bit closer.

Anna questioned Kath about the pain medication and asked her to bring in a basin in case Angel needed to throw up. Kath let her know she had everything covered. Angel just closed her eyes again and waited for the nausea to pass.

Kath and Angel were alone the next time Angel woke up. She groggily made her way to the bathroom with Kath holding on to her good arm. From there she insisted on going into the living room. "I can't believe a flesh wound could cause so much trouble. It hardly even hurts."

"I imagine the pain medication is making you woozy. I could make you a piece of toast."

Angel nodded. "That sounds good. I'd better try some of my mom's soup too."

Angel managed to eat and felt better but was too tired to stay up. "Good thing I didn't try to go home by myself."

Kath smiled. "Somehow I don't think your family or Callen would have let that happen."

Angel yawned and with Kath's help made her way back to bed. Kath adjusted the pillows and headed out of the room.

"Would you mind staying for a while?" Angel asked.

"I'm not going anywhere."

"No, I mean here. Talk to me." She moved her legs to give Kath room to sit down.

"What about?"

"Tell me about you and Callen and your family."

Kath did. Angel liked hearing her voice as she told of her husband and teenage daughters and how they'd given her the gift of a week at the beach with Callen. How she was Callen's older sister and often felt more like a mother. How their own parents had been into drugs and alcohol and how they'd lived most of their lives with their grandparents.

Kath talked about Callen's marriage and how hard he'd taken Karen's death. All in all, she painted Callen as the caring, sensitive, loving man Angel knew him to be. Not the angry man she'd caught a glimpse of Friday night.

216

The following morning, Angel awoke to the tantalizing smell and the sizzling sound of bacon. Voices coming from the kitchen reminded her that she was still in Callen's house.

"Did you get anywhere with your interviews yesterday?" Kath asked her brother.

"Right now I'm just weeding out the people who didn't kill Christy. The car's owner has an ironclad alibi. He was here in Sunset Cove the entire time. Same goes for his employees. Looks like none of them did it. I'm still looking at Mitch's two youngest sons."

Angel grimaced with pain as she swung her legs over the edge of the bed.

"Better see if our guest is ready to eat," Callen said. "I think I hear her stirring around in there."

Kath appeared in the doorway. "Need some help?"

"Maybe." Angel stood still for a moment, waiting for the room to sway, and when it didn't she ventured forward. "I think I'm okay."

"How's the arm?"

"Hurts some, but I'm sticking with Tylenol today. The stuff the doctor gave me makes me feel like I've been rolling around the ocean in a storm."

"I know what you mean." Kath walked with her to the bathroom and waited outside while Angel used the facilities and washed her hands. Lifting her good arm, Angel finger combed her hair. Not that it did much good. A gray complexion didn't do much for her appearance either. Kath had loaned her a pair of pajamas with legs that trailed along on the floor behind her. She tried rolling up the cuffs with one hand and gave up. They'd just have to drag.

Callen and Mutt appeared at the sliding glass door just when Angel got to the table. "You're looking good this morning." He dropped a kiss on her cheek and hung up Mutt's leash.

"Liar."

"Compared to yesterday." He washed his hands and dished up breakfast. "Did you sleep well?"

She nodded. "I'm ready to go home."

He looked disappointed. "I'm not sure that's a good idea. Why

217

don't you hang around here for another day. Kath could use the company and—"

"Callen." Kath gave her brother a look of warning and turned to Angel. "Tell you what. Have breakfast with us, then shower and get dressed. Once you do that you'll have a better idea of what you can handle."

"Sounds fair enough," Angel agreed. "And if I feel good enough to go home?"

"I'll take you, of course." Kath poured orange juice into three glasses. "And we'll have to figure out a way to get your car home."

"Your car's taken care of," Callen said. "Your brothers took it over to your folks' place." He frowned. "I'm not sure that going to your apartment is a good idea. Not just because of your arm."

"You think whoever shot at me will come back?" Angel hadn't really been awake enough since the shooting to think much about the shooter or his motives.

"That would be my main concern, yes."

She replayed the fourth email message in her head. "I doubt it. Dragonslayer didn't want to hurt me, remember? He just wanted to get me out of the way for a while, and he certainly did that."

Callen didn't seem convinced, but he didn't argue either.

"I overheard you mention that you'd cleared Mitch and his employees and that you were still looking at the sons?"

"Yeah, why?"

"The youngest one is still in high school. I didn't mention this the other night, but I think he drove Gracie out to the farm the day Jenkins was killed. She said she had to go out to get some papers and insists Phillip was alive when they left." Angel nibbled at a piece of multigrain hazelnut toast. "That's why Candace confessed. She knew Gracie had been out there."

"That's a pretty important piece of information." Callen didn't seem too pleased.

"Yeah, well, what I'm trying to say is that he couldn't have been in Florence. He was here."

"Jenkins was killed on Tuesday, right?"

She nodded.

218

"Well," Callen went on, "we found the car that day and we figure the victim had been dead for a couple days at that point. The guy had a head start on us. We think he left the area on Sunday."

"Oh." Angel felt sick. "I left a message for Nick about the Bailey kid. It'll be easy to check him out since he goes to the high school. In fact, that was on my agenda today—to talk to him about his trip out to the Jenkins's farm that day. Do you really think Justin stole his dad's car and killed that girl?"

"He's been in some trouble lately," Callen said. "Skipping school, partying. I'll be taking a hard look at him." Callen didn't say the words out loud, but Angel knew he didn't want her anywhere near Justin Bailey.

She wasn't too crazy about meeting Justin either, especially if he'd been the one to kill Christy. "I'm having trouble connecting the dots between Jenkins and the Grant girl. Do you really think there's a connection? It doesn't seem feasible that Justin would kill her and then show up at the farm the same day Jenkins was killed."

"No, it doesn't." Callen finished off a glass of milk.

"Hmm. I just had a thought. Remember what I said about the women in the support group hiring a hit man?" She reached for a jam jar.

His eyes narrowed as he tried to follow her line of thought.

"What if Gracie hired Justin to kill Phillip? Maybe she knew about Christy." Angel had trouble believing her own suggestion. She'd suspected Gracie all along but couldn't imagine her condoning the death of a girl her own age. Gracie just didn't seem that hateful.

Callen rubbed the back of his neck. "Tell you what. I'll question him about Jenkins at the same time. Find out exactly what he's been up to for the past two weeks."

Angel managed a smile. "And you'll tell me, right?"

"If you promise to stay out of trouble."

"I have no intention of getting into trouble." And she didn't. Unfortunately, though, she had no way of knowing that trouble would find her.

Callen left as soon as he finished eating. Kath secured plastic wrap around Angel's dressing, sealing it in a waterproof cocoon. By the time Angel had showered and gotten dressed, she was too exhausted to do anything but go back to bed.

"You knew this would happen, didn't you?" she said to Kath.

Kath smiled. "I had a hunch."

Angel awoke at around 1:00 in the afternoon. The house was oddly quiet. Angel used the bathroom and ventured into the living room. Kath and Mutt were gone. A note on the table told Angel that they'd gone exploring at the northern end of the beach in the tide pools and that if Angel wanted lunch, Kath had made a chicken salad sandwich for her.

Angel devoured the sandwich and, feeling much better, decided to walk over to her parents' place to pick up her car. *"Gone home,"* she wrote on the bottom of Kath's note. *"Thanks for everything. Angel."*

No one was home at the Delaney house, so Angel secured her keys from the table near the front entrance and drove back to her apartment.

The activity left her feeling exhausted, and she headed for the bedroom to take another nap. Her cell phone rang, and Angel retrieved it from its pocket in her bag.

"Hello?" The caller sounded out of breath. "Angel?"

"Yes, it is. Who is this?"

"Gracie."

"Are you okay?"

"No. I think I know who killed that cheerleader in Florence. I need to talk to you. Please meet me . . . at the school. Hurry. I'm afraid he might . . . I gotta go."

The line went dead. Any residual weariness fled. Angel grabbed her keys and arrived in front of Sunset Cove High School five minutes later.

TWENTY-NINE

———

Callen pulled into the lot of Mitch's Auto Body. As he'd told Angel, he felt the owner and his employees were telling the truth; their alibis had checked out. Now he wanted to focus on Mitch's two boys.

"Detective Riley." The man was cordial enough, but Callen could tell that underneath the smile and proffered hand, the man clearly didn't want him there. Callen didn't blame him. He was there to talk about the man's sons.

"Come on into my office, detective. What can I do for you?"

The office was a small cubbyhole smelling of grease and looking like it might have looked fifty years ago. There was a current calendar on the wall, next to a picture of a pinup girl from the fifties.

"I have a few questions." Callen eased onto the plastic chair that had seen its share of grime.

The day before, Mitch had indicated he'd noticed the car missing on Saturday before last. Christy hadn't come home Friday night. Callen reminded him of that and asked, "Do you know where your sons were at that time?"

"I wish I could tell you. Justin said something about going to the track meet, but I don't know that he did. I'm thinking if he had, he'd have taken his pickup. When I first noticed the car was missing, I thought maybe one of my boys took it, but neither one of them owns up to it. Best I can tell you is that some stranger came along, saw the keys in it, and took off."

"Let's back up a minute. You first thought one of your kids might have taken it?"

"At first. Justin uses it sometimes when his truck is in the shop. He's getting ready to paint it. Jimmy has used it too."

"Jimmy?"

"The middle boy. He's twenty now. Jimmy comes and goes pretty much as he pleases. I got to where I don't pay him no mind. Wanted to throw the bum out two years ago, but the wife says to leave him be. He ain't a bad kid." Bailey poked his tongue into his cheek to dislodge a wad of chewing tobacco, which he spit into a can at the side of the desk. "Turns out Jimmy hadn't used the car either."

Or he wasn't admitting to it. But then who would? "When did you talk to Jimmy?"

"Last night. He'd been in Portland visiting a friend and just came home."

"What's the friend's name?"

Mitch shrugged. "Probably Rob McKenzie."

Callen wrote the name down. It was very possible that Jimmy had taken the car and been forced to come back to Sunset Cove without it. After all, he couldn't very well bring back a car in which he'd stowed the body of the missing girl.

"I just hope he was telling the truth, you know, about not taking the car. Jimmy might be a rabble-rouser, but he ain't no killer. He has plenty of girls running after him. He didn't have to . . . you know . . . take that girl."

"Did Jimmy say anything about how he got to Portland?" Callen asked.

"Says he hitched a ride. He'd planned on taking the car, but it was gone. I wish I could be more specific. Best I can tell you after talking to the boys is that someone must've taken it during the night."

"I'd like to talk to your boys myself. Can you tell me where to find them?"

"Justin would be in school. Jimmy's working today. I saw him out in the shop just before lunch."

Callen talked to Jimmy and collected a DNA sample via a mouth swab. Jimmy swore he had nothing to do with the Florence girl's disappearance. He brushed long hair out of his eyes. "I was in Portland. You can call my buds. They'll verify it."

"Okay, I'll do that."

"I haven't been anywhere near Florence," Jimmy said again.

Callen nodded and thanked him for his time. The kid was a drug user, and Callen doubted his alibi would hold up. Still, he would call the Portland office and ask to have a uniform trooper check out the names and phone numbers Jimmy had given him. "We'll check out your alibi, and in the meantime, I'd like you to take a polygraph test."

He shook his head. "I don't know about that. Those things are kind of scary."

"Nothing to worry about, Jim. So long as you're telling the truth."

"I guess that would be okay, then. When do you want me to take it?"

"I'll set something up in the next day or so. I have to bring a specialist in from our Salem office. Mitch, just to be sure, I'd like your younger son to take one too. I'm not suggesting they had anything to do with the crime, just whittling down the list of possible suspects."

"I understand. We'll cooperate. What about my mechanics?"

"We've checked them out already. Their whereabouts can be accounted for. In the meantime, I'd like to hear a little more about Justin."

Again, he got little more from Mitch than a reluctant admission that Justin had missed a lot of school recently.

"The boy likes to go fishing," Mitch offered. "Wants to be a commercial fisherman and don't care much about finishing school. Me and the missus told him we wanted to see him graduate."

Callen went home after the interview, wanting to check in on Angel, and was surprised to find both his sister and Angel gone. He read Kath's note and the scribble at the bottom from Angel.

He hurried back outside and drove past the Delaney house. Her car was gone. Callen dialed her cell phone and got a busy signal.

"What are you doing, Angel?" he spoke to the phone as he folded it. "You're supposed to be resting." He had no time to track her down. He straightened his shoulders. Maybe he was worrying over nothing. Angel could just be enjoying her daily latte over at Joanie's.

He really needed to quit obsessing over her every move. She was an adult, after all. If she felt well enough to go home, she must be okay.

You should be thankful she was able to do that. And he was, on one hand. On the other, he feared she might take up where she left off on the investigation. After the shooting, the Sunset Cove PD had sprung into action, investigating the banker's disappearance as well as the shooting incident involving Angel. They were looking closely at the emails Janet Campbell had received but had made no headway there.

Callen tried to put Angel out of his mind. He had to focus on his own investigation. He fixed a sandwich with the chicken salad he'd made the day before. With Mutt lying at his feet, waiting for crumbs, Callen called the high school. The principal was more than happy to talk to him. It seemed that Justin Bailey was in big trouble. He'd been truant so often he was in danger of not graduating. "I talked to him last week, and he's promised to try to make it up. I guess his parents bribed him with the down payment on his own fishing boat if he'd stay in school until graduation."

He thanked the woman and hung up. If it turned out that Justin had taken his father's car and killed Christy, all the fishing boats in the world wouldn't do him any good. Callen planned to do some fishing on his own. Time to set the hook on the boy and reel him in and see what the DNA evidence turned up.

His pager vibrated as he slid into his unmarked Crown Victoria.

He glanced at it and frowned. Pulling his cell out of the console, he dialed Angel's number. Still busy.

As she headed toward the school, Angel called Rachael and Callen, leaving a message for each of them. Gracie wasn't waiting out front like she said she'd be. Angel stopped and climbed out, scanning the area. A number of kids were milling around. Angel asked several of them if they'd seen Gracie. They had earlier but had no idea where she was now. One had talked to her at her locker. "She seemed, I don't know, scared, I guess. Said she needed to get home right away."

"Who was she with?" Angel asked.

"Uh, no one . . . except . . ." She frowned. "Justin came up to her right when I was leaving. He wanted her to go with him. She told him she had to wait for somebody. I'm sorry, that's all I heard."

Angel talked to several other kids, but no one else seemed to know anything. Growing frantic, she ran inside, looking down each of the empty halls, then back out to her car. She grabbed her phone and called Callen. Busy. She didn't have his beeper, so she had dispatch put her through to him. He called back within a few seconds.

"Angel. What's going on?"

"Gracie. She called and asked me to meet her, said she knew who killed the cheerleader. She sounded scared. I got here as fast as I could, but she isn't here. One of the kids said they saw her with Justin. I'm driving around the school to see if his pickup is still here. If not, I'm heading out to the farm." Angel put the car in gear and eased onto the road.

"You think she went with the Bailey kid?"

"I don't know. One of the girls told me she was anxious to get home and he was with her."

"Somehow I don't think that's where he's headed. Stay where you are. I'm on my way." He hung up before she could object.

Angel drove past the school and back again, parking on the other side of the street. The crowd had thinned out. There was no gray, primed pickup in the parking lot. Angel was torn. Should she head out to the farm or wait for Callen? He'd asked her to, but why?

225

What had Gracie learned? She and Justin Bailey were obviously friends. If Callen was right, and Justin had killed that girl . . .

Please, God, don't let Gracie be the next victim.

Callen pulled up behind her, and she climbed out to meet him. "Gracie said to meet her right here. Did you find out anything about Justin?"

"Plenty. He wasn't in school most of last week—his folks suspected he'd been skipping school to go fishing. I've got Nick checking his story out now. Haven't gotten hold of Justin yet. I wanted all my ducks in a row before talking with him directly."

"That's what I was afraid of. It may be too late." Angel raked both hands through her hair. "If Justin killed Christy, and Gracie found out about it, she could be in danger too."

"When did she call you?"

Angel checked her watch. "About fifteen minutes ago."

Callen reached into his car and pulled out his radio and asked dispatch to put out an all points bulletin on the boy's truck, taking the description and license plate information from Angel's notes. As he climbed into his car, he said, "You need to go back to my place. I'll keep you posted."

Angel got into his car instead. "I have no intention of going to your place. Gracie asked me to meet her. She's in trouble, and I'm not going home until we find her."

Callen started to argue, then stopped. "All right, but I want you to remember, you're a civilian, not a cop. And you've been injured. No matter what happens, I need you to do what I tell you."

Angel agreed. She whipped the seat belt around herself, forgetting for a moment that she'd injured her arm. She bit into her lip, almost drawing blood. She wasn't about to let Callen see how much pain that little movement had brought her. Not now. Callen started the car, not seeming to notice her discomfort.

Dispatch reported that an officer had seen the pickup heading out of town toward the Jenkins place.

"Is he sure?"

"Affirmative. The deputy knows the kid and the vehicle."

"I'm on my way."

"He's taking her to the farm?" Angel asked.

226

Callen nodded. "It's isolated and the main road goes straight into the forest. Easier to get lost there than on the coast highway."

Angel hung on as Callen made a U-turn and headed back the way he'd come.

"You'll have to give me directions." He placed the light on top of the vehicle and flipped on the siren. "I've never been out there."

Angel focused on the road, trying to keep her arm from hitting the door as Callen squealed around the corners, breaking speed records in getting out to the Jenkins's farm. Callen told the deputy who'd been following them to go straight out the main road in case they kept going, but as soon as they saw the pickup in the driveway, Callen called for backup.

The pickup was the only vehicle parked in the driveway. Candace's parents were probably still in town with the younger children. Angel hoped they stayed there. "This is weird. If he was abducting her, why come here?"

"Maybe Gracie talked him into stopping. She might have been stalling for time."

As they pulled in beside the pickup, Callen unbuckled his seat belt and ordered her to stay put. When he opened the door, a gunshot came from the barn. Callen ducked, using the door as a shield.

"Stay where you are and you won't get hurt!" someone yelled. "Just don't make me shoot you."

Angel had heard that voice before, but it wasn't until she saw the motorcycle at the side of the barn that she put two and two together.

"Gracie!" Angel yelled.

"Angel, help us!" came the muffled cry. It too had come from the upper level of the barn. The sliding door had been closed to within six inches.

"It's Darryl," Angel said. "He must be the one Gracie was talking about. Darryl must've stolen the car from Mitch. I don't know why it didn't occur to me before. I knew he'd left his motorcycle here and came back to get it on Tuesday."

Callen got on the radio to dispatch. "Looks like we have a hostage situation out here." He gave them the necessary information and requested additional backup.

"What do we do now?"

"Wait."

Within minutes, five more official vehicles arrived, including an ambulance.

Darryl had to be close to panicking. Angel forced back the terror rising in her own chest. She hadn't been in a hostage situation since Dani.

"I have Gracie and her boyfriend," Darryl yelled. "Stay away—all of you—or I'll kill them."

"What do you want, Darryl?" Callen yelled up at him.

"I just want to get out of here. That's all. Gracie had no business telling lies about me. I didn't kill anybody, and she knows it. I tried to tell her, but she wouldn't listen."

"Okay, just calm down. We're listening to you, Darryl." Callen sounded calm and collected, but the tightness in his shoulders and neck told Angel he was anything but.

"Maybe I could talk to him," Angel suggested. "I talked to him at the casino."

"No."

"Callen, I can negotiate with him. I have the training."

"Stay put!" Darryl yelled again. "Don't make me shoot you. I said stop!" Another gunshot and a scream.

"Gracie!" Angel bolted for the barn.

It may not have been the smartest move she'd ever made, but she didn't think about that. She only thought that while Darryl was distracted, she could get inside the barn and see what was going on. Maybe she could make a difference.

"He shot Justin," Gracie hollered from the loft just above Angel's head. Her screams turned to sobs, then everything went quiet.

The other officers moved around, taking position as Callen directed. He glared at her from his position at the car, and Angel put a finger to her mouth.

THIRTY

"What are you thinking?" Nick growled at Callen. "How could you let Angel go in there?"

"I didn't *let* her." Callen's insides had turned to jelly, and he expected his body to do the same. He hadn't felt this helpless since Karen died. There was nothing he could have done then, but he could do something now. He could rush the barn, maybe getting himself or one of the other officers killed in the process. He could try to distract Darryl and get another officer in there.

But was that the best strategy? Too much chaos and Darryl might kill Gracie. He may have already killed the Bailey kid.

"I'm going in after her," Nick said through clenched teeth.

Callen clamped a restraining hand on Nick's shoulder. "Let her be."

"Are you crazy?"

"Angel's a cop."

"Not anymore," Nick insisted.

"She's still a cop inside," Callen tried to explain, "or she'd never have done what she did. Angel isn't thinking like a civilian right now. I say we leave her alone. She's a negotiator. Let her do what she's trained for and pray she knows what she's doing. Our job right now is to back her up."

Callen cringed, hardly believing those words had come out of his mouth. This was Angel. His Angel. He couldn't let her confront Darryl alone. Unfortunately, at the moment, his options were somewhat limited.

Let her go. She was destined for this. The thoughts came from somewhere outside himself. Something Tim talked about in church Sunday hit him square between the eyes. Had God chosen Angel for police work? Had he chosen her for this?

"You're crazy," Nick muttered. "I'm writing this up."

"Trust me, Nick, or better yet, trust God."

"What's God got to do with it?" Nick shook his head in disgust.

Callen thought Nick might ignore him, but then his big shoulders rose and fell. "I sure hope you know what you're doing."

"So do I, Nick. So do I." He glanced back at Angel and gave her a thumbs-up sign. Angel nodded and headed for the ladder to the loft.

Callen gave directions for the small contingency of officers to move quietly into position. He wished they had a SWAT team—or at least more officers who'd been trained in this sort of thing. He'd have preferred negotiating with Darryl on a cell phone, but that wasn't an option now. Any movement on his part might endanger Angel and the teenagers' lives.

Like soldiers, the officers dispersed, behind the barn, at the house, behind the vehicles. He posted two officers at the outer perimeter to keep out unwanted types like the media. Seconds later they were all in place, weapons at the ready.

"Darryl? Is that you up there?" Angel called out in a voice more suited for a social gathering than a hostage situation. "It's me, Angel. We met at the casino, remember?"

"What do you want?" Darryl sounded scared and unsure of himself.

"To talk. Tell me what's going on. Maybe I can help."

"You can't help. No one can."

"What if I can get you out of here?"

"Like how?"

Callen swallowed back the fear still lodged in his throat. Darryl was listening. No wonder Angel was good at this. A guy couldn't help but listen to a voice like hers.

Angel's throat was dry. She swallowed hard before speaking again. "Darryl, did you go to the police with the information you had about your uncle? I asked you to do that, remember? Did you tell them that Gracie had been here just before you and that when you got here your uncle was dead?"

"N-no. I couldn't do that. I was afraid." Darryl lowered his voice; Angel could barely hear him.

"Because of the picture in the paper?" She gripped the ladder and took one step up. "Were you afraid they might recognize you as the guy who killed the cheerleader?"

"That was an accident." Feet scraped above her and to the left. "I didn't mean to hurt her. I just wanted to have some fun."

Angel closed her eyes, trying to block out the gut-wrenching reaction his confession brought. *Don't think about it, Angel. Don't think about Christy or how sick and disgusted you feel. Focus. Get him away from those kids.*

"I know you did, Darryl." Even Angel was surprised by the sympathy in her tone. "But you gotta believe me, holding Gracie and Justin hostage isn't going to help you."

"They're my ticket out of here."

"No, they're not. I am." Angel had to convince him, had to somehow get him to let the teenagers go.

"You?"

"How far do you think you'll get? You've already shot Justin. All you have now is Gracie, and the police aren't going to be too worried about what you do to her." *Don't say anything, Gracie, please. God, keep her quiet.*

"W-what do you mean?"

"She killed your uncle, remember? You told me you saw her and Justin leaving when you were coming in. You said your uncle was dead. If that's true, then Gracie must've done it. You need to let her and Justin go so the police can arrest them. If you really want to get out of here, let them go and take me instead." She inched up another step.

"Why would you do that?"

"I'll be honest with you, Darryl. Gracie and Justin are just kids. Justin has been shot. He needs medical attention. You don't want him to die, do you?"

"No."

"Then take me as a hostage." She advanced again until her head almost reached the opening.

"Yeah, like that's gonna happen."

"You've got a much better chance with me. Trust me on this. My boyfriend is a cop. He's out there right now. Do you honestly think he's going to do anything to jeopardize my health? If I tell him to keep everybody back, he will. Honest. Let the kids go, Darryl."

He didn't answer.

"I'm coming up." Angel took a step. "You'll see that I don't have a gun. I'm being square with you, Darryl. You'll have a much better chance taking me hostage over those teenagers. They're unpredictable and—"

"Okay. Come up, but put your hands in the air where I can see them."

Angel raised her arms and took the remaining steps slowly, deliberately, her gaze scanning the baled hay. She hesitated when she caught sight of Darryl. He stood against the wall, holding one of his uncle's handguns. His gaze darted back and forth between Angel and the kids. "Get over there next to them."

Angel didn't have to be told twice. Her heart thumped in her ears, nearly drowning out Gracie's sobs. Angel closed the distance in three steps and dropped down in front of the injured boy. He'd been shot in the abdomen; his chest rose and fell, but his skin was pasty white. "We have to get him to a doctor fast." Angel glanced up at Darryl. "There's an ambulance here. Please let the police come up here to get him."

"No." He clenched his teeth together. "Nobody's coming up here."

Angel froze. "You said you'd let them go."

"I can't." Darryl was near to tears himself. "Don't you see? They'll shoot me the minute I go outside. You're trying to trick me."

"No, they won't. I'll be with you. They'd have to shoot me too, and they won't do that."

Angel took off her jacket and pressed it to Justin's wound, choking back sobs as she had visions of Dani and Billy bathed in blood. Her efforts had been useless then. "Darryl, please listen to me. If we don't get him out of here, he'll die. We can't let that happen."

Telling Gracie to put pressure on Justin's wound, Angel scrambled to her feet and went to Darryl. She grabbed his free hand. "Come with me. We'll go down together. We'll go out to your Harley. They won't shoot you if I'm on the bike with you, Darryl. They won't. As long as I'm with you, you're safe."

Her actions took him off guard, and he stared at her for a long moment. Angel met his gaze, hoping her expression conveyed the compassion she was striving for and not the contempt she felt.

"I'll be safe?"

She nodded. "We'll head east. There are a lot of trails out there and a lot of roads. They won't be able to follow us."

"Why are you doing this?"

"I care, Darryl." She pinched her lips together. "Because I care about what happens to those kids."

She pulled on his arm, and he followed her down. She walked in front of him as they reached the entrance of the barn. "Don't shoot!" she yelled as they came to the open barn door. She stepped out first, her hands raised.

"Try anything and she gets it!" Darryl shouted. His gun was pressing into her back. He inched her toward the bike. "Get on," he ordered. "You drive."

Out of the corner of her eye, she saw officers enter the barn. The kids would be safe. Her heart dropped to her knees. Her plan had worked.

Good job, Angel. She swung her leg over the seat. *What are you going to do next?*

Callen felt numb as he watched Angel come out of the barn at gunpoint. She'd done it. He had no idea how, but she'd gotten Darryl away from the kids. They were still in a hostage situation, only now the odds were better—he hoped. If they had a SWAT team, one of the sharpshooters would've been able to pick Darryl off. But Callen didn't trust any of the officers out there to put Darryl out of commission.

He'd alerted the officers to hold their fire—to wait until Angel gave them the opportunity they'd need. And she would—he had no doubt about that. He just wished it wasn't her getting on that bike.

He leaned on the hood of his car, Darryl in his sights. Other officers were doing the same.

Darryl, weapon still in hand and pointing at Angel's head, climbed on the bike behind her.

"I don't know how to drive these things," Angel insisted. "You should drive."

Actually, she had driven a cycle, numerous times. Tim had owned one in his younger days, and in Florida she'd been trained to patrol using bikes, cycles, and horses, as well as cars. She hoped she'd be able to remember the basics, because right now her latent skill was the only thing that might save her.

"And have you jump off and the cops shoot me in the back?" Darryl punctuated his comment by pushing the gun squarely against her rib cage. "The key's in the ignition. Just crank it."

Angel did as he said. If Darryl decided to shoot, the bullet would go straight into her heart.

He helped her shift it into gear. "Go."

Please, God, please let this work. Angel gripped the handlebars and gunned it. The bike leaped forward, front wheels lifting off the ground like a rearing horse. She hung on as the bike dropped back to earth, then sprang forward. She blew out a long sigh of relief and glanced back. Mission accomplished.

She could hear Darryl swearing. His free arm no longer gripped her waist, and the gun had flown out of his hand when he hit the gravel road. He was now lying on his back in the middle of the driveway, surrounded by cops. She released the pedal and braked, then turned around and headed back.

234

"Nice job, Angel." Nick patted her on the shoulder. "Where'd you learn to handle a Harley?"

"Florida," she answered.

"You lied," Darryl whined. "You said you didn't know how to ride. You told me I'd be safe with you."

"I said as long as you were with me." Her mouth grim, she added, "You're not with me now, are you?"

An hour later Angel was back at Callen's place, putting ice on her throbbing arm. The body did miraculous things when caught in a life-and-death situation. She could attest to that. She'd been aware of the ache, but it hadn't been all that painful until the ordeal was over and she had begun to relax.

Kath brought the ice bag and propped it between Angel's arm and the couch.

"Thanks." Angel took a sip of ice water and set the glass back on the coffee table.

Once she was settled, Callen started lecturing her, but it wasn't the lecture she expected. Callen didn't tell her she was an idiot for running headlong into a dangerous situation. Instead, he said, "If you're going to act like a cop, then be one. Quit telling yourself you were doing it to please your dad. I saw you out there, Angel. You weren't worried about impressing anyone. You had one thing on your mind and that was to get Gracie and Justin out of that barn and away from Darryl."

"Hush, Callen, leave the poor girl alone." Kath softened the demand with a smile. "Angel has plenty of time to think about whether or not she wants to change careers. She doesn't have to decide about going back to work today. But what I do want you to do is tell me what happened. How did Gracie and her boyfriend end up as hostages?"

Angel looked at Callen. "Do you want to tell her or should I?"

"I will. You need to rest."

"It's my arm that needs rest. Not my mouth."

"So you say."

She slapped his arm, then left her hand where it had connected.

Callen went on to tell Kath about the phone call Angel had gotten. As he spoke Angel thought about the moments after Darryl's arrest. A tearful Gracie emerged from the barn, just in front of the EMTs who were carrying Justin out on a stretcher. She made a beeline for Angel, hugging and holding her with the intensity of a child Dorothy's age, her cool aloofness long gone.

"They said he was going to be okay." Gracie hugged her even harder. "I was so scared."

"You were brave."

"You didn't really mean what you said about me killing Phillip, did you?"

"Darryl thought you had." Angel guided her out of the road and onto the porch. "Let's sit down." The suggestion was for her own benefit more than Gracie's. The adrenaline rush had evaporated, and her legs felt as though they were going to melt. "Tell me what happened."

"About Phillip?"

"That too, but let's start with your standing me up."

"I'm sorry about that. I wanted to get home. I saw the drawing on the news this morning—the one who killed that girl in Florence. He looked familiar, but I couldn't place him. After school I thought about it again. Some of the kids had a copy of the picture. I guess the cops were handing them out. Anyway, I took one and started really looking at it. That's when I knew it was Darryl." She covered her mouth with the back of her hand. "I got really scared. I wanted to go home."

"But why? All you had to do was call the police."

"No, you don't understand. My grandparents were picking up my brother and sister from school and they were going to take them to the aquarium. Darryl was there and told them he'd pick me up."

"You still could've called the police."

"I was afraid to. They put my mom in jail. So I called you. I figured you'd know what to do. Anyway, Justin saw me in the hall and offered to take me home. I told him I had to wait for you, but he said it would be too dangerous to wait around 'cause Darryl could be there any minute. All I could think about was getting home. Turns out Darryl didn't come to the school at all. He was out at the house stealing one of Phillip's guns."

"He was in the house? How did you end up in the barn?"

236

"We were getting out of the pickup when Darryl came up from the root cellar. Justin grabbed my hand and told me to run. We headed for the barn, hoping he wouldn't see us. It was stupid. Darryl came after us. He made us go up into the loft. I think he was going to tie us up so he could get away. We'd just gotten up there when you came, and he got real scared and said he was going to kill us if we said anything."

Angel knew the rest of the story all too well. She squeezed Callen's hand, thankful to be alive and grateful he had allowed her to deal with Darryl her own way.

"So the case is closed," Kath said.

"Not yet." Callen stroked Angel's hair. "We still need to get the test results on the evidence we sent in."

"And there's still Phillip Jenkins's murder," Angel said. "Gracie told me Phillip was dead when she and Justin came by to pick up her essay for an afternoon class."

"Do you think she's telling the truth?" Kath asked.

"I do now." Angel frowned. "And that lets Darryl off the hook as far as killing his uncle is concerned, since he got to the house after Gracie. Which means Candace didn't kill him either, unless she did it before she left to pick up the kids. Which she didn't do, because Becky came after she left to have her afternoon meeting with her boss." Angel rolled her eyes. "Did I say meeting?"

"So the secretary killed him?" Kath frowned. "I'm confused."

"She says he was alive when she left, so either she's lying or someone else came to pay Phillip a visit after she left."

"And," Callen interjected, "that may have been Fitzgibbon, Savage, or one of the women in your support group."

"Any of them could be Dragonslayer," Angel said. "I think he or she killed Kelsey and Jenkins. Douglas Stanton from the bank may be the next victim."

"He's still missing," Callen added.

Angel's cell phone rang. She'd set her bag on the floor next to the sofa.

"Stay where you are," Kath said. "I'll get it." She located and answered the phone. "Sure, she's right here." She handed Angel the phone. "It's Rachael."

"Hi, Rach, what's up?"

"Am I glad I caught you. Things are going from bad to worse. Janet called and said her ex was in town. She decided to do what we'd talked about, which was going to the police and turning him in for blackmail. Well, you are not going to believe this, but when the police went to arrest him, he was dead."

"What?" Angel sat up straight and swung her legs off the couch.

"What's wrong?" Callen asked.

The ice pack fell against her back. Angel got up and began pacing. "Do they know what happened or who did it?"

"He was shot—similar to Jenkins. Dragonslayer left another note on Janet's computer. All it said was 'He won't bother you again.'"

Angel glanced at Callen's worried expression. "I'll be right over."

THIRTY-ONE

Angel got the details, and Callen insisted that if she planned on going anywhere, he was going with her.

"Good. You need to be there. The same person who killed Jim Kelsey killed Phillip Jenkins and Janet's ex. Janet's ex is Charles Campbell, by the way. Now that you've solved your Florence murder, you can come back to these."

"If this Dragonslayer is real." Callen massaged his neck and tipped his head back. "And you're right. I need to go."

"Dragonslayer may be one person or it may be several." Angel carefully tugged her jacket sleeve over her injured arm. "But one thing is certain. These guys were killed because they were abusive to their wives. I have no doubt that if we don't get the killer soon, we'll have corpses stretched out from here to Lincoln City." She placed a hand on Callen's arm. "There are more abusive men out there, and who knows when this psycho will strike next."

She bit her lower lip. She had told Janet that Callen might be abusive. If Janet was behind these deaths, Callen could be next.

Don't go there, Angel. That's not likely. She had an alibi for the time Jenkins was killed.

Angel adjusted her jacket and kissed Callen's cheek. "Do you want to take separate cars or ride together?"

"Together—I'll drive. You shouldn't be using that arm."

He was right about that. Her active afternoon had caused the wound to bleed. They'd had to stop at the emergency room on the way to Callen's place to get the blood-soaked dressing changed. And she'd had to endure a lecture from the ER nurse. The nurse suggested using a sling as a reminder not to use the arm at all for the next day or so. Angel had the sling in her car and agreed to use it if needed.

She and Callen didn't speak on the way to the hotel. An odd silence permeated the car, creating a chasm between them. Angel couldn't read him. Although he didn't seem angry with her, he wasn't happy either. He seemed thoughtful and remote.

"I won't interfere with the investigation, if that's what you're worried about," Angel said. "If I should happen to find anything, anything at all, I'll let you know."

Callen nodded. "When we get to the scene, try to stay in the background, okay?"

They reached the hotel, a place in Lincoln City. Nick was there when they arrived and greeted Callen with a slap on the back. "Boy, am I glad to see you." He tossed Angel a rueful glance. "I thought you were taking it easy."

"I was until Rachael called." Angel looked past him to the wheelchair sitting in front of the window with an ocean view. A fire was going in the gas fireplace, and the windows were wide open. A cool westerly breeze wafted into the room. Crime lab techs were scouring the room for evidence and taking pictures. As a police officer, Angel would have been privy to all the details. As a private detective, she had to wait until the information was released or find out on her own. She looked around at the other officers, hoping to see a familiar face, but they were all new to her. Nick probably wouldn't have been here either if he hadn't been looking into Janet's allegations.

"The ME's already been here." Nick directed the comment to Callen. "They carted out the body about an hour ago."

"How did he die?" Callen asked, drawing his notepad out of his breast pocket.

"Gunshot to the head. No weapon that we can see. Bullet is still in the guy, so we'll get a make on it after the autopsy."

"He was shot at close range—similar to Jenkins." Nick shook

his head. "Poor guy didn't have a chance. Didn't look like he knew what was coming either. No sign of a break-in."

"Do you have a time of death?" Callen's gaze traveled over the room.

"Probably happened last night," Nick answered.

"Witnesses?" Callen stepped inside, and Angel shadowed him.

"Yeah. We lucked out there. Manager said he saw someone fitting the ex-wife's description come into the hotel around 8:00 looking for the guy. Right now she's our only suspect."

"Sounds too easy," Callen said.

Nick rolled his eyes, his gaze settling on Angel. "Don't I know it. I'm checking out all the angles this time. Campbell only made two phone calls from his room. One to his ex-wife's office at 2:00 and another at 7:00 in the evening to her home. I checked the numbers." He hesitated. "You need to come in on these killings, Riley. We just don't have the resources."

"Might not be a bad idea—especially now that it looks like all three deaths are related. I'll talk to my boss and Joe—make sure they're okay with it."

"It sure would help. I'm in way over my head." He turned to Angel. "And no comments from you."

"Is that what all this attitude is about?" Angel stood in front of him, hands on her hips. "You felt this way from the beginning and you've been taking it out on me?"

"I never meant to do that. It's just that you're way smarter about this stuff than I am."

"I am not."

"Right. Tell me you haven't aced every test you've ever taken. You're a better marksman, you could easily have passed the exam for detective. I'm having to work my tail off in these courses. And with all this work . . . I don't know. It's too much."

"Test results don't mean all that much," Angel insisted. "You're a good cop."

"I should've listened to you on the Jenkins case. I know it was stupid, but I wanted to prove you wrong."

"You two can hash out your differences later," Callen said. "Right now we should be focusing on the evidence."

Nick resumed telling Callen what he knew about Charles Campbell's death. Angel listened with half an ear, more intent on Nick's comments about Janet having been there. She was surprised to hear that. Janet hated her ex—hated the control he still had over her, but more than that, she hated what he'd done to her and her unborn baby. But enough to kill him?

Sounds like a motive to me. Honoring Janet's plea for confidentiality, Angel hadn't told Callen the whole story. She might need to now.

She excused herself and went out to the lobby, where she sat in one of the overstuffed chairs and made a phone call.

"Rachael, did Janet tell you she came to see her ex last night?"

"No, she didn't." Rachael hesitated. "You're sure?"

"No, but according to Nick, the manager saw a woman who fit Janet's description. I'm going to want a photo so we get a positive ID." Angel had a thought. Maybe someone other than Janet had been there as well. "Can you get me a photo of all the women from the shelter? There's one tacked on the bulletin board there. See if you can get a good copy and bring it to me." Angel told Rachael where she was and hung up.

The more she thought about it, the more she wondered about that diabolical plan she'd talked to Rachael about. If a group of women had put together a plan to kill their abusive husbands, wouldn't they make certain each wife had an alibi?

Candace thought she'd had an alibi, but no one saw her during the hour she was reading. Then when she got home and found her husband dead and Gracie's footprints on the floor, she had to clean things up. Angel made another call, this one to Janet.

Angel skipped the preliminaries and got right to the point. "Did you go see your ex-husband last night?"

"Who is this? Angel?"

"Yes. Did you?"

"No. Why would I do that?" She sounded shaken and tearful.

"I have no idea, but the manager here said you were here."

"I wasn't. Do the police think I killed him?"

"They haven't gotten that far. They'll need to verify if it was you. I just talked to Rachael and asked her for a photo of you and all the other women from the shelter."

"I . . . I don't know what to say."

"Did you kill him?"

"Of course not."

"Well, then who did? Who else knew he was in town?"

The silence either meant she had told no one and she was trapped or she had told someone and that person was the killer. "I need to do some checking. I'll call you back."

Angel leaned against the back of the chair, and pain shot through her arm. Her eyes drifted closed. Coming here had been stupid. Callen was right; she should have stayed home.

Callen was glad to be on another case. He always suffered a letdown when an investigation ended. Especially one as intense as this latest one. He'd hardly had room to breathe. Even though the evidence hadn't been processed, he had no doubt Darryl Jenkins had killed Christy Grant. Angel's testimony pretty well locked things up. Darryl might come back later, claiming coercion or that he hadn't made the condemning comments. But they'd get him one way or the other.

After a case had been resolved, Callen would often second-guess himself, thinking if he'd done this or that, things might have been different—he'd have solved it sooner. But this time, he could bypass much of the self-recrimination and focus on these bizarre and complicated murders.

Angel had been exhausted, and he'd dropped her off at his place a few minutes ago. She'd been more than ready to go home. She hadn't even argued when he asked her to stay at his place in case her arm started bleeding again. Kath was still there and would watch over her. He'd have some peace of mind for the night at least.

Callen worried about her injury, but what concerned him even more was the possibility that the killer she'd been so doggedly pursuing might try again. He didn't want her alone until she at least had a weapon for protection. Her own gun was still being held in evidence in another case. He made a mental note to pick up a weapon for her tomorrow.

At the hotel, Angel had told him about her call to Janet and how the counselor denied having been there. He admired Angel's quick thinking in supplying them with a photo. Rachael hadn't arrived with it until after he'd taken Angel home, so Angel didn't know that the hotel manager had made a positive ID on Janet.

Apparently the counselor had lied. Odd, though, that Janet would talk to the manager and announce her presence if she planned to commit murder. Then again, a woman who'd been through what she had might have been too distressed to consider the consequences.

By the time he left the hotel for the second time, it was 10:00. Since he wasn't feeling the least bit tired, he decided it was time to pay a little visit to Dr. Janet Campbell.

After Callen had dropped her off at his place, Angel had thought briefly about calling Janet to follow up on their conversation. She'd opted to leave before the photos arrived, and secured a promise from Callen that he'd let her know for certain whether or not Janet had been there. Weary and desperately in need of sleep and some strong pain medication, Angel went to bed at 9:00. She'd talk to both Callen and Janet in the morning.

The next day, after coffee and a shower, Angel called Janet and got the answering machine. She called the office; same thing there. Of course, the office didn't open until 9:00. Angel would go over there then. Maybe Claire knew where she was.

When she'd called to ask Callen if he'd talked to Janet, he didn't answer. She called dispatch, but the operator couldn't find him either.

Why aren't you answering my calls? "Callen, where are you?" Angel muttered.

"Did you say something?" Kath shuffled out of the guest room, making a beeline for the kitchen and the coffee Angel had made.

"I'm trying to get hold of your brother."

244

She yawned. "He didn't come home last night?"

"I don't think so—and he isn't answering his phone."

"Hmm. Maybe he's still at the crime scene. It wouldn't be the first time he's pulled an all-nighter."

Angel took a tentative sip of her coffee. "Still, you'd think he'd answer his phone or his pager."

"Don't look so worried," Kath said. "I'm sure there's a good reason. Maybe he's out of range."

"Maybe." Angel didn't think so. Something was going on. She could feel it—that ominous sixth sense that kicked in now and then. As the minutes ticked by, after she'd gotten dressed, the unnamed fear grew. Why hadn't he called back? Where was he? Had he gone to talk with Janet last night?

Angel pictured him lying in Janet's apartment, wounded or dead. With fierce determination, she put the thought from her head. Her imagination could be downright annoying at times. *He's all right*, she told herself. *Callen can take care of himself.* She chided herself for even thinking the negative thoughts.

Instead, she focused on the case. The night before when Angel had talked to Janet, Janet had said she hadn't been at the hotel, but she'd acted like she knew who had. Had someone posing as Janet gone to see Charles? Had that person stopped at the front desk to make sure the manager knew she was there, then gone to his room to kill him? Had this been an attempt to frame Janet? Or had Janet lied? Angel's thoughts were in danger of short-circuiting. There was really only one way to find out.

Angel asked Kath to keep trying to call Callen and to let him know she was going to Janet's office.

At 9:10, Angel entered the counseling offices and found Claire frantically canceling appointments. "Did you have an appointment today?" she asked, looking overwhelmed.

"No, I just wanted to talk to her."

"Well, she's sick. She left a message on the machine telling me to cancel all her appointments and to take the day off."

"Sick?"

Claire nodded. "The flu or something. I tried to call her at home, but there's no answer."

"Did you know Janet's ex-husband was murdered last night?"

Claire's large eyes grew even larger. "My gosh. You don't think Janet . . . No, she wouldn't do something like that. Last night she had group at the shelter. She talked a little about his being in town, but . . ." Claire shook her head. "Janet wouldn't do that. She told us she was having him arrested for blackmail."

"Claire, this is really important. Do you have notes on the meetings? I know you do, but do you have them here?"

"Yes, I type them up the next morning. I haven't had a chance to do these."

"I need to see them."

She glanced around, her expression desperate. "I'd like to help, I really would, but this stuff is all confidential. Dr. Campbell would kill me if I let anyone near her files."

"I understand that, but Janet may be in trouble. See, I don't think she killed her ex. I asked her last night if she'd told anyone about him being in town. Now you're telling me she told the group last night. One of those women may have killed him."

Claire placed her elbows on the table, face in her hands. "This is terrible. I can't believe what you're saying. But I can't let you see the notes. You're not even a police officer." When she looked up, tears filled her eyes. "I don't know what to do."

"Remember that day I came to group, and Heather let it slip about them hiring a hit man?"

Claire nodded and reached into her drawer, pulling out a tissue.

"I'm wondering just how much of a joke that was. How often did they talk about things like that?"

"Only that one time, and while you were there." She dabbed at her eyes and blew her nose. "You don't really think they'd do something like that, do you?"

"I don't know what to believe," Angel said. "I keep going back and forth. Did one of those women kill all of those men? Did they take turns? Did they hire someone? Did Janet kill them? Or Lorraine or Heather or Debra? Or you?" Angel leaned on the counter.

"Me?" The word came out in a squeak. "How can you say that? What reason would I have?"

"Okay, then, talk to me. I need your help." Angel had hoped to put a little fear into the woman, and she had. She needed to see those notes.

"I can't tell you anything. I know Janet wouldn't kill anyone. She's kind and caring. As for the other women, I just don't know. Sometimes they get really nasty. They say terrible things about their husbands. They've been through so much, but I can't imagine any of them doing something so terrible."

She covered her mouth with her fist as her tears continued. With her right hand, she turned back pages in the appointment book. "There is something I should tell you." She opened the book to Tuesday, May 6, the day Phillip Jenkins had been killed. "I lied to the police about Janet being here when Phillip Jenkins . . . um . . . died. It wasn't exactly a lie, I just told them she had clients and that she was here all day. I thought she was. She told me she was staying in to eat lunch and was going to take a nap."

Claire threw away her used tissue and grabbed another. "I had to leave early that day to run some errands in Lincoln City with Debra. I was gone for two hours. She was here when I left and still here when I got back. Only, there was a new name written in the book—Janet said he'd come in and was upset, so she saw him. There was no reason to doubt her. But later, when I went to bill him, I realized he didn't exist."

"The police will eventually discover the name was a phony. That makes you an accomplice."

"I didn't think about it. I just wanted to protect her. Janet's been through so much, and she's helped so many people."

"What about the morning I was shot? When did Janet come in to the office?"

Claire flipped the pages of the appointment book. "She had me cancel her morning appointments. She was going to talk to her attorney."

Angel blew out a hard breath. Janet could have done it. Things were not looking good for the mild-mannered counselor. "Do you have any idea where she is now?"

"No." Claire continued to cry. "But if you want to check her apartment, I know where there's a key. She's had me pick things up for her before. It's under the flowerpot on the second step."

Angel thanked her and hurried out of the building to her car, then drove out to Janet's condo. After finding the key where Claire had said it would be, she opened the door. Janet wasn't there. That didn't surprise her, but what she found next certainly did.

Angel discovered an open suitcase and clothes tossed all over the bed. In the kitchen, she noticed two cups and plates on the table, along with crumbs from half of a small, round, decadent-looking chocolate cake that still sat on the island. Who had been here with her and when?

If Janet had been packing, where was she now? If she'd run away, why hadn't she finished packing and taken her clothes with her? Maybe there hadn't been time. She apparently left in a hurry.

Angel called Callen again. Still no answer. She called his house, and Kath told her she hadn't heard from him and that dispatch had been trying to reach him. "I'm getting worried."

Me too. She didn't tell Kath that. "I'm sure he's okay."

Janet missing. Callen missing. Douglas Stanton missing. *What's going on?*

She called Nick. "Have you seen Callen?" she asked as soon as he answered.

"No. I've been trying to get him all morning. Last night he said something about interviewing Janet Campbell."

Angel sucked in a sharp breath. "I'm in her apartment right now. She's not here. I think you'd better get over here. Get some lab guys over here too. Someone was here with her. We need to know what happened."

"You back on duty, Delaney?"

Angel stopped pacing. "I—"

"I'm on my way," Nick said before she could respond.

Angel studied the apartment in more depth. The techs would be able to tell what had happened, if she hadn't already destroyed evidence by just walking through the scene. She looked at the carpet—her footprints marred the freshly vacuumed floor. Now

248

that was strange. Janet was in too much of a hurry to finish packing but had time to eat cake and vacuum the floor?

No way. Angel carefully made her way back outside to wait for Nick and the CSI team.

Some time later, the techs had worked their way through and were checking out Janet's computer in the loft when they found the note from Dragonslayer. Nick and Angel read it together.

Dear Dr. Campbell,

Things weren't supposed to turn out this way. I had everything planned out perfectly. You shouldn't have gone to see Charles. I never meant for you to be a suspect. It's all unraveling now, and I don't know what to do. Things are happening too fast.

Dragonslayer

THIRTY-TWO

——

Callen felt like he'd been hit on the head, but he hadn't, not that he could recall. He'd been eating cake and drinking coffee with Dr. Campbell. Now he found himself in the dark, figuratively and literally.

He tried to rub his forehead but couldn't raise his hand. Both hands were secured behind his back with handcuffs—probably his own. His feet were bound as well, and a wide piece of tape stretched from one ear to the other, efficiently covering his mouth. His captor had thought of everything.

He tried to sit up only to discover that he'd been cuffed to a metal pole of some sort. It was maybe two inches in diameter. Water lapping nearby and the faint smell of creosote, brackish water, dead fish, and rotting wood told him he was somewhere on the bay. A boathouse or bait shack, maybe, or the hold of a boat. He thought he heard a motorboat in the distance. Sure enough, a few minutes later water lapped against his new habitat and set it to swaying.

Callen's stomach rebelled at the wavelike movement. He took several long, deep breaths, willing it to calm down. Willing his brain to come up with some answers as to what had happened and why he was here.

It hurt to think. Hurt to move. He managed to sit up, almost pulling his arm out of the socket in the process. He leaned back against the pole, trying to figure out how he'd ended up here.

He remembered paying a visit to the counselor, intent on finding out what she was hiding. Janet had seemed glad to see him.

"I knew someone would be by to talk to me about Charles." She motioned him in. "I'm glad you came tonight. I couldn't sleep anyway."

He'd made a courtesy call to her on the way over, wanting to make certain she wasn't asleep or in her pajamas. She hadn't been.

"I guess my first question would have to be why you lied to Angel. You told her you hadn't gone to the hotel, yet the manager identified you."

She sighed and poured them coffee from a full pot, then sliced a piece of cake for each of them. Sitting down at the table with him, she said, "That wasn't very smart of me. I couldn't believe he'd been killed, and I was afraid my having been there would put a nail in my coffin for sure. My first inclination was to run away." She nodded toward the bedroom. "Even started packing."

Callen noticed the suitcase on the bed and clothes tossed haphazardly about. "You changed your mind?" He put a bite of cake in his mouth. The cake tasted like a piece of heaven. He'd missed dinner and could have eaten the whole thing.

"Not entirely." She cut off a small piece with her fork and put it in her mouth. "I decided that running isn't the answer. Especially since I didn't kill him."

"And you went to see him because . . . ?"

"To tell him I was going to the police. To let him know that he wasn't going to get another penny from me." She paused to take another bite.

"How long were you there?"

"Fifteen, maybe twenty minutes. He didn't believe I'd follow through on my threat. I told him he could expect a visit from the police."

Callen finished off the cake and almost asked for another slice. "Good cake." He pushed the empty plate away.

"Mm. I wish I could take the credit. I didn't make it. It was here when I got home from work. My housekeeper probably left it for me. She knows I love chocolate."

"Who's your housekeeper?"

"Heather Davis. She's one of the women from the shelter. She doesn't stay there anymore. I hired her as a housekeeper several months ago, and since then she's developed quite a business. She'll make goodies for me every once in a while." Janet yawned. "I'm sorry."

Callen couldn't remember much past that, other than feeling dizzy and light-headed. He'd tried to stand for some reason and fell to the floor like a stumbling drunk.

Thinking about it now, he realized he'd been drugged. Had Janet put something in the cake or the coffee? He closed his eyes. Stupid. Stupid. He never should have accepted the coffee and cake. But she'd eaten it too. She'd had coffee from the same pot, hadn't she?

A stifled groan told him he wasn't alone.

THIRTY-THREE

Daylight came and went. Still no word from Callen or Janet. Angel had stayed at Janet's until the lab techs left. Nick promised to let her know the test results as soon as they came in.

Angel called Rachael at 7:30 to fill her in.

"Are you hungry?" Rachael asked when she'd finished.

"Not really, but I suppose I should eat something."

"I'll meet you at the Burger Shed."

A few minutes later, they were sitting in a booth, placing their orders.

"You have no idea what happened to them?" Rachael asked.

Angel sipped at her water. "None."

"You don't suppose they've gone somewhere together?"

"Callen and Janet?" Angel shook her head. "Callen wouldn't do that. Besides, both their cars are gone. I think they might have been abducted. I know that sounds crazy. He's big and strong and he carries a gun. Still, something is just not right about the whole thing. Maybe he never made it to her place. Maybe he's out there somewhere . . ." She bit her lip, thinking once again of her conversation with Janet in which she'd said she suspected Callen might be abusive. She told Rachael about that conversation. "If Janet is the Dragonslayer, she might've gone after Callen."

Rachael stared at her. "You actually think Callen is abusive?"

"No . . . I don't know. The point is, I told Janet I thought he might be."

"What did she say?"

"Her first reaction was like yours—surprise. Then she told me to take my time to be sure one way or the other."

"Doesn't sound vindictive."

"No, but I didn't tell anyone else. And I don't think with all her confidentiality issues she'd tell anyone either." Angel leaned back when her burger and fries arrived. She topped her burger with all the condiments and took a large bite. Rachael worked on her fried chicken. "Something just doesn't fit," she told Rachael.

"What do you mean?"

"Janet. I mean, yeah, she was abused. Her husband caused her to lose her baby, then turns around and blackmails her. Major trauma. It wouldn't surprise me if she'd snapped."

"Is that what you think? That she's working as a counselor and killing off abusive men in her spare time?"

"That's what I mean. In a twisted way it makes sense. Only, then again, it doesn't. Callen is missing. Janet's gone and so is her car. But she left her clothes and her purse and a chocolate cake."

"A chocolate cake?" Rachael's head snapped up. "Now, leaving the suitcase and the purse behind, I can understand, but what woman would voluntarily flee without taking her chocolate cake?"

"Be serious."

"I am. Angel, I talked to that woman for several hours the day she came to see me. My take? She's no killer. And she's not a quitter. Personally, I don't think she'd run. She might think about it, but I'll bet she's the type to stick around and see it through."

"So what happened to her? And where is Callen?"

"Did you ever get a look at those notes she kept from the support group meetings? Maybe we need to take a closer look at those and talk to these other women."

"Claire wouldn't let me near them," Angel said. "Janet has her well trained in the area of confidentiality."

"Well, Claire isn't there now, is she?"

"You want to break into the office?" Angel gasped.

"Of course not. You're going to get us in."

"And just how am I going to do that?"

"Doesn't your ex-boyfriend have an office in her building?" Rachael gave her a wicked grin.

"Oh no." Angel rolled her eyes but moments later found herself asking Brandon for a favor.

"No way," he said. "I can't believe you're asking me this."

"Brandon, this is important. Janet Campbell is missing and so is Callen. She may be the person who killed Jim Kelsey and Phillip Jenkins. Helping find the real killer will vindicate Michelle."

Michelle seemed to be the magic word, because after a short pause he agreed.

From the Burger Shed, Angel and Rachael walked the three blocks to the building where Janet had her practice. Lights were on in several offices. The front door was locked, but the security guard opened it when they knocked. He smiled when they told him who they'd come to see. "Mr. Lafferty is expecting you. Go on up."

Brandon was waiting just inside the law offices. Angel and Rachael took turns greeting him with a hug and thanking him for his help.

"Don't mention it." He scowled and picked up a file. "Bring me the keys when you're done, and I'll get them back into the janitor's closet."

They took the elevator to Janet's suite of offices and easily gained entrance. They spent over an hour searching but could find no record of the notes Claire had taken. Discouraged, Rachael and Angel returned the keys, thanked Brandon for his help, and left. Back at the Burger Shed, the two women got into their respective cars and headed home.

Angel called Nick to see if they had made any headway on finding Callen, Janet, or Doug Stanton. All available law enforcement agencies were on the lookout, but so far, nothing.

It was late. Angel's arm hurt. She felt bone tired, but how could she give up with Callen out there somewhere and very likely in danger? She had no doubt that Claire had taken those notes home with her, but why would she do that? Was she protecting someone? Had Claire been in contact with Janet? Maybe Janet had asked her to bring them to her. Angel glanced at her watch. Nine o'clock. It had been twenty-four hours since Callen had dropped her off at his place and she'd kissed him good-bye. She should have insisted on staying with him.

The missing files put things into a different perspective. Angel hadn't thought much about Claire being a possible suspect. But now she wondered. Did Claire type up notes of Janet's private sessions as well as the support groups? Had Janet told Claire that Callen might be abusive? Maybe the two women were working together. If Claire were meeting Janet, where would they go? Claire's place? Angel tried to remember the conversation she and Claire had during the break at the support group meeting. Had she mentioned where she lived? Angel couldn't recall.

She stopped by an all-night market for some coffee and borrowed a phone book from the clerk to look up Claire's address. She lived in one of the older homes along the south side of the bay. Angel drove over to check it out. This home, like a number of others, had a yard sloping out to the water and a boathouse alongside a private dock. Trees and overgrown shrubs made the house almost impossible to see from the road. Angel almost drove past without stopping, but she caught a glimpse of Janet's car parked in the driveway off to one side. Angel stopped and cut the engine and the lights. She pulled out her cell and called dispatch, asking the operator to have Nick meet her out here. After giving her location, Angel stepped out of her Corvette and quietly closed the door.

A light arched behind the house, flickering through the tree branches. A flashlight. Angel sneaked around to the back, where she noticed two crouched silhouettes heading toward the dock. The person bringing up the rear had a gun. From her vantage point, it looked as though the first person was being held at gunpoint.

They disappeared inside the boathouse. Angel stayed in the shadows until she reached the dock, then moved stealthily toward the boathouse. Upon reaching it, she crouched beside it.

"Get in the boat." A woman's voice. Sharp and angry.

"This is wrong. Can't you see that?"

It didn't take long for Angel to determine who the voices belonged to. Claire and Janet.

"There's no other way," Claire said, her tone softening.

"Please don't do this," Janet pleaded.

A loud gravelly moan emanated from inside the boathouse. Masculine. *Callen?*

"You shut up!" Claire spoke with such vehemence that Angel feared she'd use the gun.

As much as Angel wanted to step inside, she couldn't—not yet. She needed to determine what was going on. Besides, she didn't have a weapon and would be useless with her injured arm.

"Please, Claire," Janet spoke again. "I understand why you felt you needed to kill those men, but why kill Detective Riley? He's not an abuser." Janet's voice wavered.

Kill Callen? Angel thought she was going to be sick. But wait. Hadn't she just heard him in the boathouse?

"You're the one who gave him the cake," Claire said. "That was only meant for you."

"Why, Claire? Why are you doing this?"

"For someone who's so smart," Claire answered, "you can be extremely dumb. What else am I supposed to do? Give myself up? Get into the boat."

More shuffling. Angel found a crack between boards that gave her a partial view. The only light came from a small lantern that now hung from a nail near the entrance. The boathouse was open at the front, accessing the bay. Janet climbed aboard.

"Inside the cabin," Claire ordered. Once Janet was inside, Claire went aboard and closed the cabin door.

Angel eased closer to the boathouse door. She had to find a way to stop Claire. Maybe there was a way to sabotage the boat. Keep her from taking Janet and Callen out to sea. She hadn't said as much, but Angel surmised that was her plan. Dump their bodies at sea and keep going.

She heard a creak behind her and, thinking it was Nick, turned around, holding a finger to her lips to silence him. But it wasn't Nick.

The first thing she saw was the faint glistening of the gun barrel. The second thing was the hard, cold look in her captor's eyes.

Angel hadn't been that far off with her diabolical plan theory. She just wondered how many of the women were in on it.

THIRTY-FOUR

———

S o you weren't joking after all." Angel's gaze shifted again to
the gun.

Debra waved the gun to the side, indicating for Angel to go
inside. "We thought about hiring someone but decided we could
use the money ourselves. It wasn't that hard."

"Debra, is that you?" Claire called out.

"Me and an uninvited guest. Looks like we have another one."
To Angel she said, "Open the door. We're going for a boat ride."

"What if I say no?" Angel swallowed back the tide of fear
threatening to engulf her; with much more bravado than she possessed, she called Debra's bluff. "What are you going to do, shoot
me? Looks like you're going to kill us one way or the other, so what
difference does it make?"

"None at all to me, except that you might have a chance out
there." She nodded toward the ocean.

Angel wasn't falling for it. A person wouldn't survive more than
a few minutes in the frigid water. "So you're saying you don't mind
shooting me or having neighbors hear a gunshot and noticing my car
is out there. The police are on their way. They know I'm here."

"Just get on the boat," Debra growled between her teeth.

"No. I'll take my chances out here. Shoot me. Go ahead." Angel
felt as if her heart were turning over faster than the boat's motor.

259

"I can understand you wanting to get rid of those abusive men, but Janet?"

"Janet." Debra spat out the word as though it were poison. "Janet was going to turn us in to the police—she thought everything could be settled without violence. But she was wrong. Violence begets violence. We never meant for anyone else to get hurt other than the abusers. But you and your boyfriend had to interfere. Now we have no choice."

"Yes, you do. You can turn yourselves in."

"What, and plead insanity?"

Angel caught her gaze. "Give me the gun, Debra."

She waved it again. "No way."

"Debra," Claire called out, "get on board now." The motor sputtered, then died.

"I hear sirens," Angel said. "Turn yourself in before—"

"Debra, please. The police," Claire pleaded.

"I can't just leave her here."

"Then shoot her." Claire started the engine again, and again it died.

In one swift move, Angel stepped away and jumped off the dock. The gun went off.

The water, still fresh from mountain runoffs, took her breath away. Not daring to surface, she managed to turn and swim under the dock. She felt her way along the pilings and under the boathouse walls, coming up at the prow of the boat.

"Where is she?" Debra screeched as she pumped more bullets into the inky water.

"Never mind her. We have to get out of here now." Claire's pitch rose with each word. The motor roared to life.

Debra entered the boathouse and climbed aboard. Claire eased the vessel forward.

Angel worked her way alongside the boat until she reached the stern. She grasped the ladder that extended up and over the rail, fighting the water churned up by the propeller. Within seconds they'd head toward open water. Only about two feet of water separated the boat from the deck inside the boathouse. Angel looked around for a board or something to shove into the propeller blades to stop them. Nothing. Not even a piece of driftwood. She tugged at her shoe, yanking it free after what seemed an eternity. She'd shove the shoe into the blades. If it didn't work, she could lose an arm. But if she didn't try, she'd lose Callen and Janet. Angel took a deep breath and let go of the ladder. At the same moment, she pushed the tennis shoe into the blades.

Something snagged her arm as she went under. She bobbed up and caught the edge of the dock. The boat had cleared the boat-house, its motor silent as it drifted a short distance and bumped against the end of the pier.

Footsteps pounded on the dock. *The cavalry. Thank you, God.*

"Police!" someone shouted. "Don't anybody move."

Nick yanked her out of the water as if she were a rag doll. She was too numb to protest. Seconds later he had her wrapped in a wool blanket and was carrying her toward the house.

Angel didn't get to hang around long enough to find out what happened. She didn't really need to. Nick had everything well under control.

The emergency room was crowded that night, for at least a few hours, while doctors checked out everyone for injuries. Angel had not lost an arm or even come close. The wave action had knocked her into a piling, breaking open some stitches and opening her wound again. The nurse cleaned the wound and steri-stripped it closed. She was just finishing up when Callen brushed aside the curtain and stepped into the room.

Haggard and unshaven, he leaned down to kiss her forehead. She smiled and poked a hand out of the warming blankets to caress his face. His gaze caught and held hers.

"I understand you saved my life." Callen stroked her cheek. "Along with Dr. Campbell's and Doug Stanton's."

"Stanton?"

"He was in the cabin with us. Trussed up and awaiting execution."

Angel winced. "I didn't do anything you wouldn't have done."

He smiled. "Are you sure about that?"

"Yeah. I was so worried about you, Callen. What happened?"

"Long story, but we'll have plenty of time to talk about it later."

She smiled and closed her eyes. Callen was safe. Candace was out of jail and back at the farm with her family. And the bad guys had been rounded up. It had taken a long time to warm up after her flirtation with hypothermia, and now all she wanted to do was sleep.

The next afternoon, Angel and Anna Delaney were stretched out on beach lounges, catching some sun, watching the waves roll in and out. Seagulls squawked overhead. Mutt lay between them, watching their every move, concern written in his liquid brown eyes.

Callen stood at his barbeque, grilling thick T-bones, while Paul and Rachael followed his orders to set the table and bring the food he'd prepared earlier out to the table. Tim and Susan had taken the girls for a walk on the beach and were just coming back. Peter was heading for Portland, where he would catch a plane to the Bahamas to deal with some sort of emergency at the resort there. Nick had picked up Rosie and was on his way over.

"It's hard to have someone else taking care of dinner." Anna turned her head in Angel's direction, sunglasses hiding her eyes.

"Mmm. Enjoy it, Ma. You'll be back in the kitchen soon enough." Angel hadn't really talked with her mother since her father's death. Truth be told, she'd been avoiding it.

"Angel, move in with me."

"What?" Angel wasn't sure what she expected, but not this.

"You heard me. With your father gone, the house is too big and I hate being alone."

"I don't know what to say."

"Just think about it. The boys say I should sell and move into a condominium, but I don't want to do that."

"You shouldn't have to—sell, I mean. It's too soon anyway."

"Angel," her father had told her before his open-heart surgery, *"if anything happens to me, take care of your mother."*

Anna nodded and looked back at the water. "I miss him."

262

An old familiar lump made its way to Angel's throat. She didn't cry this time. She'd done far too much of that already. "I miss him too." Eventually, she would have to deal with all the unfinished business that had gone on between them. The funeral had helped. So many people had come up to her—especially people he worked with—telling her how proud he'd been of his little girl. She just wished he could have told her—shown her.

"Come get it!" Callen yelled.

Angel set aside her thoughts and helped her mother out of the chair. How ironic that they would both end up with arm injuries. Fortunately, neither was serious enough to keep them out of commission for long.

Dinner provided a perfect opportunity to watch Callen as he interacted with the people she loved most. How could she have thought him abusive? Her heart swelled to twice its size as it filled with love for him. She could hardly wait for dinner to end and for conversations to fade and their guests to leave.

At 8:30 she got her wish. She and Callen were alone. He would be taking her home soon, but she had him to herself for at least another hour or two.

He turned on the dishwasher, hung up his apron, and joined her on the couch. She curled her fingers in his hair. "That was quite a performance. We'll have to start calling you Emeril."

He smiled. "Enjoy it while you can. As soon as that arm of yours heals, I plan to recruit you as my chief cook and bottle washer."

"In your dreams."

He leaned over and planted a sweet, lingering kiss on her lips, leaving her breathless and wanting more. He tipped his head back and slouched down on the couch, closing his eyes in the process.

Angel brushed his hair from his forehead.

"I suppose you're itching to know how everything turned out." He smiled as though he didn't mind telling her.

Angel hadn't planned to ask, thinking her curiosity could wait a day or two. "Now that you mention it, I suppose I am. There are still a lot of unanswered questions. Like how you managed to get yourself abducted."

Callen told her about his talk with Janet. It had been Claire, not Heather, who'd brought the cake, a cake laced with a powerful sedative that had knocked both Callen and Janet out. Claire came back with Debra, thinking they'd find Janet passed out, only to find they had to deal with Callen as well.

"Why would she use a sedative rather than poison?"

"Like her note said, things were happening too quickly. They had to find a way to get rid of their victims. They couldn't afford to have any more bodies turn up—at least not around Sunset Cove. She and Debra planned to take us out to sea and dump us."

Angel ran a hand through her hair. "What about Charles? They left his body in the hotel in Lincoln City."

"Who knows? Her note said things were unraveling. I don't think either of them were thinking too clearly."

"It's hard to believe they would actually devise such a devious plan. They both seemed nice and fairly well adjusted." She frowned. "So who was Dragonslayer, or did they write the notes together?"

"Debra didn't know anything about the notes. In fact, she about went ballistic when she found out."

"Do we know why Claire sent them?"

Callen shook his head. "Not specifically. Serial killers will often leave clues—the murdering becomes a sort of bizarre game to them."

Angel shivered. "Do you know who shot me?"

"That was Debra. She figured you wouldn't suspect her with Doug missing. In fact, Debra's the one who actually killed Kelsey and Jenkins. We recovered the bullet Debra fired at you and it matches the one used to kill Jim Kelsey."

"But she used Phillip's own gun to kill him?"

"Right. We don't really know why. Maybe to throw us off the track."

Angel frowned. "But what about the receipts that put Debra and Claire at the outlet mall in Lincoln City?"

"Claire was at the mall, but Debra had given her one of her credit cards to use, so they could establish an alibi for both of them."

"And Charles?"

"Claire admitted to killing him. She thought she was doing it as a favor to Janet and apparently didn't realize that Janet had gone to see him. Claire, of course, didn't talk to the manager like Janet had."

Angel blew out a long breath. "I still don't get it. Seems like Claire and Debra thought they were helping these women. Claire killed Charles so Janet would be free of him, but then why would they decide to kill Janet?" She thought about the conversation she had with Janet after Charles's murder. "She knew. Janet was on to her."

"I'm afraid so," Callen said. "Janet should have come to us, instead she started asking questions. They didn't want to kill her but didn't know what to do. I think they actually believed they could get her over to their side. Janet said they talked to her about coming with them. And of course she refused."

"Claire told me about her abuse as a kid. It must have been horrendous to mess her up like that."

"Mmm. I think we've just skimmed the surface where she's concerned."

"You mean she's killed before?"

"We're looking at the possibility. She kept journals, and either she's one heck of a fiction writer or she's a serial killer."

"She seemed so quiet and unassuming." Angel shifted her shoulder for comfort.

"They're the most dangerous." Callen wrapped an arm around her and brought her close.

"What about Debra? I know her husband was abusive—"

"Actually," Callen interrupted, "he wasn't."

Angel twisted around to get a better look at his face. "Are you serious?"

"Turns out that Debra was the abusive one in that relationship. Doug was leaving her. And she wasn't about to let that happen."

"So she was going to kill him?" Angel was still having trouble assimilating all of it.

Callen nodded. "I'm afraid so. Better that than have the whole town find out her dirty little secrets."

They sat in silence for a while. Angel tried to absorb the truth about the women she'd come to know. Her mind traveled from them to Candace and Janet and Michelle, wondering if they'd had any inkling as to what Claire and Debra had done. Had they been protecting them? She asked Callen about it.

"We haven't seen any evidence to indicate their involvement. I really don't think they had a clue until Janet began to suspect Claire."

"If Debra was the abusive one, why would she go to the women's shelter—why be part of the support group?"

"Oddly enough, Debra saw herself as the victim in the marriage. She's still claiming that she was being abused—I don't know—maybe they were abusive toward one another, emotionally, at least."

Angel was quiet for a moment. "I've made a decision," she said, changing the subject.

"About . . . ?"

"My job."

Callen smiled. "Good."

"I want to be a detective."

He leaned back. "With the PD?"

"I'm not sure about that part. I like working with Rachael."

Callen didn't respond; he didn't have to.

"I know you don't like private investigators, but I'm hoping you'll adjust your thinking where I'm concerned."

"Angel." He kissed her. "I'll support you no matter what you decide to do."

She grinned and snuggled up against him. "I also have an offer to teach law enforcement at the community college."

"That's great."

"And Joe called to ask if I was coming back once my leave ended. I guess Nick decided not to continue the detective classes—he prefers just being a cop. Joe offered to let me go through detective training if I wanted."

"What did you tell him?"

"Same thing I'm telling you. I have a lot of options and a lot to think about."

"I have another option for you." He kissed her nose.

"You want to offer me a job?" Angel met his gaze.

"Not a job, exactly, though if you ever want to work for the state police, you have my vote." He tucked a finger under her chin and lifted her face, lowering his lips to hers for a toe-curling kiss. "I'd like you to think about marrying me."

"Callen, I . . ."

"Not for a while," he added quickly. "I'd just like us to see one another exclusively with the idea of marrying in a year if we both agree."

Angel sighed and linked hands with her favorite detective. She did indeed have a lot of options. Whatever she decided, she would remain in law enforcement. Being a cop was part of who she was, deep down, inside and out. Angel couldn't imagine anything, not even marriage, changing that.

She wondered what her father would think, and which direction he'd want her to go.

Would he approve of Callen? Definitely.

Would he be proud of what she had done? Of course.

Would he be okay with her being a detective? She smiled. Probably not, but two out of three wasn't bad.

ACKNOWLEDGMENTS

———

Thanks to my editor, Lonnie Hull Dupont, who has believed in Angel since the beginning. Also to Kristin Kornoelje and other editors and readers at Baker Books.

A special thanks to Travis and Belinda.

To my round robin pals for their prayer and encouragement.

Thanks to my husband, Ron, for his help, encouragement, and support as I exit life and enter my fictional world.

Thank you to God, who makes all things possible.

Patricia H. Rushford is an award-winning author, speaker, and teacher who holds a master's degree in counseling and is a prolific writer with over forty books to her credit and more than a million copies sold. Patricia was nominated for an Edgar Allan Poe award for her book *Silent Witness*. She conducts writers workshops for adults and children and has appeared as a featured guest on numerous radio and television shows. Her books include the Angel Delaney Mysteries, the Helen Bradley Mysteries, and the popular Jennie McGrady Mysteries for young readers, as well as the McAllister Files, which she writes with a detective for the Oregon State Police to create CSI-like mysteries.

Books by Patricia H. Rushford

Fiction:

Sins of the Mother
The Angel Delaney Mysteries
    Deadly Aim
    Dying to Kill
The Jennie McGrady Mysteries
The Helen Bradley Mysteries
The McAllister Files
    Secrets, Lies & Alibis
    Deadfall

Nonfiction:

Have You Hugged Your Teenager Today?
It Shouldn't Hurt to Be a Kid
What Kids Need Most in a Mom

For details see Patricia's website at www.patriciarushford.com

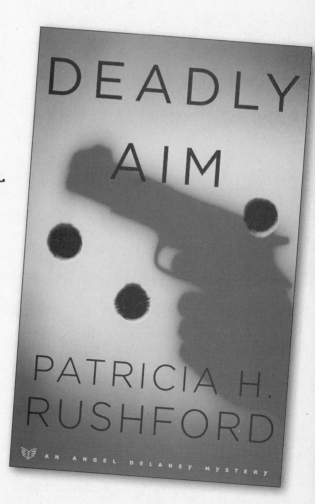